BLUE
RIDGE

VIKING

75 years

BLUE RIDGE

T. R. PEARSON

VIKING

VIKING

Published by the Penguin Group

Penguin Putnam Inc., 375 Hudson Street,

New York, New York 10014, U.S.A.

Penguin Books Ltd, 27 Wrights Lane,

London W8 5TZ, England

Penguin Books Australia Ltd, Ringwood,

Victoria, Australia

Penguin Books Canada Ltd, 10 Alcorn Avenue,

Toronto, Ontario, Canada M4V 3B2

Penguin Books (N.Z.) Ltd, 182–190 Wairau Road,

Auckland 10, New Zealand

Penguin Books Ltd, Registered Offices:

Harmondsworth, Middlesex, England

First published in 2000 by Viking Penguin, a member of Penguin Putnam Inc.

1   3   5   7   9   10   8   6   4   2

PUBLISHER'S NOTE

This is a work of fiction. Names, characters, places, and incidents either are the product of the author's
imagination or are used fictitiously, and any resemblance to actual persons, living or dead,
business establishments, events, or locales is entirely coincidental.

LIBRARY OF CONGRESS CATALOGING IN PUBLICATION DATA

Pearson, T. R., date.

Blue Ridge / T. R. Pearson.

p.   cm.

ISBN 0-670-89269-6

I. Title.

PS3566.E235 B58 2000

813'.54—dc21   00-025826

This book is printed on acid-free paper.

Printed in the United States of America

Set in Garamond 3

Designed by Betty Lew

For Joy
with gratitude

BLUE
RIDGE

He was still two hours shy of Knoxville by the time he stopped, well past midnight at a motor lodge along the interstate. The place was rampside and overgrown, twenty dollars a night. Ray rousted the night manager, a whiskery old coot in a beltless housecoat and tartan undershorts, and filled out a guest card in the puny eyesore of a lobby which was dominated by a decorative electric fireplace—red fiberglass brick, brown fiberglass logs, a lightbulb for a flame. A gaudy chintz settee with a hideous dust ruffle sat beneath the lone window. A vase on the wormy side table was shoved full of dusty artificial magnolia blossoms.

As Ray shifted about to hand over his card, the all-weather carpet crunched like cellophane underfoot. The night manager read the thing at arm's length.

"Mr. Ray Tatum. I'm going to need an address of some sort."

"I just left a job in Mobile. I'm headed for one in Virginia."

"Whereabouts?"

"Hogarth. Up around Lexington."

"All right, then." That gentleman produced a golf pencil from his bathrobe pocket and licked the lead in advance of making a laborious notation. "Now," he said, "about this dog of yours."

Together they watched Monroe sniff a settee bolster. She was black with gold markings and inordinately wirehaired, a squat and unbecoming marriage of terrier and retriever.

"Me and the missus don't have much use for dogs. I'm going to have to charge you. Say ten."

"Dollars?" Monroe made a tentative exploratory lick at the fiberglass hearth, sniffed the logs and eyed suspiciously the sixty-watt inferno. "I didn't have to bring her in, you know? Could have just left her in the car."

Monroe shifted about to consider a choice bit of decor on the far wall, a paint-by-numbers rendition of a schooner under full sail heeled over in the wind. A geometric wave in four graduated tones of gray broke across her bow. Monroe grumbled, lowly, deep in her throat.

"Don't," Ray told her.

She glanced at him as she weighed his wishes and made her canine calculations, as she determined that she would prefer, in fact, to bark—at the painting and the settee, at the plastic flowers and the wheel-hub lamp, at the cheesy electric fireplace. She bounced on her front feet, yapping.

Ray had already hoisted his canvas duffel from the floor by the time the night manager had settled on a course of action, had moved to unceremoniously rip Ray's guest card into pieces. "I think he's half crazy."

As Ray swung open the lobby door, a little bell attached to the jamb gave a tinny tinkle. He paused to indulge in brief but baleful study of the room. "Just opinionated," Ray declared and followed Monroe into the lot.

She waited by the driver's door of Ray's thirdhand Grand Marquis and, once Ray had opened it for her, bounded gracelessly onto the seat. Ray pitched his duffel into the back among his boxes and sacks, his lone piece of sky-blue hard-sided luggage. Monroe circled twice and dropped onto her folded beach towel with its seahorses and sand dollars, its undifferentiated dog grunge.

"Nice going."

Monroe snorted and shut her eyes, comfortable, content, altogether impervious to censure.

Ray drove through the night, fueled by acrid convenience-store coffee and orange Nabs, kept himself awake with blasts of air from his wing window and late-night radio at full volume— bilious talk for malcontents, lite variety, twangy country ballads, Jesus, Jesus, Jesus. The sky was just brightening to the east as Ray pulled into a rest stop north of Abingdon, Virginia, where he dropped open the glove-box door and drew out his service revolver, a nickel-plated .357 wrapped in an oily rag. Monroe had her nose in his back, shoving him, before he could swing fully out of the sedan.

They wandered a grassy hummock between the car lot and the truck lot in the chill June air. Long-haul drivers napped in their cabs, their running lights lit and their engines rumbling.

A young man raced in off the interstate in a chopped-down pickup, jolted to a stop and lurched out from beneath the wheel to relieve himself in the lot.

"See that?" Monroe ignored Ray, circulating slowly, sniffing each tuft of fescue with scrupulous deliberation. "For the love of Christ, pee!"

A groggy semi driver crawled out of his sleeper and onto the passenger seat of his cab. He rubbed his eyes and stretched, wiped the night's condensation from his side window with his sleeve and spied a man in the grass by the drink-box shed with a shiny revolver in hand, watched a scrawny black mongrel urinate at gunpoint.

To hear him tell it, Lowell had connected again. With a waitress this time. Blond. Lithesome. An employee of the ersatz saloon in the clutter and scree along the bypass where the cuisine is all batter-dipped but for the cheesecake and the patrons are frankly encouraged to leer. He described her to me—the hand-tooled boots, the willowy legs, the brief denim shorts, the gauzy cotton tank top snug against her downy skin.

"And I do mean straight out of the melon patch," Lowell assured me. "That girl was just plain gifted."

I was perched on the end of Lowell's credenza, looking out his office window. He has a view of the entire professional park, from the auto glass shop out by the traffic signal clean across to the chiropractic center on the rise before the woods. With the leaves off the trees, I could even make out a little of the Roanoke skyline—the DoubleTree hotel, the boxy retirement high-rise, the thicket of burger signs on stalks where the interstate runs through.

"My fork had some crud on it," Lowell told me. "So I asked her for another one, and she did like this."

Lowell raised a hand and beckoned to me. He was clear across the room, had rolled himself over to the shelving by the door.

"Come here."

Lowell motioned again from his desk chair. He gave a slight accommodating shove that rolled him halfway to me before he braked himself with his shoe heels.

Lowell has taken to riding his desk chair in a recreational sort of way, backward usually with his right foot for a tiller. He keeps a can of lubricant in his file drawer for the casters, and with a trifling push off the wall by his coat tree, he can pass into a hallway, span it at a headlong clip and clatter across the threshold into my office—those occasions anyway when I have failed to see him coming and have neglected, consequently, to swing shut my office door.

Lowell laid his hand lightly to my forearm. "'I'm so sorry.'" His voice but a breathy whisper which might have been a little stirring from a leggy blond waitress but proved unsettling from a pudgy actuary.

"And hell, I mean I was looking right down her shirt. Could see clean to her belly button." Lowell set in on a tour of his office, rolling backward and musing lasciviously while, for my part, I retreated to his credenza by the window. "I wish you'd seen the way she smiled at me. We had this thing, me and her."

I could see down on the grounds the new girl from reception, the brunette with the ever-evolving coiffure. It's up. It's down.

It's braided. It's teased. It's curled. It's straightened. And always, somehow, it's ill-suited and unbecoming.

I watched her stalk along the circular path through the water garden—provided, that is, that a quarter-acre of hardpan that's host to a puny vinyl pool, a pair of orange koi and a couple of scraggly beds of creeping juniper can actually qualify as a water garden, even if that is what they call it upstairs. Of course, they also insist that the food in the cafeteria is "Mediterranean."

She was smoking a little ruthlessly and clutching herself against the February chill. Ribbons, I noticed. Pigtails.

"We're going back tonight," Lowell said.

"You and Erlene?"

He nodded.

While I watched that girl flick her smoldering butt into the water feature, Lowell prattled on about his leggy waitress as if he were wholly wanting in crippling romantic impediments, as if he weren't afflicted with an actual wife, a combover and a gut. Some fellows get crud on their forks and probably do go home with a waitress, but Lowell is the sort condemned to fresh flatware instead.

Lowell was busy concocting, it appeared, prospective suave maneuvers in his head when he glanced across the hallway toward my office door and called out, "He's in here."

I was expecting Ronald from downstairs. Hotshot, underwriter, cologne addict and full-time medical miracle—both brain-dead and gainfully employed. Ronald is evermore stopping by with questions, usually pretty much the same questions he stopped by with the week before. Ronald takes no notes, has no memory to speak of, no grasp much of policy provisions or standard insurance English. Apparently, he succeeds instead on dopey charm and a near debilitating miasma of British Sterling.

Over by Lowell's window, perched on his credenza, I was steeling myself for the confectionary onslaught of Ronald's cologne when I caught sight of the uniform sleeve, the holstered Glock, the unnaturally shiny oxfords.

"Mr. Tatum?" He said it just generally into the room.

He was of the standard police build and type. Strapping, I'll call it, and square-headed, with high-school football in his background and probably a little juvenile thuggery.

"Over here."

"Mr. Paul Tatum?" He read my name from a scrap of paper. I nodded. "Could I speak with you, sir?"

He gestured for me to join him in the corridor and retired from the doorway. Lowell grinned at me as I passed, winked, and asked loudly if I was knocking over liquor stores again.

Officer Hayes, his tag read, and he had assumed already his veneer of professional sympathy by the time I joined him—the slight smile, the downcast glance, the undermining insincerity. "I'm afraid I have some bad news, sir."

I recall how unnaturally calm I was as I cataloged my family members and acquaintances. Clearly, somebody was dead—my brother maybe in Topeka, or his insufferable wife, or one of their wretched children, or Uncle Trent the dowser and crackpot with the tar-papered cabin on the Cape Fear River, or my cousin Ray, the deputy sheriff in Mobile.

I left to Officer Hayes all of the wincing and the huffing, watched impassively as he ran through his repertoire of compassionate tics. Finally he told me with a shake of his head, "It's your son, sir. He's been killed."

I didn't respond straightaway, didn't quite know what to say. Politely, funereally, Officer Hayes considered the floor tiles until I'd managed at length to speak.

"Who?"

It was hardly the manner of reply Officer Hayes had anticipated and made provision for. He lifted his head and looked dully at me, consulted his scrap of paper.

"Your . . . uh . . . son, sir. You are Mr. Paul Tatum of 3418 Wycliff Road?"

I nodded.

"Johnathan Troy Everhart." He was reading again. "Your son, right?"

"Oh," I said. "My son."

He followed me into my office where I dropped into my desk chair while he remained standing opposite.

"What was it? A car wreck?"

Officer Hayes shook his head. "Homicide, sir."

"Where?"

"New York City, sir."

"You know, he's not really my son," I said.

Officer Hayes considered again his scrap of paper. "They've got you as next of kin."

"What about his mother?"

"Dead since ninety-eight."

"And her husband? That Everhart?"

"Ninety-six." He creased the scrap and shoved it into his trouser pocket. "So, he's not your boy?"

"Well, I guess I'm technically his father, but I never even knew him, only saw him once or twice."

"So he is your boy?"

"His mother and I had a . . . thing. We were like nineteen." I gestured helplessly. "She wanted to keep the baby."

Officer Hayes nodded, curtly and disapprovingly.

"I got a picture once around Christmas. I talked to him a time or two on the phone. He stopped by maybe three or four years ago here at the office, but I never really knew him."

"They need an ID on the body, sir."

"Isn't there a wife or something? A girlfriend? A neighbor? A buddy?"

He shook his head. "Why don't you come downtown and talk to my lieutenant? I'm sure we can work something out."

"Right now?"

Officer Hayes nodded. "I'm parked out front. I'll drive you over."

I glanced significantly at the paperwork on my desktop and groaned as if I were, in fact, professionally put upon and mired up. "Five minutes?"

Officer Hayes nodded again and retired into the hallway. I could hear the squeak of his shiny oxfords, the mechanical shiver of the water cooler just up the corridor as he had himself a drink. Lowell put his feet to the wallboard by his coatrack and gave a shove. He streaked backward across the office, his chair casters chattering, as I stepped around my desk and shut my door.

Officer Hayes had precious little to say to me on the way into town, so I was free to listen to the staticky chatter from his cruiser radio. The professional park and the station house are hardly fifteen minutes apart, but that proved time enough to establish Roanoke as a lawless fleshpot of the mid-Atlantic. The Roanoke PD was busy rousting hookers from the bus depot. They'd intercepted a man with Connecticut tags hauling cocaine on the freeway, had collected the perpetrator in a pair of convenience store robberies, were closing in on a fellow wanted in a barroom pistol-whipping and had run across a load of unbonded liquor in a paneled furniture truck.

"Is it always like this?" I asked Officer Hayes as he wheeled down the ramp off the bypass into center-city Roanoke.

Like most southern towns of any size, the place looked evacuated—no pedestrians to speak of, little traffic, a few office towers, sandwich shops, vacant storefronts, abandoned warehouses, unlimited parking. Officer Hayes eased up to the curbing before the police station—grimly modern and foreboding, a marriage of steel and raw cement.

"Like what?" he said as he shed his harness and shoved the shifter into park.

He pointed me to an orange plastic chair in an upstairs hallway.

"The lieutenant'll be out in a minute," he told me and indicated with the pitch of his head an interrogation room across the way from where I could hear a pair of fellows lavishing obscenities upon each other.

Straightaway a woman came by and put to me a question. She was some manner of civilian employee with a heat-lamp tan and prehensile fingernails, and she wanted to know if it was my Chrysler Brougham they'd fished out of the quarry.

"I drive a Cavalier," I told her, which she made, for some reason, a note on her palm about prior to lingering to take in with me a heated exchange from across the hall. There was rancorous dispute just then as to who was the bigger motherfucker.

I sat around in that corridor for probably an hour before the lieutenant finally came out shoving before him a fellow in handcuffs who looked little more than a boy. Wiry and blond, he was lavishly tattooed and had an appreciable funk about him, smelled of sweat and cigarette smoke, refuse and neglect. The lieutenant called in a uniformed officer to usher that boy along the hall, but he wheeled about and jerked free by the drink box so as to dredge up, while glaring our way, a mighty gob of phlegm that he made a vile show of discharging upon the linoleum.

"Mr. Tatum?"

I nodded, and the lieutenant motioned for me to walk with him. He was beefy and black and unshaven.

"Sorry for your loss," he told me with arid constabulary compassion.

His name was Rucker. Lewis. He had his own office on the far end of the squad room at the head of the hall, his own drip coffeemaker, his own ratty settee, his own endearing nickname. Lulu, they called him, or rather, Lieu-Lew.

His signature, as it turned out, was in feverish demand. He'd hardly pointed me to a chair and settled in behind his desk before the pageant began—clerks and secretaries, officers and detectives, all of them with releases and requisitions, with arrest reports, with file transfers, with warrants and wants. They'd tap on the door frame behind me. "Hey, Lulu," I'd hear.

So I sat and waited further while he signed and initialed, while he answered questions, while he dispensed advice and trafficked in cordial interoffice insults. He was obliging a detective with

his initials by the time I noticed the fax. It was a grainy transmission on slick curling paper with "NYPD" in bold black letters at the top, but the typewritten message was indecipherable
from where I sat. Beneath it was a reproduction of a driver's license with its photo murky and poorly resolved. The state of
Florida, I could see that much. Johnathan Troy Everhart.

The lieutenant made triplicate notations on tissuey requisi-
tion sheets and shoved them at the detective who was hardly
into the squad room proper before I heard a light insistent tapping on the jamb from the next supplicant.

"Lulu?"

"Give us a minute, will you?"

Rucker tidied up the clearing on his blotter. He plucked the
curling NYPD fax sheet from the disheveled stack of papers on
the front corner of his desk and offered it to me.

"The officer filled you in, right?"

I nodded.

"They found that in his pocket."

The license had been badly photocopied to begin with and
then muddied further in transmission. I could read Troy's name
and height and eye color, could barely make out the Florida state
seal and a scrap of the signature of the commissioner of motor
vehicles.

"Did he get robbed or something?"

"Hard to say. A neighbor found him dead in his apartment."

"He had an apartment?"

The lieutenant nodded.

"In New York?"

Rucker consulted an open notepad. "Thompson Street, somewhere around Canal. This is news to you?"

He watched me and waited, would prove singularly accomplished at waiting which, doubtless, was the key to his professional success. I'd been earwitness to his talent for salty profanation, but that was plainly just a sideline and a manner of release. His true gift, as it turned out, was for silence, wholly unperforated and nagging. He just sat there and said nothing but in a way that was inviting, almost insistent really. So I obliged the man. I talked.

I told him everything I'd told Officer Hayes, but with enlargements and unconsidered elaborations. I spilled out the shoddy unbecoming details of my dalliance with Troy's mother, auditioned assorted extemporaneous excuses for my sundry failings as a father, took pains to inform the lieutenant I'd sired the boy back in '73 when people were freer with their ardor than lately they'd become.

Rucker gnawed his lip by way of gloss and response, loosed the occasional noncommittal neck noise as I prattled on, cobbling up further mitigations and allowances for myself, until I'd wearied of talking, until I'd given entirely out of personal clemency. Only then did Rucker trouble himself to speak.

"What do you say I call up there and tell them you're coming? Probably won't take but a day."

I think I must have nodded, believe I even managed to grunt my assent. It was the residual shame talking, I suppose, seeping out as best it could. He jotted a name and a number on a sheet of notepaper, ripped the page free and offered it to me. I heard a sharp pecking on the door frame as I took it.

"Hey, Lulu," somebody said.

The town of Hogarth, Virginia, lay gathered snugly in the bowl of a steep and secluded valley with the Blue Ridge Parkway, the Appalachian Trail, and tens of thousands of acres of national forest rising to the west. To the east was a spur of the uplands given over to apple and nectarine orchards and, beyond it, the James River and the Lynchburg pike. A lone roadway entered Hogarth from the south through a gap in the ridgeline and passed directly through the heart of town, continuing but a half dozen miles north where it went to gravel and then hardpan before giving out entirely at a pipe gate by a tractor shed overgrown with climbing roses.

Ray Tatum slanted in before the sheriff's headquarters in the old post office by the courthouse. He wore one of his generic khaki uniforms, his leather utility belt, his nickel-plated sidearm.

Ray climbed from the car and stood by while his Grand Marquis dieseled and sputtered and came, at last, to its usual consumptive stop. Clumps of lavender bloomed on the manicured plot of ground before the courthouse. As Ray adjusted his shirttail and hiked his trousers, he sniffed the fragrant air and, in keeping with his custom, declared aloud that it was freighted plainly with promise.

The squad room was as he'd imagined, which is to say jumbled and cluttered and charmless. The walls were hung with police notices and FBI fliers, with a topographic map of the county and a Shell Oil map of the state, a New Testament calendar and the stuffed head of a brown bear. The far wall was graced by a sizable oil portrait of a barrel-chested man with a spectacularly bushy mustache who was identified on a brass plaque affixed to the gilded frame simply as "Colonel Hogarth." He wore a broadcloth suit and a shimmering glaze of hair pomade, held some manner of rodent in his arms.

"Are you Mr. Tatum?"

A woman in civies—a print blouse and extraordinarily snug jeans—smiled up at Ray from her desk.

"Yes. Ray."

Gazing at him still, she dropped her jaw and shouted, "He's here, Chief!"

Ray had yet to meet the sheriff, had only corresponded with him through the mail and spoken to him on the phone. The sheriff's wife had personally arranged for Ray's ramshackle rental house with its shabby furniture and musty throw rugs, its scorched saucepans and mangled flatware. Ray had arrived prepared to praise it with a smile.

The sheriff emerged from his office. His given name was

Brady Wilfred Quinn, but nobody much called him anything but "Chief." He proved as beefy as Ray had imagined, though he was remarkably light on his feet, seemed to glide across the squad room and offered one hand for shaking while he clapped Ray stoutly on the back with the other.

"Well, well. In the flesh." He squeezed Ray's neck with nearly therapeutic force. "Did you find that house of yours all right?"

"Yes, sir. And please do thank your wife for me. It's just ideal." Ray's grin felt ridiculously toothy to him.

"Good. Good." The chief laid an arm full about Ray's shoulders and steered him through the squad room. "Come on and meet the crew. I believe you've spoken to Ailene. This is Carl."

Carl was thirtyish and soft around the edges. His haircut looked to Ray self-inflicted.

"Walter, our parking revenue man."

Walter was ashen and wheezy. From his chair by the wall, he waved at Ray with his tire-chalking stick.

The chief squired Ray toward a third deputy, who rose from his desk as they approached. He was severely thin, agitated, grim.

"And this is Larry."

Larry glanced only sidelong and curtly at Ray before stalking across the squad room toward the back hallway where he entered the toilet and slammed the door shut behind him.

"Don't mind him," the chief said. "He's just torn up about his wife. She ran off with a dentist from Blacksburg—what was it—three, four years ago?"

Carl and Ailene shrugged and nodded irresolutely while Walter brandished his chalking stick like a scepter. The chief sorted through the jumble of papers on Larry's desk and came away with a postcard which he handed to Ray. It was printed across the front with a smiling cartoon molar holding a toothbrush in its tiny gloved hand.

"He still gets hot about it whenever he comes due for a cleaning."

The chief snapped his fingers twice at Ailene, and she fished a platinum badge out of her in-basket which she handed to the chief who shoved it at Ray. "Why don't you ride with Carl? He'll show you the ropes. It's pretty much like I told you on the phone. We serve a few warrants—bad checks mostly. We write a fair amount of traffic citations. We've got your garden-variety thieves, a little bootlegging. There's a patch of pot in the timber here and there. We get a couple of domestics a month and our share of bar fights, but then you've see all that down in Mobile."

"Yes, sir. I guess I have."

"Chief."

"Right. Chief."

"There's a fairly rough lounge out past the quarry at the motor hotel, a colored roadhouse down on the river. But, all in all, there's usually nothing too awful gaudy afoot."

The chief tapped on Carl's desktop with his knuckles. "Take Ray here around. Show him the hot spots, and I don't mean Little Ruth's and the goddamn Chuckwagon!"

It was Carl's practice to ride low in the cruiser seat, to drive with a lone finger curled around the wheel and with an arm stuck out the window to dangle down the door panel. As Carl rolled slowly south on the main street, Ray could hear the rhythmic clicking of the wheel bearings.

Carl twitched his head as he spoke. He pointed exclusively

with his nose. "Videorama." There were no pedestrians about, no traffic much along the street. "Feed and seed. Five-and-dime."

Spindly water-starved geraniums languished in raw cement planter boxes along the sidewalk. Faded royal blue banners flapped from the lightposts, each imprinted with the golden silhouette of a gnarled fruit tree. The roots snaked about to form the words "Hogarth Apple Butter Festival—1988."

"Hardware. Hair Palace. NAPA. The IGA's just up the road."

Carl turned onto a side street, where he motored past a branch bank and a vacant warehouse, a defunct and abandoned service station. He crossed a creek on an iron bridge that groaned and popped alarmingly, and they rolled into residential Hogarth, tony Hogarth, old-money Hogarth. The roadway was lined with ancient white oaks. Their canopies met and intertwined overhead, and their roots had ruptured and buckled the concrete sidewalk. Windfall limbs littered the street.

"Had us a hell of a storm the other night. Look at this mess."

Carl ran over a tree limb, snaring it on the undercarriage and dragging it loudly along the road. He rolled to a profane stop by the curbing just before a pair of massive ornate cemetery gates.

Ray climbed out for a look around as Carl plunged under the vehicle, and Ray was frankly surprised by what he saw, had hardly expected tasteful prosperity here in the middle of nowhere much. The cemetery was bordered on two sides by five grand antebellum houses, four of which were in excellent repair. Their front gardens were abloom, their lawns immaculate, the structures themselves stately and imposing. The fifth, however, was overgrown and slightly tumbledown, conspicuously neglected.

"Pretty over here," Ray said.

Carl wriggled out from beneath the cruiser, a knobby oak branch in hand. "Mostly old timber and lead-mine money. That was Colonel Hogarth's place." Resorting to his nose again, Carl indicated the grandest of the homes which was flanked by ancient silver maples and crape myrtles in glorious bloom.

"Chief's aunt's in it now. Hell, it's all widow women through here." Carl glared uncharitably toward the house in disrepair, with its weedy gardens and its cluttered and overgrown yard. A window screen lay on the porch roof. A cement birdbath had toppled into the shrubbery. There was some manner of abstract sculpture on the lawn that looked like rusting shipyard salvage.

"Some Yankee woman in there." Carl shook his head disapprovingly as he climbed back into the cruiser. "Thick as flies anymore."

Carl backed the cruiser into a well-worn slot in the scrub and the bushes, just where the Lynchburg pike bottomed out at the base of a precipitous hill. He switched on his Vascar deck as a furniture truck blasted past them off the slope, and Carl checked his LCD screen. Seventy-two miles per hour. A Buick sedan motored past. Sixty-eight.

Carl unrolled the throat of a white paper sack on the seat between them which was translucently grease-stained and rested upon a road atlas so as to spare the upholstery. He fished out a pasteboard tray of onion rings and settled it onto the dash, pulled out a hamburger wrapped in oily waxed paper and handed it to Ray.

Ray worked the paper loose to find the bun was soggy with

meat juice and milky coleslaw seepage. Chili grease dripped onto Ray's trousers. Carl drew from the bag a burger for himself, ripped away the wrapping and nipped off a quarter of the sandwich at a bite. His chin glistened, and chopped cabbage dribbled down his shirtfront.

A pickup truck rolled past. Sixty-four.

"Now, Walter," Carl said, chewing, "he swears by the double-cheese when any fool knows the chuckwagon's the way to go." Carl raised his burger to make educational use of his gnawed patty. "Chopped steak," he said. "That double-cheese, it's all hoof and suet. What do you think?"

A greasy nugget of chili dropped into Ray's shirt pocket. "I think I'm going to need a shower."

A midnight-black Cadillac raced past doing seventy-three. "The ophthalmologist's wife," Carl said, indicating the driver with an onion ring. "That woman's got some legs on her."

A dinky, battered Datsun truck zipped by them, racing down the hill at sixty-nine. "The least Hayes girl." Carl shoved the remainder of his burger into his mouth, working it over exhaustively. "She's a tramp."

A candy-red tow truck roared past. Seventy-one. "Randy from the Sinclair."

Ray slyly dropped the remainder of his hamburger out the cruiser window as a massive maroon Delta 88 came yachting off the hillside. Carl caught a glimpse of the Florida front tag and checked his LCD screen. Fifty-eight. He fairly roared out of the shrubbery. "Goddamn snowbirds!"

Ray watched from the passenger seat as Carl approached the driver's door of the Oldsmobile. Through the rear glass, Ray could see the octogenarian behind the wheel, that part of him anyway that cleared the front seatback—his bony withered hands on the steering wheel and the liver-spotted crown of his head.

Carl lectured him through the open side window, leaving, Ray noticed, his palm to rest upon the hilt of his revolver. Ray shook his head and groaned, dug chili from his shirt pocket. He could not, for the moment, find much trace of promise in the air.

Monroe stood waiting for him on the front porch of their shabby house. She didn't yip and bark with pleasure in the way of most dogs, failed to writhe and wriggle with affection. Instead she merely sat on her haunches and watched Ray roll in his Grand Marquis through a gap in the autumn olive hedgerow and into the yard.

Once he'd climbed the steps and had mounted the porch, Monroe nudged his thigh with her nose, once and firmly, a little punitively even. "Back at you," Ray told her.

Ray made do for dinner with a packet of nuts and chuckwagon burger combustion. He set up his television on the dinette table and labored fruitlessly for the better part of an hour to pick up a station before he elected to sit quietly in the gathering darkness instead and listen to the cattle, restless in the pasture alongside the house, to the mice in the walls, to Monroe as she stood in the front room barking at their homely camelback sofa.

Ray shed his khaki shirt, his trousers, and dropped them on the bedroom floor, crawled onto the squeaky iron bed in his faded paisley boxers. His cotton spread was fresh from the five-and-dime and still creased. His new sheets were stiff and dye-

scented. Ray switched on the bedside lamp, and the bulb at-
tracted immediately some manner of minuscule green bug that
swarmed about the shade. Beetles and crickets rebounded off
the window screens with startling force.

Ray read from a local history of Hogarth and environs presented to him by Ailene at the end of his shift which was little
more than a pamphlet, stapled together and crudely printed.
The author was identified in busy gothic script as Mrs. Ted
Hogue, and she held forth at windy and rhapsodic length on the
gracious natural bounty of the local countryside.

She enthused over the climate and the dramatic upland terrain. She identified both products of local manufacture: carpet
backing from the plant on the Lynchburg pike and pressure-
treated planking from the lumber works upriver. Mrs. Ted
Hogue supplied a fractured impressionistic tour of town which
was long on bubbly turns of phrase but largely barren of particulars. She proved to be keen on the massive rock courthouse and
fonder still of the stately Baptist sanctuary. The town cemetery
was decidedly less to her liking as the effect of the place had
been spoiled for Mrs. Ted Hogue by a particularly tasteless
marker which she found unduly showy.

Monroe, as was her custom, leaped onto the bed to circle and
settle, to sprawl at the foot of the mattress with a throaty groan.
She leaned heavily against Ray's legs, crowding and shoving
him as Ray came across a brief biography of Colonel Hogarth,
timber merchant and smelting furnace magnate, husband of
Lila, father of Jean and Orville, proud owner of Silas—a three-
legged muskrat—which Mrs. Ted Hogue offered up without
the scantest trace of enlargement.

Ray tossed the pamphlet onto his night table, switched off

the bedside lamp and drew up his scratchy top sheet with its penetrating chemical stink. The air was clammy but cool, and the night was profoundly dark. Ray shifted and sidled beneath the bedclothes. Monroe, grumbling, followed him across the mattress and pitched heavily against him.

A man up the road called, Ray had to figure, to his dog—anxiously, loudly and with a palpable hint of exasperation. "Queenie!" he shouted. "Come on here, Queenie girl!"

The style of my house, I've been told, is abbreviated ranch. That anyway was the realtor's phrase of choice. Stunted bungalow would probably be more accurate. The place is small and boxy, squat and shallow, indifferently put together. The clapboard siding is made of presswood which swells and rots and flakes. The windows are balky and aluminum. The shutters are ebony wood-grained plastic. I have an unadorned stovepipe for a chimney and a frost-blasted slab of cement for a front porch.

I can't say I ever really wanted a house, wouldn't even have been shopping for one if Lowell hadn't visited on me a mortgage deduction calculation. I'd been happily renting for years, had a frumpy little duplex apartment off the freeway past the airfield with a fenced-in paved patio out back. My carpet was amber deep-pile, my icebox avocado green. The place came with a full-time landlord and weekly lawn-care service. The only tool I needed to have on hand was a phone.

But then Lowell went and took a dogged interest in my personal tax burden, and he talked me into a homestead and a half acre of weedy yard. These days I caulk. I paint. I clean out my gutters. I track roof cement onto the rug.

I can't say I'm much on yard work. It's been four years now since I first intended to take shears to my shrubbery—my sprawling forsythia and leggy mock orange, my sweetspire and thorny pyracantha. I'm prone to let the lawn become immoderately unsightly before I trouble myself to mow. I raked leaves once a couple of years back but didn't take to the ordeal.

Accordingly, my lot tends to be a bit of an eyesore, but only partly on account of neglect. My dogwood trees are blighted and failing through no fault of my own. My lone white oak was disfigured by ice, and a sumphole is slowly forming in my side yard. The seepage from it is slightly frothy and tartly aromatic, looks suspiciously iridescent in the sun.

I've little doubt that my neighbors resent me. They are young couples for the most part, house-proud and horticulturally ambitious, are evermore beautifying and renovating, weeding and mulching. Twice a year, without fail, they all fertilize and lime. I catch them sometimes glancing direly at my property as they jog along the street.

Inside it's a different story as I'm a pretty formidable housekeeper. My rooms are evermore neat and uncluttered. My knickknacks are artfully situated. My surfaces shine. In truth, I'm afflicted with a bit of an overactive interest in housework, which I'll allow anymore is within hailing distance of a clinical compulsion.

I don't just vacuum and dust and tidy. I routinely indulge as well in a strain of domestic trigonometry, am given to altogether senseless adjustments to the furnishings about the house. The fluted edges of my cherrywood end tables must run parallel to my couch arms. My oscillating fan has to be precisely centered within its coil of excess cord. I require my interior doors to rest snugly against their rubber stops, and I prefer that all of my lampshade seams face north.

I won't even mention the custodial care I take with my book spines and magazine bindings, the time I devote to my stacking Bakelite coasters. Suffice it to say that while my yard has the look of uncultivated savannah, my house inside would appear to be maintained by an order of monks who've taken together a vow of anal retention.

Now I'm aware, of course, that I could do with a more profitable enthusiasm, and a few months back I attempted to act on a scrap of therapeutic advice that I came across in the *Roanoke Times and World News*. Twice a week or so they run a syndicated column by a woman who gives herself out as a counselor and a healer. In truth, she's just a ceaseless scold with a gossamer New Age turn of phrase, a Californian, that is to say, by psychiatric disposition.

She'd run a letter from "Fussy in Phoenix," who'd had a troublesome fixation, was unnaturally preoccupied with toilet bowls and toilet rings and water closets in general. He was evermore disinfecting them, was scrubbing and scouring and buffing, and he allowed that but for the fact his house had only a bath and a half, he'd hardly know the leisure to go outside.

I'd endured by then a few episodes in my front doorway when I was off for work and would notice a shifted lampshade seam or a magazine askew and get drawn back in for a spot of domestic triage, so I was prepared to be attentive to what that columnist advised.

She opened by berating Fussy in Phoenix for a paragraph or two which tends to be her technique and her method. Then she diagnosed him, identified, that is to say, his issues which proved in fact subliminally colonic. She followed with a smattering of gauzy healing talk, and by way of a cure, she urged Fussy in Phoenix to procure for himself a cat.

She assured him that he would find cat ownership edifying as cats are better organized than the majority of people and are reliably more democratic about their compulsions. They'll bathe. Then they'll nap. Then they'll frolic maniacally which they'll readily dispense with for dinner, and that columnist suggested that Fussy in Phoenix might profit from the exposure.

Like most spectacularly specious advice, this cat business struck me as penetrating and sensible at first. I was convinced straight-off that a fellow helplessly scrubbing his toilets in Arizona might, after all, realize improvement from the company of a cat. Moreover, I figured my case was sufficiently benign that I could probably take a cure from no more than a rented feline.

They seemed, however, at the animal shelter reluctant to engage in a lease for a cat. They did show me a seven-year-old male in precarious health who wasn't, they told me, likely to last through the year. At their insistence, I held him on my lap and stroked his head as instructed which prompted him to spear my finger on an incisor.

I came home, consequently, with a dog instead, a gangly wire-haired mongrel named Luther. He had enough terrier in him to make him uncommonly unsightly but sufficient hound to render him sedate. I'd noticed him fluffing his little dog bed there in his animal-shelter cage, and he'd worked and shoved it until it fit at handsome angles in the corner. Then he'd left off with the thing entirely to plunge his snout in his water dish which had struck me as a healthy indication of Luther's divided interests.

Of course, I should have come away with just a finger bathed in iodine.

For a dog, Luther wasn't remotely troublesome or destructive. He'd only ended up at the pound because the woman who'd owned him had died, and she'd been, I was told, feeble and decrepit there at the end, so Luther had grown accustomed to sprawling about and making his own amusement. As healing and edifying pets go, then, Luther should have been ideal. The advice, however, I got from that woman in the *Roanoke Times and World News* proved as incisively effective as newspaper therapy ought to be. I didn't show, that is to say, any measurable improvement though the dog grew remarkably worse.

I was accustomed to mounting my own transgressions against the scrupulous order of the house. I'd neglect sometimes to swing the bathroom door full back against its stop, or I'd allow my coiled phone cord to get kinked and twisted. But, like most compulsive people, I'd developed a satisfying knack for chiding myself and being simultaneously contrite. Luther simply served to throw my cycle out of balance as he foisted on me the obligation of correcting him as well.

When I'd snap at him, however, for shoving his food bowl off his mat or for knocking the braided throw rug before the kitchen sink out of true, he'd peer up at me with a blend of generic canine guilt and quivering bewilderment. So not only didn't Luther function as a therapeutic mitigation, he antagonized me, and his habits played on my nerves. Consequently, the evening he nosed the door and I turned him into the yard and then neglected to let him back into the house, we were likely not between us terribly overwrought about it.

I'll admit to a hint of anxiety when I couldn't locate him in the morning, but it dissipated steadily throughout the course of the day. He wasn't, in fact, much on my mind by the time I rolled up in the evening, and I had my key already in the lock when I heard my neighbor shouting at me.

She calls me Bill which I tend not to answer to since it's not, after all, my name, but she's been calling me Bill for so long now it would be awkward to correct her. Furthermore, as I'm usually slow to respond, she's decided I'm hard of hearing, and the woman has taken to shouting at me whenever we have a chat.

I turned to find her standing in her carport with my dog from where she siphoned off an appreciable dram of air. "Is he yours?" she yodeled at me.

I looked at Luther who looked at me, and we came together to an understanding.

Hers is the sort of family typical to my street—middlingly affluent and neatly nuclear. She has a husband who departs each morning in the dawning and returns home in the dusk, carries a canvas briefcase, invariably wears chinos and high-mileage nubuck shoes. They have two children. The girl is blond, sevenish and blisteringly disrespectful, while the boy, maybe five, is loud in a far-reaching and adenoidal sort of way. When contradicted, he tends to drop to the ground in a wailing heap. It would appear that he and his sister run the enterprise next door which seems devoted to their happiness and ceaseless transportation.

I shook my head, eyeing Luther. "Never seen him before," I said.

"He came in the cat door last night. Millie and Brandon just fell in love with him." She scratched Luther's ear, and he nuzzled against her, watching me. "He doesn't have a collar."

"You ought to keep him. Seems nice enough."

We heard together a baritone thump from inside her house, which was followed by the sound of glass breaking and a hoot of laughter from her son. She wheeled and dashed onto her screen porch and in through the side door. "Honey," I heard her call in that rising tone of tremulous diplomacy that has supplanted the belt and the hairbrush, the bare legs and the crape myrtle switch.

Left alone, Luther and I considered each other in silence for a moment before he rose from his haunches, tucked his tail and set about to bark. He fairly howled at me, showing his teeth, and chased me up my walk. I was full in the house with the door shut behind me before he saw fit to shut up, and it has been his habit and avocation ever since.

I came home early after my visit to the Roanoke police department, was avoiding Lowell chiefly, was putting off the interview he was bound by nature to conduct, the detailed explanation he'd require. I eased into the drive to find the children next door dismantling their latest conveyance, some manner of Dodge, I could tell, from the medallion the boy had snapped off the hood to chew.

Apparently they'd given over dressing Luther to pillage their mother's vehicle. Luther had a linen table runner tied around his neck like a scarf and so felt, I guess, more intrepid and dashing than normal, bold enough anyway to pursue me clean onto my stoop where he lingered for a considerable spell yelping.

I hadn't, even by then, decided just what I'd do. The shame I'd felt at the precinct house had, like shame will, evaporated, so I was back to thinking myself a paternal technicality which allowed me to take the whole wretched business for an imposition. I even managed to fume a little in the mirror on my closet door as I shed my tie, uncreased it and returned it to its peg.

I didn't know I had need of my Bostonian shoe box full of photos until I'd fetched the thing from the coat closet shelf and had settled it onto my lap. It was a small matter for me to lay my hand upon his picture as it was filed precisely where I'd left it, just there between the snapshot of Clovis, the piebald schnauzer I'd owned as a boy, and the Polaroid of my mother's brother's girl in her dress whites. It was in, that is, with the animal attachments and the relations once removed.

I don't suppose he was but seven or eight when it was taken. He was sitting on a curbstone in a scarlet cowboy shirt, in black trousers with ivory fringe along the seams. He was smiling, grimy and immoderately toothless.

I remember when it came, was working out of Marietta at the time. The thing had been forwarded twice, and the envelope was tattered and taped. I'd stopped by then even thinking of them at all, so it was a startling item to fish from my rusty little postbox by my apartment door, an authentic shock, I recall, as I spied it among the bills and the bulk-rate clutter.

There was a sort of a note on the back of the picture, brief and in pencil, an accusation, I was tempted to believe. "I hope you are well," she had written. "We are."

I had rubbed it away with my dampened thumb and had trimmed down that photo to fit in my billfold. Frequently after the bourbon and steak, the strippers and draft beer, back when I was entertaining clients almost nightly, we'd pass inevitably through a besotted maudlin interlude. They'd moistly show me pictures of their kids, their houses, their cherished sports coupes, their wives.

I'd respond with my solitary snapshot. I'd fix my mouth and tell them, "My boy."

I considered him there on his curbstone with his cowlicks, his gritty fingers, his hazel eyes, his gummy smile. I carried him with me into the kitchen where I settled him onto the dinette as I dug in my trouser pocket for the crumpled sheet from Rucker's pad. He seemed to watch me—a child still, alive still, my son.

The cord hung, I noticed, pleasingly unkinked from the wall phone as I took up the receiver and dialed the 212 area code.

3

He spat his breakfast at me, puny atomized flecks of it that he broadcast with velocity every time he spoke. Naturally, he was a tireless talker, bellowing over the drone of the engines, peppering me with reconstituted eggs and damp airborne crumbs from a granola bar. His name was Willard, but he insisted I call him Hank. He was in paints and primers, stains and shellacs. As he was far too blubbery and sizable for his airline seat, he'd raised the arm between us and was migrating in my direction.

"Don't even have to sand it," he shouted moistly into my ear. "No sizing. No priming. Won't fade, chalk, blister, or pop. Dries in half an hour—winter, summer, rain or shine."

He laughed, shaking his head in wonderment as I blotted myself dry with my crumpled napkin.

"Goddamn latex enamel miracle, if you ask me." He took up his plastic cup from his tray table and shook it until the ice in it clattered and rattled like rocks in a can. "Oh, nurse!" The stewardess up along the aisle glared at him, at me. "I'm parched, sugar."

She stalked toward us, her lips fixed in a grim smile. She looked a little too old for the job, a touch too matronly, decades removed from her perky and chipper years.

Hank shoved his cup at her. "Smirnoff," he said. "Two times." He winked as she dabbed a grainy speck of granola from her cheek and examined it on her finger end.

I became aware of a mechanical whirr, felt a slight but decisive jolt and looked out past Hank to see the wing quivering, the flap retracting. I heard a staticky pop overhead and the voice of the captain addressing the cabin. I was seized, as is my custom when flying, by irrational mortal terror.

"Morning, folks. This is Captain Billings up in the cockpit . . ."

That was all I could make out before a shift in cabin pressure stoppered up my ears as the nose of the plane dropped out of level. I glanced uneasily at Hank and swallowed hard to clear my earways.

". . . forty-two degrees. Wind out of the northeast at twelve knots. Visibility, three miles . . ."

I lost him again to the shifting pressure and so made up my own calamity which is what I do when I fly instead of sleeping or reading or eating. I twitch and fret and fully expect to perish.

"We've got us a raging inferno in the cargo hold. Blinding smoke in the cockpit. That's Cape May off to your left."

The unfortunate news is always delivered in that languid commercial-pilot drawl. I tend to blend the scraps of what I can hear when my ears clear with what I'm disposed to imagine.

"We're coming up on catastrophic hydraulic failure, about one hundred and sixty miles south-southeast of LaGuardia. We'll be plunging shortly into the Atlantic, so feel free to wander about the cabin."

"What's he saying?" I asked Hank and pointed as casually as I could manage toward the speaker overhead.

Hank spilled closer to me still. He laughed. "Pretty windy myself," he told me and fanned the air before his face. "It's that goddamn granola. Hardly fit for a goat."

Hank grabbed my upraised finger, squeezing it tightly in his doughy palm. He cackled. He tugged.

We approached out of the east, vectoring well out over the sea at Sandy Hook and sweeping in directly above the Verrazano Bridge. We descended through broken clouds, following the eastern shoreline of the harbor over the Brooklyn shipyards and the clotted expressway traffic. The plane quivered and bucked, and our pilot made a folksy indecipherable announcement. The stewardess lurched by with a plastic sack and snatched Hank's cup from his hand.

"See if you can buckle up," she told him with a doubtful shake of her head and a vile little sneer, plainly persuaded there wasn't webbing enough to span him. As Hank watched her work her way forward through the pitched cabin, he leaned over and spritzed me with a merciless remark.

We followed the East River north along the entire length of Manhattan. I caught glimpses of the bristling skyline beyond Hank through our window. Planes lifted off from Newark to the west. Barges and ferries dotted the harbor. A yellow blimp advertising spark plugs drifted sluggishly above the Hudson.

Flying out of Roanoke, we had traveled for a time north along the spine of the Appalachians, passing over hundreds of thousands of acres of uninterrupted hardwood forest. From twenty-eight thousand feet, the bare treetops had looked plush and wooly. The woods had draped the ridges and the hollows like a blanket flung onto the ground, and the sight had been impossibly serene, unavoidably belittling. The Blue Ridge Parkway, parting the treeline and conspicuously manufactured, had made for a stark intrusion in that wilderness, had done duty as a scar.

Descending into LaGuardia, everything was different. Reversed. I spied the odd scrap of greensward in the Bronx—separating apartment buildings, bordering motorways—sparse beleaguered clumps of trees, the exotic perfection even in winter of the manicured outfield of Yankee Stadium. The rest was roads and rooftops, smokestacks and bridge towers, the scummy chop of Flushing Bay.

We banked steeply, nosing down into a sharp descent. I heard the pinging of an electronic duotone, an unintelligible declaration from the pilot. We touched down with a jarring thud, and our stewardess announced the local time as if we had just winged in from Dar es Salaam and had need to reset our watches.

Hank and I had agreed to share a cab into the city, but that had been a while back, over the Chesapeake. Apparently Hank had reconsidered his options since then, and we parted company in the concourse, halfway to the terminal. It was an altogether informal sort of leavetaking. Hank simply veered into a bar as if drawn there by magnetism. He dropped his satchel and grip on the floor and settled onto a stool, meaning plainly to linger and stay.

I can't say I much minded as I was damp enough already, and I accounted myself streetwise and fit to make my way around. Not, of course, that I actually was, but I had visited New York a few years before and had ridden in Lowell's K car pretty much all over the city. Naturally, we were lost and disoriented the bulk of the time, but I had successfully put that from my mind in the intervening years.

Lowell and I had come up for an actuarial conference, and we had decided to stretch our per diem by staying in a New Jersey motel rather than joining the other conferees in the pricey hotel in town. Or rather, Lowell had decided for us and had picked our digs as well, had veered off the roadway without consultation. The establishment was in Weehawken on the way to the Lincoln Tunnel, and it sat perched upon a sooty hunk of rock above the highway from where it advertised rooms by the hour on an illuminated sign.

The parking lot was full of trash and low-slung sedans, and the building itself was uninviting and dowdy, but Lowell declared that we would only be sleeping there, after all—or lying awake listening to rutting moans and traffic, as it turned out.

The manager, a swarthy little man in a cubicle behind a sheet of Plexiglas, was shrieking at a customer as we entered the motel office. The two of them were disputing the bill and making violent threats upon each other.

The way I recall it, the customer—who had the dainty aspect of a pipe fitter and was wearing a slate gray shirt with his name in an oval above the pocket—had taken a room for an entire sixty minutes but had discharged prematurely because the woman he'd hired in the motel office had continued to stimulate him well after he'd instructed her to stop. He felt that he qualified, as a consequence, for the thirty-minute rate, and he argued the girl they'd supplied him had been, in a manner of speaking, defective.

That swarthy little manager was of another mind altogether, and the atmosphere in that motel office was ripe with ugly high feeling, so I was inching back toward the door and trying to slip into the lot when I heard Lowell say, "Excuse me, Tony."

The customer wheeled on him with a murderous glare, studied Lowell up and down and determined he'd never so much as clapped eyes on him before, appeared, in fact, prepared to believe that Lowell was possibly clairvoyant. I don't think he ever noticed that he had his name stenciled on his shirt, and he couldn't have known Lowell for the sort who routinely prefers to be familiar.

"Me and him," Lowell told the manager. "Three nights," which proved sufficiently intriguing to prompt that swarthy little fellow and the customer both to consider us in studious silence for a time. They were helplessly constrained, I have to think now, to imagine me and Lowell engaged together in some manner of middle-aged white-boy sexual congress, seventy-two prepaid hours of swampy actuarial love.

Our room was entirely enclosed against the weather which is the best thing I can say about it. Otherwise, it was cramped and dirty and shabbily furnished and, while the HBO—as advertised—was free, you had to pay with quarters for electricity to the television. There wasn't even anything to pilfer, no ashtrays or coasters or stationery or tiny packets of hair-care products, nothing anyway readily visible to the naked eye.

We did carry home, we discovered later, a healthy dose each of lice.

As it turned out, we didn't even save any money. We had to pay four dollars for every trip through the tunnel into town, and no matter how we studied the parking signs, we still collected seven tickets. So we spent about twice what we would have if we'd stayed in the midtown hotel with the other conferees who were content to attend the workshops and socialize in the mezzanine bar, but Lowell insisted we needed to be out on the prowl.

He'd come armed with a list of lounges and nightclubs he wanted us to visit, but we never in fact actually found one of them. We enjoyed instead an uncanny knack for coming across the sort of place where the whiskery patrons at the bar would lift their heads off their forearms and glare at us as we passed through the door.

By sheer happenstance, we wandered one evening into a lower Broadway bar with an ample supply of seemly young women in it. The place was bordering on deafening what with the music and the chatter, and it was cramped and inordinately crowded. Most everybody there was dressed in stylish lower Broadway black but for me and Lowell who looked like we'd just dropped by for an audit.

Lowell was gazing about, I recall, trying to catch some young lady's eye and persuade her with his best worldly smirk that he, in fact, was desirable when a girl slipped up beside me and spoke flush into my ear.

"Why so sad, little man?" she said.

She'd hardly allowed me occasion to fumble about for a response before she laid a palm to my cheek and kissed me full upon the mouth. She was maybe twenty, and she tasted of cigarettes and tequila. Once she'd pulled back, she giggled and lurched into the bowels of the bar.

Lowell saw the whole thing and dragged me outside to dissect it, so we stood there on the corner of Broadway and Broome, away from the music and the clamor, and engaged between us in an explication of that girl's motives and intentions, a thoroughgoing and futile study of my possible allure. I'd been driven, we decided, to look bewitchingly forlorn by the countless water rings upon the bar.

Lowell reasoned he could stand to look more gloomy himself, so from that point on Lowell indulged about the island of Manhattan in a hangdog expression that suggested a blend of fresh grief and psychosis and, naturally, served to get him nowhere much.

By one or two in the morning, we'd be ready for Weehawken and would set out on our search for the Lincoln Tunnel entrance. We learned to depend on West Side prostitutes to point the way, and on our last night there, Lowell tried to hire one out of desperation. She had on a shiny wig that looked to have been made from shredded tarpaulin, and she was noticeably less grimy than her girlfriends. But once Lowell had acquainted her with the name of our motel, she proved entirely too revolted to go.

So based on little more than three days of semidrunken disorientation, I'd deemed myself acquainted with New York. Consequently, I waited in the queue for cabs outside the terminal at LaGuardia with precious little in the way of trepidation, and once I'd piled into the back of my taxi with my grip, I barked out my destination as if I might know where it was.

"Duke Hotel," I said. "Waverly Place."

The telephone number Lieutenant Rucker had given me had connected me with a detective in the first precinct. Doogan, his name was, and I'd asked him to recommend a modest hotel in the city. He'd come up with the Duke and had named for me the park that it was near which I'd not seen fit somehow to jot down.

The driver eyed me in the rearview mirror. He was plainly not from New York, wasn't even from North America. "Manhattan?" He said it only three times before I understood him.

I shrugged, and he told me something in Farsi, I believe, which, as comments go, was probably unsavory.

He had a little book, a five-borough gazetteer, that he consulted as we raced toward the city and in through the Midtown Tunnel. He lost interest in the thing whenever we were stopped in traffic, would busy himself instead with senseless jockeying and blowing his horn. Sometimes he'd chatter out the window with one of his fellow cabbies alongside us who, like him, had left his home and traveled halfway around the world to sit on a New York City cross street in a yellow Crown Victoria. Then the light would change, and he'd stomp the gas and begin again to read.

It turned out that the Duke Hotel was just off Washington Square Park at the southern terminus of Fifth Avenue, and it was a passable improvement on our Weehawken motor inn. The desk clerk's sheet of Plexiglas was a bit less greasy and smudged, and my room was not, I learned at length, infested with parasites.

I had a television that I didn't have to pay pocket change to watch, a handsome plastic bronze ice bucket though I could never locate the machine, a miniature sewing kit in a basket on the vanity counter along with two ounces of wintergreen mouthwash and a packet of cream rinse. The walls were painted a deep oppressive brown, and the furnishings were of that ponderous faux-distressed variety. There was a clock radio on one bedside table and a black metal coinbox on the other for purchasing quarter-hour interludes of vibrating Magic Fingers.

My lone window afforded predominately a view of a dingy airshaft, though I could see in a gap across the way, beyond a rusting downspout, the bare limbs of a plane tree bordering the park.

I immediately unpacked my grip, refolded my clothes and stored them away in the bureau drawers as I am one of those people who actually uses motel dressers. Then I perched on the mattress and studied the printed instructions on the face of the phone. I was convinced still that the entire enterprise would be simple and straightforward, was feeling even a little fatherly now that my son was dead. I could smell on the air scorched peanut oil—the pervasive stink of Chinese takeout—felt up into my shins the lurching thump of a guest along the hall and heard what I took at first for the muffled burbling of a pigeon.

The sound was coming through the bedside wall, and leaning to press my ear to the plaster, I heard a woman in the room next door who sounded to me to be weeping.

They sent a cruiser for me, and I was waiting out front under the awning as it pulled up, a blue-and-white, dinged and battered, filthy.

The driver rolled down his window. "You Taylor?"

"Tatum," I told him.

"Yeah, right. Hop in."

There were two patrolmen up front, a white one and a black one. They talked only to each other, mumbling back and forth across the seat while I sat ignored in the back behind a steel-gauge divider. We moved easily through traffic, heading cross-town, east toward First Avenue and the morgue. The black officer kept the radio mic in hand and cleared our way, when need be, with the aid of a loudspeaker on the roof.

"Pull right. Pull right. Move it, pal." And the cabs and sedans and panel trucks would grudgingly ease clear a path for us. At signal lights, he'd give a yip on the siren and we'd roll cleanly through the intersections, stopping traffic on the avenues.

I don't believe they were in any particular hurry. I certainly wasn't, heading like I was for the morgue after all. I got the impression that was simply the way they traveled through the city—moving as they pleased, indifferent to right-of-way and the ordinary courtesies of driving. Clearly, to their way of thinking, that stuff was for civilians who didn't count for nothing exactly but counted plainly for less.

Detective Doogan was waiting for me, him and his partner, a vain clotheshorse named Vitale. They were leaning against the trunk lid of their navy Chevy as we pulled up to the curbing. The black officer pointed them out through the windshield with his mic hand as the driver, wordlessly and with the click of a button up front, unlatched my door.

They proved to be an odd pair, Doogan and Vitale, seemed together to thrive on frivolous interpersonal contention and argued vigorously about most anything that came to hand. As I approached them, they were hard at a dispute on the topic of some film that had lately opened and they neither one had seen which hardly prevented them from debating the cup size of the actress in the lead and disagreeing as to the order of her assorted former husbands.

I stood by for a moment while they picked and nattered at each other. From up the avenue, I heard the sharp amplified voice of the black patrolman instructing a motorist in what fashion precisely to get the hell out of his way.

"Mr. Tatum?" Doogan offered his hand. "We spoke on the phone. Thanks for coming." He jabbed his thumb and, by way of introduction, informed me, "Vitale."

Vitale smoothed his hair with his palm and flicked a speck of lint from his suitcoat, favored me with a head twitch and a wink.

"I'll go tell them we're here," he said.

Vitale crossed the walk and climbed the brief stairway before the building opposite, pausing to admire his reflection in the door light. He was fit, impeccably groomed, passably handsome. Vitale gave off self-satisfaction like a scent.

Doogan was another case altogether. He heaved himself upright from the trunk lid with a groan. He had fairly walked out of his homely black wing tips and had secured the fraying hem of a trouser leg with a half dozen staples. His dress shirt had been white once but not recently, and the jacket sleeves of his blazer left off well before his forearms did.

"Tough duty," he said as he took hold of me at the elbow and steered me across the walk. "Lost my boy a while back."

"I'm sorry," I told him.

"Ahh." Doogan waved off my compassion with a swat of his

hand. "What are you going to do?" He drew open the door for me and swept me ahead of him into the building with a courtly flourish.

We took an elevator car up to the eighth floor. It moved slowly, creaking and shuddering, clattering up the shaftway.

"Duke all right?"

"Yeah. It's fine."

"Stayed there a month once," Doogan told me. "Trouble at home," he added, pressing his lips together and nodding grimly.

Vitale was waiting at the landing, checking his tie knot in the chrome finish of a fire extinguisher as the doors slid open, and they had a simmering conversation as we walked. It concerned some piece of precinct business that meant nothing to me, but it was, I noticed, a normal sort of chat for the pair of them, routinely contentious give-and-take over the pneumatic whine of a bone saw from up along the corridor and in spite of the extraordinary odor of the place, a noxious and nearly intolerable blend of chemistry and decay.

My hand shot to my face, covering my nose and my mouth. I must have vented some manner of disgusted grunt because Doogan straightaway drew a handkerchief from his pocket and left off with Vitale to offer it to me. Like his shirt, it had probably been white once as well. I declined it with a shake of my head, chose instead to make do with my bare palm and the spicy residue of Skin Bracer.

The room they took me into was bright and cold and empty but for an unsightly little settee and, above it, a truly wretched painting of a Parisian street scene, worse than most dentists would hang. The large window opposite the door was covered by galvanized louvers, and we drew up squarely before it.

"Ready?" Vitale smoothed his jacket front as he spoke.

I certainly considered that I was ready. I had seen, after all, any number of bodies—my parents, their parents, my cousin with the ruptured spleen, my neighbor's child from up the street with the incurable blood affliction. As it turned out, though, I had discounted the dignified burial clothes, the handsome satin-lined coffins, the mortician's art.

I nodded, and Vitale threw a toggle switch by the window casing that caused the louvers to swivel open and reveal, on the far side of the glass, a corpse laid out on a metal table. The thing was naked and translucently white, was bloated and hairy and hardly looked to have ever been alive.

"Take your time now," Vitale told me. "Look him up and down. Any distinguishing features. Moles. Birthmarks. Scars. Anything at all."

That struck me as altogether senseless advice, since I only had to see his face to know that it was Troy. I think I might have even favored Vitale with a cutting sidelong glance before I ran my gaze up the length of the corpse and discovered, consequently, just a jagged stump of bone where a head should have been. The skin about it was ragged and hacked, was stained and mottled with gore. I'm reasonably certain that I managed to point, feel sure that I hinged open my mouth and was intending as well to speak, but I lost just then my gumption and my bearings both together.

They were looking at me, Doogan and Vitale, as I set about collapsing, were watching me as they declined, in storied New York fashion, to get involved. So I dropped unchecked to the floor in a fairly comprehensive faint, and I recall still the tang in the back of my throat as my head bounced off the tiles.

Carl drove at his customary stately velocity with his lone finger draped over the wheel, past the puny branch bank and the
abandoned rolling mill, over the railroad siding, beyond the
dowdy motor hotel at the junction and onto the hilly Lynchburg
pike.

"Wave to Grover," he said.

Carl lifted a hand in salute to a fellow on the roadside who sat
in a web-bottomed lawn chair perilously close to the blacktop.
He wore green twill trousers and brogans, a white cotton shirt
buttoned snug up to his throat, sat grinning deliriously as he
flailed both arms over his head.

"He's a little scrambled."

Ray waved as they passed and then turned to watch Grover
visit a giddy spot of semaphoring upon the driver of a Snap-on
tool truck just behind them.

They ascended on switchbacks toward the spine of the ridge
as Carl accelerated in pulses, swinging them sharply in and out
of the turns on the soft cruiser suspension. Ray could feel beads
of perspiration breaking out on his upper lip. His stomach
churned and gurgled, and he tasted in the back of his throat a
sour blend of Nescafé and Wheat Chex. Ray braced himself
with both arms and gulped the cool upland air while his skin
took on a pastel minty hue.

"Where the hell does this woman live anyway?" he barked as
they yawled around the final bend and gained the level spine of
the ridge.

Carl glanced toward Ray. "Look at you." He brought the
cruiser to a lurching halt in the roadway where it was still sway-

ing on its soggy springs as Ray rolled out of the passenger seat to wander through the ditch, dabbing at his brow and inhaling deep therapeutic breaths of air.

They were almost upon Ray before he heard them, before he caught a flash of scarlet through the leaves and the rhythmic clatter of a cup upon a pack frame as the first of the hikers stepped into the roadcut from the woods. He was lanky and shirtless. A rolled foam bed mat was strapped to the top of his pack, and he held in his hand a trail map, tattered at the creases.

"What did I tell you?" he shouted back over his shoulder as he cleared the ditch with a jangling hop and stepped into the road.

His companion emerged from the trees sucking on a grimy plastic water bottle. His pack was hung thick with laundry—socks and briefs, mud-stained shorts, flannel shirts, a dank rolled-neck sweater. He vaulted the ditch and gained the roadway as well.

"Hey, man, is this six-eighty-two?" the lanky, shirtless one asked Carl and pecked at the blacktop with the toe of his boot while clawing at a bug bite on his forearm.

Carl nodded.

"Told you." The shirtless hiker continued across the road, leaped the far ditch, and wheeled about to walk backward, to gloat.

"Yeah, yeah." The one draped with laundry followed him, fanning at a swarm of gnats thick about his head. He stumbled through the far ditch and down a weedy slope before plunging into the woods along the throat of a narrow trail marked by a swath of white blazing painted onto a sweetgum trunk.

"A.T.," Carl told Ray. "Twenty-five hundred miles of the grubbiest sons of bitches the Lord ever let breathe." Ray drew open the passenger door and slipped into the cruiser while Carl, for his part, lingered in the roadway and gazed toward the trailhead, the forest. "Ain't no chopped steak in the wilderness," Carl declared, nodding gravely, philosophically even.

Carl turned off the blacktop onto a narrow gravel side road and wheeled into a cleared lot in a crease of terrain, drawing up before a ramshackle trailer encrusted with additions—porches, stoops, sheds, lean-tos. A woman stood in the yard in a quilted housecoat and sneakers. She sucked violently on a cigarette and was talking already to Ray and Carl before the cruiser had rolled entirely to a stop.

"I just got a little weepy. Went through a spell of flashes and such."

"Is that her?" Ray asked.

Carl shook his head. "Crowder woman from across the road."

"No, sir," she said, "I can't hardly see that there's call for such as this."

As they stepped over to join her on the lawn, Ray and Carl heard shouting from the trailer, saw together a woman pause before the front screen door, a large woman, irate and shrieking.

"'Cause I told you to, that's why! And I ain't washing no more of these damn things!"

She pitched a dinner plate out of the trailer without troubling herself to open the storm door first. The saucer punched cleanly through the screen wire and clattered down the rickety front steps to shatter on a hunk of cinder block in the yard.

"Her?" Ray asked.

Carl nodded grimly. "Myra Jean Tuttle."

"What's her problem exactly?"

"Female," the Crowder woman offered. She shoved a fresh Carlton between her lips but couldn't manage to raise a flame from her childproof disposable lighter. "These goddamn things!" She hurled the lighter across the lot into a patch of thorny scrub. "Give me a match."

Carl and Ray patted their pockets, shook their heads.

"Well, shit." The Crowder woman struck out across the lawn and waded directly into the underbrush.

"Myra Jean claims to be going through the change," Carl informed Ray. "It's got her hormones up. "It's made her—"

As Carl struggled for an apt description, Myra Jean Tuttle reappeared in the doorway with a slender gentleman in hand. He was wearing a pair of emerald green coveralls and a sweat-stained meshweave cap, and Myra Jean Tuttle gripped him by the back of his collar and the seat of his pants. She flung him with remarkable force, failing again to trouble herself to swing open the screen door, and he punched out the rest of the ragged wire, carried it with him as he tumbled down the steps and came to rest chin foremost in a patch of clover by the bottom landing.

"—peevish," Carl said. "It's made her peevish. Hello, Harold."

Harold jerked his head and grunted at Carl, kneaded his shoulder joint.

"Are you all right?"

"I guess."

Harold struggled to his feet, brushed himself off and adjusted with meticulous sartorial care his bright brass coverall zipper tab.

"Harold, have you got a match?" the Crowder woman called,

thigh-deep in the thorny scrub at the edge of the yard. Harold dug through his pockets and pulled out a squashed and tattered pack.

Myra Jean Tuttle stalked the length of the trailer in her bare feet, thumping about on the wall-to-wall. Each time she passed the open doorway she threw an item into the yard—a serving platter, a clock radio, a curling iron, a brindled house cat.

"Mangy fucking bastards, whole pack of you!" She took aim and fired the TV remote at Harold who ducked and dodged, but it still caught him blunt-end foremost just above his ear.

"Ouch," Harold said, not with any enthusiasm or anguish but just with appreciable practice, it sounded to Ray.

"Why don't we call in the game warden?" Ray suggested. "Have him bring her down with a dart?"

Myra Jean Tuttle sailed, one by one, a half dozen soup bowls into the yard. They shattered on the rickety stairs, on the stepping stones and stray cinder blocks, on each other. "Shut up!" she shrieked at Harold who had not so much as offered to speak.

Larry rolled in off the road in his cruiser, his beacon pulsing. "Boys," he said, strolling up. "Myra Jean off her feed again?"

"It's a bad one," Harold allowed. "Worst I've seen. We ain't going to have nothing to eat on."

"What do you think?" Larry said, chiefly to Carl.

"Not a thing for it but to go get her."

Larry inhaled deeply and sucked spit through a tooth gap in a show of back-hollow resignation. "Well," he said, "all right then."

Carl unholstered his revolver and handed it to Harold. Larry did the same as Ray looked on. "Rather get bit than shot," Larry told Ray as he mounted the stairs.

"What do you want me to do?" Ray asked them.

"We'll holler for you when the time's right," Carl said and followed Larry up the stairway where together they dodged a hail of teakwood salad bowls. Myra Jean Tuttle shouted at them from the doorway, allowed hotly that she was down at the moment on men.

Ray drew his nickel-plated .357 from his holster and handed it to Harold who shoved it into the waistband of his pants. "You'd best watch your jewels," Harold volunteered, and it sounded to Ray like experience talking. "She's got one hell of an aim."

Ray was only just mounting the lowermost tread as Carl and Larry charged into the trailer and fell together upon Myra Jean. They shouted at her, lavishing her with abuse, and she responded with glorious freshets of profanation. They grappled violently, the three of them. Sizable and estrogen-depleted, Myra Jean Tuttle lurched about the trailer home carrying Carl and Larry on her back. A Jim Beam Christmas decanter came to hand as they tussled through the front room, and she swung it vigorously at the pair of them in turn. They responded together with uncharitable commentary.

Ray had gained the porch proper and was malingering at the doorway as the radios began to squawk from the pair of cruisers in the yard.

"Hey, mister." Harold pointed across the lawn with Carl's pistol. "Somebody's calling you."

Ray looked to see the Crowder woman sitting beneath the wheel of Carl's sedan. She was shouting into the unkeyed radio mic. "What!?"

"Anybody there? Carl? Ray?" It sounded to be Ailene.

The Crowder woman laid her lit cigarette on the dash. She drummed the microphone against the steering wheel and then raised it again to her mouth. "What!?"

Ray peered into the trailer as Myra Jean stumbled back along the narrow hallway, barking Carl and Larry against the paneling. Carl gave her a halfhearted tap on the skull with his lacquered nightstick, and she replied with a searing remark before vanishing with the pair of them into the tiny bathroom.

"Carl? Ray? Anybody?"

"What!?" The Crowder woman was pounding the microphone on the cruiser door frame as Ray relieved her of it and reached in to adjust the gain.

"Go ahead, Ailene. It's Ray."

"I've got something for you."

"Oh, yeah?"

"Something juicy."

Ray met them at a bedraggled little gas station and country grocery back along the ridge where they sat together on a weathered bench, swatting gnats and drinking sodas. They had left their packs at a shelter, had backtracked at a run along the trail and down the road, were winded still and rose to their feet as Ray rolled in off the blacktop.

Ray carried those boys to the trailhead and followed them

into the woods. He'd never walked the Appalachian Trail before, not any scrap of it, and was surprised it wasn't grander
somehow, wider at least and less weedy and overgrown, something more than just a path in the forest.

The shirtless hiker assumed the lead and guided Ray down a
side trail beyond the shelter toward a spring that bubbled and
percolated out of a rude rock basin. The overflow trickled along
a mossy slot that plunged down the hillside. They left the path,
slipping between two basswood trees, and continued along a
fold in the terrain toward the trunk of a fallen locust.

"I was taking a crap," that shirtless boy said by way of explanation.

Ray saw them before those fellows had even pointed them out
as they were glaringly conspicuous among the fern fronds and
the rotting leaves, were scoured of meat and tissue, sinew and
flesh, were pocked and bleached and brittle, were jarringly out
of place. Ray squatted alongside them. He pulled a ballpoint
pen from his shirt pocket and ever so lightly touched the index
finger with the chrome tip of it, causing the thing to snap off
cleanly at the second joint.

Ray scratched carefully about the bones, dredging and exca-
vating, clearing away the clay. He revealed a thumb and a carpal
bone, the knobby head of a radius, somebody.

"Maybe a bear got him, or a bobcat. I hear there're even
cougars up here." The shirtless hiker looked to his buddy, who
nodded, who scratched.

Ray rose to his feet and peered into the murky half-light of
the old-growth forest, at the towering tulip and ash trees, the
gnarled oaks and redbuds, the serviceberries and laurels. A gray

squirrel chattered from a limb above the springhead while, well back along the ridgeline, a woodpecker drummed for grubs.

"Yeah," Ray said, exposing those boys to his thin and frankly patronizing law-enforcement smile. "Maybe so."

Ray waited at the roadside where he could hear them struggling up the rise, creaking in and out of the switchbacks. The chief's Country Squire wagon was hardly built for mountain travel, was low to the ground and absurdly front-heavy, useless off the blacktop and a four-door sled in the snow. The chief nosed the thing into the ditch by the roadway where his muffler hung up with a metallic groan.

The hikers were waiting at the trail shelter. "Tell them," Ray said, and the shirtless one set in with his narrative, electing to begin in Georgia where they had gotten out of their car.

The chief tolerated that boy nearly into the Smoky Mountains before he interrupted, before he inquired, "Just who was taking the crap?"

The shirtless hiker raised his hand.

"And you looked down and saw them?"

"Yes, sir."

"Hell of a thing," the chief said, shaking his head.

The shirtless hiker nodded obligingly and then jabbed his grubby companion who nodded as well.

Ray stepped between the basswood trees with the chief just behind him while Walter struggled along with a camera bag and a shovel. Ray had taken a stick to the bones and scratched away more clay with the pointy end of it, revealing three ribs, a portion of sternum, a bit of collarbone, the entire skull. The chief lumbered to a stop on the steep hillside, braking himself against the fallen locust trunk.

"Might want to watch where you step," Ray suggested, even as the smell hit them both, foul and fecal.

The chief lifted a shoe, caked along the sole, and swore with considerable vigor and variation.

"I figured they might have brought him up from the pasture," Ray said. He pointed downslope to a slight break in the trees where a trace of fence line was visible.

"They who?"

"Whoever did him in. Could have brought him down from the shelter too, but the pasture's a little closer."

"Let's just slow down here, Ray." The chief lowered himself to his haunches and knocked a clod of dirt from a rib, cleared away a bit of leaf mulch from a femur. "Nobody had to kill him for him to get dead. He's not all that deep. Hell, maybe he was just out here hunting and burst a seam, fell down and died. Leaves covered him up. Ground washed over him. Did you think of that?"

"He fell down and died all right." Ray kneeled alongside the chief and lifted the skull free from the loam to reveal a pair of fractures on the backside of the cranium, two jagged spots where the bone had been shattered and punched through. "But he had a little help."

The chief shoved his finger through one of the holes and exhaled loudly, put-upon and irritated. "Get out the camera," he said to Walter, "before we lose the light. Me and Ray'll turn him up for you."

With that, the chief took up the shovel where Walter had dropped it and handed it to Ray. He then reached into Walter's shirt pocket and helped himself to a cigarette before perching on a rock to smoke it and watch Ray peck with the shovel blade at the roots and the clay and the quartzite. Ray shortly turned up a trio of shirt buttons, a trouser clasp, scant pocket change, a pair of molded sneaker soles, and rotting scraps of leather upper.

"Has anybody gone missing around here?" Ray asked Walter, the chief.

"There was that Tally girl," Walter offered.

"She turned up," the chief told him.

"How about that banker down in Lynchburg? The one that made off with all that money?"

"Turned up."

"And that preacher? Remember? Ran off with the organist."

"Turned up."

Ray scratched up a manner of comb, a pick actually, with long and slender teeth and a black plastic handle fashioned in the form of a clenched fist. He tossed the thing to the chief.

"I could have told you," the chief muttered. "These goddamn people."

Ray discovered a ring, lumpen and caked with clay, and cleaned it, scratching at the dirt with his fingernail. It was light and cheap, pewter or plate, and manufactured to fit two fingers at once. Raised on the face were the letters *RAJ.*

"Ring a bell?" Ray tossed it to the chief as well.

The chief considered the ring on his palm and shook his head. "Work many homicides down in Mobile?"

"One or two. Of course, they all had meat on them."

"Good enough for me." The chief stood from his rock and stretched as if from a nap. "Won't be much behind it. That ilk'll kill each other over any damn thing. You'll put it together or you won't."

The chief plucked another cigarette out of the pack in Walter's pocket and set about whistling a jaunty tune which Ray recognized straightaway as the theme song from that Tuesday-night sitcom about the happy-go-lucky investment banker and his dyspeptic Siamese cat.

4

My lone cube of ice was melting in a trickle down my forearm as I held it, wrapped in a soggy paper towel, to my head. The Chevy interior stank of stale cigars, and the velour backseat was lavishly stained, dappled with encrustations. Vitale drove, dodging ruptured asphalt and sunken manhole covers as he raced south along Second Avenue. He'd adjusted the rearview mirror so that he might watch himself watch the road.

"I'm going to call that son of a bitch," Doogan declared hotly. "See if I don't."

"I would," Vitale said, veering around a bus.

"Didn't I tell him, 'No hands. No head'?"

Vitale nodded. "I heard you."

"Didn't I say it looked like some kind of mob shit? Didn't I tell him that?"

"That's what you told him."

Doogan turned to eye me over the seat back. "And he was supposed to tell you. Told me he'd tell you. What was that sorry bastard's name?" Doogan asked, glancing at Vitale.

"Lieutenant Rucker," I said.

"Yeah, Rucker. The minute we get back, I'm calling Richmond."

"Roanoke," I said.

Doogan glared at me. "Head all right?"

I examined my soggy paper towel, pink with diluted blood, and felt the tender knot, touching it lightly with my finger.

"Not really," I told him.

"Good."

We took Houston Street west across town, stopping briefly at a bakery off Mulberry so Doogan could pick up some manner of confection which was flaky and cream-filled and dusted with powdered sugar. He fished it straightaway from its bag and ate like he'd gone unfed for days as we raced south down Varick. Vitale preferred a different bakery and another manner of confection which he apprised Doogan of as prelude to a debate.

The First Precinct house was situated on a curious piece of Manhattan real estate, faced a narrow cobbled street just below Canal that gave onto the roundabout where the Holland Tunnel disgorged its ceaseless stream of traffic. The inner median had been made into a sort of park with statuary, staked saplings, and the odd slatted bench. A pedestrian bridge, encased in fence wire, crossed over the motorway. I spied a woman in the park, saw her as we nosed in before the precinct house. She was sprawled on a bench, sleeping perhaps, or dead from the exhaust.

The precinct building itself was ancient and crumbling. It was attached still to a working stable for the mounts, Vitale told me, of the officers who patrolled Battery Park and the grounds around City Hall. The squad room was perfumed, consequently, by the rising stink of dung and hay and ammonia.

Vitale and Doogan had it all over Rucker and his crew when it came to quasi-bureaucratic uproar, and they led me back to their desks through what looked like an active insurrection. Detectives were barking at each other, at civilians and handcuffed suspects, were shouting—a few of them—into their telephone handsets. Vitale's and Doogan's desks sat side by side facing a windowless wall that was dingy and institutional green, puckered and flaking, an ideal candidate for Hank's latex enamel miracle. Doogan cast about the squad room for a chair and, finding one under a grungy perpetrator across the way, removed it by main force. As he approached with the thing, Doogan did me the courtesy of swabbing the seat with his nasty noserag.

"Now then," Doogan said, settling the chair before me and motioning for me to sit, "let's see that picture of yours again."

I reached for it in my topcoat pocket, had showed it to them in the morgue once they had managed to revive me, once they had settled me onto the settee beneath the hideous Parisian street scene. They had shared, at the time, a glance between them—weary and put-upon—which they revived once Doogan had relieved me of the photo, once they had spied again young Johnathan Troy Everhart perched in his cowboy outfit upon the curbing.

"And this is the only one you've got?"

"Like I said, I never even knew him."

"Did you tell that shithead in Richmond?"

"He thought I ought to come anyway."

Together Vitale and Doogan spewed breath and swung their heads from side to side. "I'll just bet he did," Doogan told me and pointed to a file on Vitale's desktop. "Did you know your boy had a jacket?"

"A what?"

"A sheet," Vitale said as he flipped open the folder and shoved it at me.

The top page was some variety of police form, a smudged carbon, and Doogan reached over to point out the pertinent lines. "Three arrests. Two convictions. Simple possession. Possession with intent. He did eighteen months."

"Drugs? That's what this is about?"

Vitale shook his head. "Money," he told me. "That's all any of it's ever about anymore."

"Think you'll find the guy?"

"Maybe," Doogan allowed, "once we've got a positive on the body."

"How about his friends? His neighbors? They'd know him better than I would."

"There was a girl up the hall who thought she could ID him, but we figured we ought to start with you. Protocol, you know."

"Might be some pictures back at his place," Vitale suggested. "We could go poke around, maybe pick up"—Vitale drew a notepad from his pocket and flipped it open—"Miss Sykes. Carry her over to the ME's."

Doogan nodded. He groaned and rose from his chair. "We'll have somebody run you up to the Duke."

"I want to go with you," I told them. "I want to see where he lived."

Again they indulged in snorting and head wagging. "No," Vitale assured me, "you don't want to see that mess."

But I was insistent in my way, not that I actually wanted to go with them, not that I was legitimately anxious to see where he'd lived, but I felt demeaned and diminished as a father, marginally insulted and inconsequential, was anxious to display a paternal interest in Troy now that he was murdered and dead.

"I want to go," I said. "I need to go." And it sounded, I suppose, so very much like something a father might say that Vitale and Doogan failed to spew breath between them, neglected to shake their heads.

So we rode the short distance uptown to Troy's apartment building which sat opposite a parking garage on a quiet block of Thompson Street, just up from Canal. The super—plump and balding—let us into the lobby, where he was shoving trash around with a broom, and I followed Doogan and Vitale up the stairwell which was steep and poorly lit. We climbed to the fourth floor and slipped in single file along a cluttered corridor where Vitale stopped before an apartment door, pulled out a key from his jacket pocket and sliced with it through a length of yellow crime-scene tape along the jamb.

I don't know that I can do justice to the stench and the gore. The smell of the apartment was thick and putrid, and the near wall was generously splattered with gristle and effluvia. A piece of bound carpet before the TV was comprehensively stained with blood which had gone brown and powdery once it had dried. It had seeped across the hardwood flooring and had pooled against the quarter round, had leached, Doogan informed me, through the plaster of the ceiling downstairs.

Doogan probed the carpet edge with the toe of his shoe. "A

juicy one all right." He said it with what struck me as admiration.

I continued to the lone window on the back wall, raised the sash and stuck my head outside. It was a short trip, as the apartment consisted of a single cramped room with a Pullman kitchen, but the air proved hardly better in the back alleyway, tainted like it was by the reek of Dumpster seepage and incinerating fuel oil. I could see a man across the way through his apartment window. He was standing before his television in his undershorts, was massaging his scrotum as he swilled translucent skim milk from a gallon jug.

I drew back inside to find Doogan sifting through the clutter of the only closet while Vitale removed the drawers from the built-in bureau by the bathroom door and dumped their contents onto the sofa cushions—mail mostly, discarded bills, catalogs, grocery coupons, a faded Polaroid of Troy's mother.

"Know her?" Vitale asked, showing it to me.

"His mom." She'd grown jowly, and her hair was cropped close and highlighted. She was standing in front of a run of board fencing, alongside a spruce the color of bread mold, was grinning slightly and looked tired to me, looked a trifle disappointed.

"How about her?" Doogan had emerged from the closet with a glossy eight-by-ten in hand, a photo of an arrestingly shapely woman in a bikini who cradled a speargun in her arms.

"Ursula Andress," I told him.

Doogan flipped the thing over for a closer look. "Oh."

The rest was just rubbish and clothes. A wallet, use-worn and empty but for a video rental card, a box of Rice Krispies in the kitchen cupboard, a jar of dill spears in the icebox, shoes, trousers, a couple of topcoats, a bale's worth of newspapers, and about a bushel of magazines—*TV Guide*s chiefly, and glossy celebrity piffle. They gave up, Vitale and Doogan did, and ushered me into the hallway.

"Four-D?" Vitale asked, and Doogan nodded, pointing up along the corridor. I followed them, lingered behind them as Vitale rang an apartment chime. I could hear jaunty insipid music from inside. A woman drew open the door.

"Sorry to bother you, Ms. Sykes." Vitale pitched against the jamb and shoved a hand suavely into his trouser pocket. "Got a minute for us?"

She was perspiring, and she raked with her fingers a strand of damp hair from her face. "No bother." She stepped out of the doorway, and I followed Vitale and Doogan inside.

She wore some sort of shiny black exercise outfit which fit her snugly and left her bare at her midriff. Remarkably, it flattered her in the way that form-fitting ensembles rarely seem to suit the women who see clear to tug them on, but she was lanky and sleek and could stand to be constricted. She was more handsome, I noticed, than beautiful, more wholesome than openly beguiling.

"This is Mr. Tatum." Doogan jabbed a thumb my way. "The decedent's father."

Ms. Sykes's bearing and expression transformed precipitously, and she became straightaway a study in heartfelt compassion.

"Oh," she told me, touching my arm, favoring me with a dewy gaze. "You poor man." As a reaction, it was almost too apt and a little troubling in its timely perfection.

"Ms. Sykes here—"

"Lizzie," she insisted.

"Lizzie," Doogan said, "was a friend of your son's. She found the body. She's an actress," he added.

And I do believe I might have actually uttered aloud, "Ah."

She was an actress in the way that some people are pigeon-toed or color-blind, was an actress, that is to say, every day and all of the time. Consequently, most everything she did had the hint of a performance about it, felt a little scripted and rehearsed, naggingly plastic at bottom.

"I'm so sorry," she told me. "He often spoke of you."

"He did?"

She bobbed her head and laid a hand to her throat. "Such a world," she said and turned stage left, toward the television.

Doogan and Vitale were together fixed upon the screen where a trio of young women were aerobicizing on the grassy margin of a dazzling California beach. They lunged and juked and twisted to the sort of music that people anymore call jazz. The girl in front, the blondest one, invited Vitale and Doogan to feel with her a telltale tautening of their gluteus medii while the other two hooted and yipped. They were, all of them, unnervingly brawny.

"Sit," she told us, and we plopped down together on her sofa like a gaggle of trained chimps. "Now, what can I do for you gentlemen?" Like most everything she said, there was frank innocence on the surface with a vaguely salacious underlay.

"We might need you to make an ID on the body after all," Vitale told her.

"Oh?" Again she laid her hand to her throat and then wandered away from us toward her kitchenette. Together we involuntarily lavished admiration upon her derriere until she turned and caught us. "You couldn't identify him?"

I realized presently that she was speaking to me. "He didn't have a—" I pointed what I hoped would be instructively toward my ear.

"Head," Vitale supplied.

"I never really—" I shrugged.

"Knew him." Vitale again. He stood and shoved a hand into his pocket in that fashion he'd apparently decided was debonair. "Still think you can do it?"

She deliberated solemnly for a moment, her fingers to her lips, and then nodded. "May I shower and change?"

"Yeah, sure." Doogan lounged back onto the settee as he spoke, settling in.

Vitale glanced about the apartment. Hers was but a studio as well. "Maybe we should wait out in the—" Vitale half pointed toward the door.

"Don't be silly, Lieutenant." She touched his arm as she spoke. "I'll only be a minute." And with that, she slipped into the bathroom and very nearly shut the door.

"A chubby *and* a promotion," Doogan declared from the couch. "Not bad, *Lieutenant.*"

Vitale eased over to where he could see a revealing bit of her in the vanity mirror while Doogan kicked off his oxfords and rubbed his feet together, groaning like a hound. I did what I usually do when left unsupervised in other people's homes: I snooped, rising from the couch and strolling about the cramped confines of Lizzie's apartment.

Her place was far cozier than Troy's. Her furniture was scaled to suit, and her knickknacks and coasters and magazines were well dusted and pleasingly tidy. One wall was given over almost entirely to photographs, framed and artfully hung, which were, without exception, pictures of Lizzie: Lizzie in costume onstage, as a sequinned flapper, a Chekhovian spinster, a scarlet-lipped chorine, a whiskery tabby. There looked to be nearly a decade's worth of head shots, a graduated history of Lizzie's cosmetology and coiffures.

I paused before a poster for a summer-stock production of *Sweet Charity*. Below the title and the names of the leads, the director and producer, the composer and the lyricist, the choreographer and set designer, was the name "Elizabeth Sykes" far left of center in scanty fourteen-point type. Beside the thing hung a black-and-white photograph, a landscape of sorts, which featured Lizzie artfully posed upon a massive boulder in a stream. She was quite naked, was reclined with her back arched and her vulva on exhibit.

She stepped out of the bathroom wrapped indifferently in a towel, her legs beaded still with water, her shoulders powdered with talc. She threw open the lone closet door and waded in to scoot her ensembles vigorously along the rod, coming away with a stately black frock that she emerged in soon enough from the toilet with her hair drawn back severely. Her heels were low and her bearing businesslike and grave, perfectly fitting for a woman who'd been enlisted to identify a body. I recall wondering to myself at that moment how she'd avoided becoming a star.

Doogan drove, permitting Vitale to ride in the back with Lizzie. I sat up front, clinging to the door arm and braced against the dash as Doogan demonstrated a taste for heedless velocity that made Vitale's driving, by comparison, seem meticulous and stodgy. Vitale held Lizzie's hand in both of his as we raced along the cross streets and up the avenues, as we bounded through the intersections and honed in on the potholes.

"It's just a little room with a couch in it and a window." Vitale stroked Lizzie's hand as he spoke. "When you're ready, I'll open the blinds, and he'll be on the other side of the glass, on a table."

Lizzie nodded and swallowed in such a way as to confirm her apprehensions and misgivings.

"You'll want to look for any distinguishing features. Scars. Birthmarks. That sort of thing."

"He had a mole," she said. "Right here." With her free hand, Lizzie drew back Vitale's jacket flap and laid a finger to his rib cage. "It looked a little like a bean." She left her finger, I noticed, to lie for far longer than was strictly necessary.

Doogan offered Lizzie his dingy noserag as we emerged from the elevator, but she produced one of her own—baby blue and lacy. They escorted her, one to either side, along the corridor while permitting me, the decedent's father, to follow along as I pleased. We waited together in the chilly anteroom as an intern rolled the body into place.

"Ready?" Vitale supported her at one elbow, Doogan at the other. Lizzie inhaled deeply and nodded, and Vitale threw the switch.

She gasped once the louvers had hinged open, quivered conspicuously as she examined the corpse. She then pointed toward the torso and cried out, "Oh, Johnny!" which was just before the vapors seized her and she lapsed into a manner of graceful senselessness that put my clunky faint to shame.

As Doogan lowered her to the floor, Vitale stripped off his jacket and balled it up to lay it beneath her head. Even limp and unconscious, she managed to sprawl most becomingly with the drape of her dress splayed out elegantly about her. Doogan patted her hand to revive her while Vitale, who claimed to be trained and certified, suggested resuscitation.

I stepped past them toward the window for another peek at the corpse, noticed this time that the chest hair was predominantly gray, that the paunch was appreciable, that the feet were flat. I spied a mole upon the rib cage that looked a little like a bean.

The brass coachlights had been lit. The protective plastic sheeting had been removed from the divan in the parlor. The table in the dining room had been set with her linen mats and runner, with her late husband's mother's silver, with her own grandmother's china.

She stood at the window looking out between her heavy brocaded draperies and through her gauzy sheers, watching her nephew, the chief, what of him she could see anyway as he lay beneath the front end of his Country Squire wagon, as he tugged at hoses and examined seals. When he finally crawled out and rose to his feet, he barely brushed himself off at all.

Evelyn McClendon fetched her broom from the basement stair landing off the kitchen and intercepted the chief on her front porch where she swept him clean with what impressed him as uncommon vitality.

It was his custom to take dinner with his aunt on Tuesdays, the night his wife attended her Christian Circle meetings. The protocol was always the same. Evelyn would make him a toddy straightaway, even though he detested toddies, but it was what her daddy drank and his daddy before him, and her recipe was ancient and effectively sacred. So she would bring him the tall glass and then return to the kitchen to cook, leaving the chief to wander the parlor and sip feebly at the thing.

She'd given him a prickly broomstraw scrape on his neck, and the chief rubbed at it as he strolled about the room. He choked down a couple of swallows of his cocktail, had poured more than a few of them into his aunt's potted persimmon in the corner alongside her highboy until the plant had begun to fail. The chief could smell the fatback from the kitchen. He could hear his Aunt Evelyn clapping her pots together and singing her scraps of hymns as she cooked, knew her to be actively occupied incinerating the greens, desiccating the cubed steak and scorching the gravy.

As he roamed the parlor, he paid little notice to the sumptuous decor, to the blood-red sateen wallpaper and hand-knotted Chinese rug, to the assorted Civil War artifacts on display in curio cabinets and glass-fronted cupboards—the disintegrating minié-ball pouch, the moth-eaten corporal's tunic, the gaudy presentation saber, the Sam Browne belt with its brass CSA buckle, the tin canister of unspent grapeshot, the pocked and fissured cannonball.

The chief paused briefly before his aunt's massive oil portrait of Generals Stuart and Lee, each nobly on horseback, the sky dark and tumultuous behind them. A lone shaft of glorious sunlight bathed them both in a ridiculously golden glow.

"Brady, sweetie, let's eat."

The chief's Aunt Evelyn smiled at him from the dining room doorway as she untied and removed her apron, smoothed her dress front with her hand. She was his late mother's sister, his only living blood kin. She was flinty and opinionated, an adamantine Baptist, a hopelessly uncharitable gossip and an abominable cook.

She allowed him the privilege of the seat at the head of the table and insisted they toast with sweet scuppernong wine. "To family," she said as the goblets rang together.

"To family." The chief only splashed a little wine on his lips as the stuff was sweeter even than the toddy.

"So tell me all about him."

"Who?"

"Your new deputy. Mr. Tatum."

"Not much to tell. He came up from Mobile. Looking for a change, I guess."

"Married?"

"Divorced. Seems they lost a child."

"Where are his people from?"

The chief forked in a mouthful of chopped turnip greens which proved bitter and burned, aggressively saline. They caught in his throat, and he was obliged to sluice them down with treacly scuppernong wine.

"Kentucky maybe, but he's worked pretty much all over. He started out down in Carolina. Around Charlotte, I think."

"Nice boy?"

"Nice enough. He's got a good head on him. I put him on this homicide." The chief hacked off a crusty morsel of cubed steak, shrugging as he chewed. "Probably a dead end."

"Those people," she said. She shook her head and gazed wearily toward the ceiling.

The chief grunted, labored to swallow and reached at last with dreary resignation for his goblet of sweet wine.

Ray's portable television played on the kitchen countertop. Although he had exhaustively adjusted the aerials and had encased them each in foil, he still picked up two network newscasts weakly and simultaneously. One came out of the Shenandoah to the west, the other out of Tidewater to the east. The anchormen rolled vertically and surged and faded with the wind, with the air traffic, with the alignment of the stars. They glossed and contradicted each other, yielding at virtually the same instant to identical antacid commercials.

Ray switched off the set and opened a clasp envelope, spilling onto the dinette table the assorted effects from the shallow grave—shirt buttons, pocket change, the trouser catch, the comb, the ring, a moldy scrap of sneaker sole. Cattle bellowed from the adjacent pasture. A truck rolled by, pinging gravel off its fender wells, and from just up the road, Ray heard again a fellow calling for his dog.

"Queenie!" he shouted. "Queenie girl!"

Ray stepped onto the front porch and spied that gentleman through a gap in the autumn olive where he stood in the road ditch opposite the pasture. His hands cupped to his mouth, he yelled into the woods, "Queenie! Come on here, Queenie girl!"

Ray crossed his yard and followed his drive through the hedge and out into the road. He looked maybe seventy, Ray figured, was tidily dressed and rigorously trim, a taut little spindle of a fellow with close-cropped hair and a starched white cotton shirt. He wore impeccably tended brogans, and his poplin trousers were crisply pleated and creased.

Ray called from across the road so as not to startle him. "Lose your dog?"

The fellow nodded, gesturing helplessly with both hands toward the woods. "Damned if she didn't run off."

"Chasing something?"

"Deer probably. Rabbit." He shrugged and turned back toward the tree line. "Queenie! Queenie girl!"

"I'm Ray. Tatum. I'm renting that place there."

"Lyle."

The man pointed to a puny house up the road with a painted slab porch and shingled siding. The lawn was neatly clipped and the shrubs manicured. Boxwoods, Ray noticed. Azaleas.

"She'll come back," Ray assured him. "Mine was gone for nearly a week once. Ran off in a thunderstorm."

"Yeah," Lyle allowed. "Maybe."

"What's she look like, in case I see her around?"

"I've got some pictures at home."

Lyle took a last searching glance along the tree line before leading Ray up the road toward his house where he stalked across his slab porch and stepped inside, holding the screen door open for Ray who followed him into the front room. The furnishings had a generic motor-lodge look to them—coordinated but impersonal. There was the smell of scorched Crisco in the air. Lyle fished through a side-table drawer and came away with a snapshot that he offered to Ray.

"She don't bite or nothing. She'll eat a little white bread if you've got it."

In the failing light, Ray took a cursory look at the photo as Lyle followed him through the doorway and across the porch. He drew up before the railing and whistled. "Queenie!" he shouted. "Queenie girl!"

Ray was stretched out in his undershorts on his bed before he'd troubled himself to look at that photo in proper lamplight. It featured Lyle in a metal porch chair wearing a wide-wale corduroy suit. He was raven-haired and smooth-skinned, possibly shy still of fifty, while the dog in his arms was rheumy-eyed and grizzled.

Ray flipped the thing over to find a date stamped on the back: October 1972.

Doogan did me the courtesy of hailing a cab, of instructing the West Indian behind the wheel precisely where to take me. They had helped Lizzie already, tremulous and woozy, into their sedan, had laid her out on their stained encrusted backseat, and meant to carry her down to the precinct house to draw up an affidavit.

I know now that he was watching us, had been trailing us most of the day. He was wholly inconspicuous behind his smoky window glass in his midnight blue Lincoln Town Car as Manhattan is fairly overrun with the things. There are fleets of them for livery, more common even than cabs, so what was one more blue sedan idling before the precinct house, before Troy's apartment building, double-parked hard by the morgue? They eased in just behind me as I climbed out of my taxi at the Duke, and I heard their sidewalls squeal against the curbing.

The knock came only moments after I'd entered my room. "Yes," I called through the door.

"Message for you, sir." The voice was low and rumbling, slightly accented.

I drew open the door as far as the nightlatch would allow and had even almost begun to speak when the gentleman in the hallway twitched. That's what it looked like anyway. He was massive, Samoan as it turned out, and he simply shifted a bit and bumped against the door with his shoulder, prompting it to shoot open and buck me backward across the floor. The brass bracket departed from the jamb, and the night chain separated from the keeper to sail past me and clatter against the dresser mirror.

He had snatched me up from the floor, had fished my wallet from my pocket and had set me firmly onto the bed before I noticed the other one—black, elegantly dressed, undeniably in charge. He entered and carefully, slowly, shut the door behind him. He tugged at his shirt cuffs, smoothed his jacket front and plunged a hand into his trouser pocket.

Cosmetically at least, he was something like Vitale but with actual taste, with better clothes, a keener sense of style. There was a Spectravision menu atop the TV by the door, and he paused, I noticed, and troubled himself to straighten it.

His name, I know now, was Giles. Mr. Giles. He smiled at me as his colleague handed him my wallet. It was an authentically winning smile. Giles had developed a skill, as it turned out, for seeming pleasant and utterly harmless. He looked to be thirty maybe, was whip-thin and wore a tiny diamond stud in his left earlobe. I watched him as he opened my billfold and sifted through my credit cards.

"Take it," I told him. "Take whatever you want."

"Do I look like a thief to you"—he extracted my driver's license as he spoke and glanced at it—"Paul?"

As I'd never actually seen a thief, I shrugged and shook my head.

"So," he said, drawing toward me until I was bracketed by the pair of them, "they tell me you're his father."

I looked at him rather dully, I imagine, and he glanced at his associate who cocked an arm and hit me, smacked me with his open hand flush upon the jaw. The force knocked me onto the floor, and my entire head went numb. The big one gathered me up and set me again on the bed.

"You are his father, aren't you?" Giles asked me again, pleasantly still.

I succeeded in assuming he meant Troy and saw fit to nod.

"Then perhaps you can fill me in, Paul. Was it him?"

I took his meaning, recollected the unearthly pallor, the wiry chest hair, the mole in the shape of a bean. I glanced toward the other one, the big one, and shied reflexively. "I don't know."

"You don't know?" Giles perched beside me on the edge of the mattress. "You couldn't recognize your own flesh and blood?"

I divided my attention between the pair of them, between Giles, that is, and his associate's beefy hand. I did nothing whatsoever by way of response which was not, I came to learn, an acceptable course of action.

"Jumbo," Giles said, glancing toward his colleague, and I got hit again, with a closed fist this time, with knuckles the size of road gravel.

Giles himself picked me up from the floor. My mouth was

bleeding, and he offered me his handkerchief—pressed, starched, brilliant white. I was reluctant to take it, to stain it.

"Go ahead," he told me. "I suppose it was a bit of a shock. I hear he was in pieces."

"They'd cut off his head," I said. "His hands. He was so . . . white."

Giles rose from the bed and rested a comforting palm on my shoulder in a fashion that seemed, remarkably enough, sincere. Jumbo looked to him for instruction and closed, I noticed, his meaty right hand into a fist, but Giles stayed him with a slight shake of his head and set about on a leisurely tour of my hotel room.

He considered the impressionistic landscape above the headboard in its tasteless gilt frame, the homely chest of drawers and dressing table, the TV remote secured into its bolted swivel. He troubled himself to smooth out the tuck where the spread draped over the pillows.

"And the woman?" he asked me.

"His neighbor. Some actress."

"What did she think?"

I nodded.

"But not you?"

"I didn't really know him."

Giles strayed to the far side of the room and subjected the upholstered chair across the way to a spot of disapproving study. He said at length, "I see." Then he fastened his jacket button and tugged again at his shirt cuffs as he crossed the room to pause before me at the foot of the bed. "I wouldn't mention our little chat."

Without instruction of any kind, without so much as a prompting glance, Jumbo drew open his sport coat to reveal a holstered pistol slung beneath his arm. It was flat black and boxy, and Jumbo's eyes brightened in such a way as to permit me to know that he would fairly delight in meeting with cause to press the bore of the thing to my cranium and discharge it.

I nodded. Giles smiled and shoved a hand into his trouser pocket. He came out with a couple of quarters which he carried to the nightstand to feed into the Magic Fingers coin box. The mattress quivered to life, and Giles shook his head, grinning still, as he let himself out the door.

Left unsupervised, Jumbo put on display his dingy jagged teeth and, in the spirit of sadistic recreation, he cocked his arm once more and leveled me, was long gone by the time that I woke up.

5

"So she's dead?" Ray asked.

"Aw, now, who's to say?" Carl grinned at him.

The chief stepped from his office with a scrap of paper in hand.

"Ray here's been out looking for Queenie," Carl informed him, smirking.

"No shame in that." The chief approached Ailene's desk. "Walter walked with Lyle nearly to Sycamore Springs once."

Walter nodded. "Nineteen eighty-six."

"So Lyle's nuts?" Ray directed the question to the chief who deliberated over a response.

"Lyle lost his people all in a clump. His wife. His momma and daddy. Had a niece to get hit by a car. All of them right there together, and then that dog of his ran off."

"When?"

"Seventy-three. Seventy-four," the chief said.

"So he is nuts."

"Grover's nuts," the chief told Ray. "Lyle's a little confused."

The chief stepped over to show Ailene his scrap of paper. "How did this fellow with the Park Service know to call me?"

Ailene fidgeted in her seat. "I sort of talked to him yesterday evening."

"Sort of talked to him why?"

"Well, Ray said you found those bones on federal land, Appalachian Trail right of way. He said we were obliged to call them."

The chief pivoted about to consider Ray, who nodded. "We are."

"Well, they're sending some snoop down from D.C." The chief read from his scrap of paper. "Kit Carson. He'll be here this afternoon."

"Kit Carson?" Ray asked.

"I guess his daddy wanted an Indian scout. Once he gets here, he's all yours." The chief shoved the scrap of paper at Ray. "Walk him through what you've got, and send him the hell home."

"Can't say I've got awful much to walk him through just yet."

"Then you'd better get cracking," the chief told Ray as he glided across the squad room and vanished into his office.

The local professional park consisted of a pair of one-story frame buildings on a cul-de-sac in a pasture. The site had been landscaped with wiry saplings and spindly rhododendron bushes that looked to be expiring from steadfast neglect. As Carl unlocked the cruiser trunk and lifted out a black plastic leaf bag by the neck, the bones inside rattled and clattered against each other.

He and Ray were shown down a brief back hallway and into an examination room where Carl swung the bag up onto the metal table while Ray attempted to sit in a tiny side chair and got wedged fast between the arms.

"What kind of doctor is this guy?" Ray asked, freeing himself by main force.

Carl wandered about the tiny room, studying the pictures on the wall. A cartoon goose with an ice pack on its head, a cartoon house cat with its paw in a sling, a rosy pink cartoon pig with a thermometer shoved up its bunghole.

The door opened with a squeak, and the doctor entered in a polka-dotted lab coat and brilliant red sneakers. "Christ," he moaned, "it's wall-to-wall earaches out there." He lit a cigarette and gestured with it toward the sack on the examination table. "Ailene called. This him?"

Ray nodded, and the doctor rolled down the neck of the sack. He sorted through the bones, drew out the skull, and examined the pair of jagged punctures in the cranial plate. "Fractures here and here. Potentially fatal. Your proverbial blunt instrument."

He extracted the pelvis and showed it to Ray and Carl. "Definitely male." He pulled out a tibula that caught his notice. "Broke a leg once." He traced a hairline fissure in the bone with his finger and then returned his attention to the skull. "A little bridgework. Gold backing on a couple of these eyeteeth. There's really not much else I can tell you."

"How long in the ground before he'd go to bone like this?" Ray asked.

The doctor peered into the sack. "No tissue anywhere?"

"Nope."

"Depending on the moisture in the soil, parasites and such— a year or two. Maybe a whole hell of a lot longer. I'm just guessing. Where'd you find him?"

"Off the trail," Carl said, "up past Poplar Camp, back in the deep woods."

The doctor gave a dire little groan and raised the skull on his palm to consider it eye to eye. "Hell of a place to end up."

The examination room door opened with a squeak, a slight towheaded boy clinging to the knob. He wore only his cotton briefs and a dusting of silt on the back of his neck and yelped violently at the sight of the fractured skull, tugging the door shut, banging it against the jamb.

The doctor looked from Carl to Ray as he shrugged and crushed out his cigarette. "Whoops," he said.

Kit Carson's spruce green Park Service Blazer sat in a far corner of the parking lot, just before a Cracker Barrel restaurant in New Market, hard by the interstate exchange. Standing at a phone box on the cinder margin of the asphalt, Kit pivoted to eye the landscape, the receiver to her ear. The rise of the Appalachians and the Shenandoah National Forest lay to the east. To the west, immediately across the highway, was the grassy sprawl of the New Market Civil War Battlefield with its quaint stacked rails, its granite monuments and its batteries of cannon.

"Yeah, I'll hold."

A blue Ford Torino, late seventies vintage, rolled into the lot riding low on its springs, dappled with Bondo and flaking with rust. It stopped, idling. A man stuck his head out of the passenger window and openly leered at Kit. He was stubbled and grit-smeared, sweat-streaked. His denim shirt was frayed at the collar and punched out at the elbows, was fouled with sawdust and gasoline and chain oil.

"Well, well," he said to his buddy behind the wheel, and the blue Ford continued slowly across the lot. Together the men studied Kit as they rolled toward her. The smart green uniform, impeccably creased. The plump breasts. The firm round flank. The smooth brown skin, deepest mahogany and achingly exotic. Federal, black, female—they salivated together at the prospect of indulging their leading animosities all at once.

The Torino eased in beside Kit's four-by-four and stopped. The grubby passenger flattened his hair down with spit and climbed out of the car.

"I'm at a pay phone in the north end of the valley. Headed for some burg." Kit produced a scrap of paper from her trouser pocket and glanced at it. "Hogarth," she said into the handset.

Kit heard cinders grinding beneath brogans and turned to see a lanky yokel, a logger by the looks of him. He leaned against the adjacent phone box and winked at her, grinning.

"I don't really have much choice, got to go where he sends me. What do you mean, how's it going to look? You want to take a date? Take a date. I don't give a happy goddamn."

Kit watched as the fellow alongside her considered her indecorously from head to toe. "Hold on a second." She covered the mouthpiece. "I'm on the phone here, Jethro. Back it up."

He obliged her, retreating very nearly a full stride, but as she raised the receiver and turned her back to him, he closed again immediately, grinding cinders.

"I'll get back when I get back. What do you want me to tell you?"

Kit pivoted to find the grubby logger repulsively close, just beside her. "Who? The blond with the tits and the inseam? You go right ahead, sugar. We're not married. I've got no claim on you."

"We was thinking we'd buy you a beer," the lanky yokel whispered moistly. "Me and him was." He jerked his head toward the Torino. "We was thinking you might like a little fun."

He had swiveled about to beckon to his buddy and draw him out of the car when Kit thrust her hand beneath his chin and clamped her fingers surely upon his windpipe. He could only manage to gurgle and wheeze by way of active objection as Kit shoved him against the side of the phone box and held him there.

"Yeah, I mean it," Kit barked into the receiver. "Maybe it *is* time for a change. So you just go on and knock yourself out." She glared at the yokel. "There are other men in this world. Believe me." She slammed the receiver into the cradle, but it clattered out to dangle by the cord.

That fellow struggled fruitlessly to free himself as Kit held him fast, compressing his airway and prompting him to flush from the chin up. He turned a lovely shade of pale blue, nearly lilac. He gurgled and managed a rattling cough. Kit drew close, seething, and brought her cheek next to his so as to speak directly into his filthy ear.

"I want you to crawl back into that rolling outhouse and get the fuck out of my life. Hear me?"

He nodded, bobbing his head as vigorously as she'd allow,

and Kit spun him around, laying her foot against his rump to help him toward the Torino. He lurched to the passenger door, massaging his throat. Coughing, glaring at her, he climbed into the car, and the Torino accelerated across the lot while Kit, for her part, pitched against the grille of her Blazer, stewing and muttering, watching and waiting, knowing it would come.

They were nearly to the roadway, were fully upon the cement apron at the far edge of the lot, when he finally accumulated the breath for it, shoved his torso out the passenger window, and shook his grimy fist. "Nigger bitch!"

I couldn't recall exactly where I was at first. I attempted to stand but discovered that I was cemented to the rug, attached by dried blood and spittle. I rolled over with some violence and came up encrusted with fuzz. The mattress was no longer aquiver, and the clock radio had switched on of its own accord, was tuned to some manner of lite FM station that was playing a variety of ballad—electric piano, synthetic strings, baritone balladeer.

"Baby, baby, baby," he sang. "Baby, baby, baby, baby."

I hoisted myself onto the bed and sat for a moment. "Lizzie!" I do believe I even said it aloud.

The desk clerk was helpful after a fashion—twitched his nose, that is, from behind his Plexiglas in the direction he thought to be south while he indelicately considered my puffy jaw, my split and bloodied lip. Ordinarily, I'd have been reluctant to wander out into the street in the small hours of the night, but it's a chore for a fellow to fear for his life more than once in an evening. I looked, moreover, robbed already and emerged from beneath the Duke Hotel awning prethrottled and unlikely to strike anyone as bait.

The park was largely deserted. There were a few joggers circulating along the bordering sidewalk, and I passed a man there by the arch just where Fifth Avenue gives out as he shoved a section of the *Daily News* beneath the rump of his Akita who simultaneously barked at me and defecated.

I had trouble getting directions once I'd passed out of the park since nobody much would talk to me on the street. What with my bruises and contusions ripening, I looked a bit of a fright, and my mouth was sufficiently mangled to prevent me from speaking clearly, so I'd be sputtering still my inquiries as people would sidestep and walk away.

I wandered south and finally got directed by a comprehensively intoxicated gentleman to Thompson Street where I found Lizzie's building by using the parking garage opposite for a landmark, and once I'd scanned the block for a blue Town Car sedan, I stepped into the alcove to ring her bell.

"Yes." I could barely hear her for the static.

"It's Paul Tatum. Are you all right?" I got only an electronic hiss through the speaker by way of reply. "The decedent's father," I added as it was the first phrase that came to mind.

"Oh! Paul!" She buzzed me in, and I crossed the modest lobby and mounted the stairs.

Lizzie was waiting for me in her apartment doorway, had changed out of her black frock into fleecy lounging togs, was barefoot and had gathered her hair on top of her head. She looked suitably somber until I'd closed on her and had stepped into the light when she spied my face and went showily aghast instead.

She ushered me inside, supporting me as if I were feeble, and she deposited me on her sofa and insisted I stretch out. She brought me ice bundled in a kitchen towel which she applied to my cheek as she ruffled lightly my hair.

"What happened? Who did this to you?"

"These guys," I told her. "They came to my room. I was afraid they might come over here."

"What guys?"

"A little black one. A big . . . brown one." I shrugged by way of elaboration.

"What on earth did they want?" She laid a hand to her cheek in a fashion that had the distinct taint of the senior-class thespian society about it.

"They knew Troy." I recalled her at the morgue in her delicate swoon. "Johnny," I said.

She rose from the settee and crossed toward the window where she rested her finger ends lightly upon the sash and gazed down toward the street.

"They wanted to know if it was him at the morgue."

"Really?" It was hardly more than a whisper.

"They didn't seem so sure he was dead."

"But you straightened them out, right?" She turned and smiled, coaching me a little, encouraging me.

I shrugged again. "Yeah, I guess."

And I mark that now as the moment when everything changed, not that I could tell it at the time, since the shift in trajectory was ever so modest, slight enough to frustrate detection but adequate to set us on a different course, to carry us where we ended up and make of us what we became.

She said nothing, lingering still by the window, and briefly, for an instant only, her expression resolved into something authentic and unapproximated. Fear, I'm prone to think anymore, simple and stark, passed through her like a chill and was gone. Then she composed herself, crossed toward the couch and improvised.

"That boy of yours." Lizzie shook her head and perched beside me, laying a hand upon my chest. "He had all the wrong friends."

"They told me drug trouble." I pointed in what I construed to be the direction of the precinct house.

She nodded and then considered me in silence for a moment, gravely almost, intensely anyway. Lizzie lingered over me for maybe half a minute—long enough, I guess, for the gestation and birth of her brand of dramaturgic love. Then she leaned close and kissed me, a bit tepidly at first but with advancing abandon and passion.

"Oh, Paul," she told me, lifting back.

It came out in hot breath and quivering emotion. Lizzie considered me tenderly, relocated a tuft of my hair and managed to seem, for all the world, smitten. I didn't trouble myself to wonder what in the hell was going on, why she seemed of a sudden to adore me. I did instead what any man would do—drew her to me, that is to say, and readily believed her.

Lizzie moaned and kissed my neck, spoke my name with breath alone. And not once, I recognize now, did she spoil the mood and giggle in the way that most women in the throes of passion will. Your average female can hardly hope to go from self-possessed career woman to wanton seductress without some stripe of transitional comic snort. So ordinarily—and I'm speculating here—a competent and capable female will find herself bedded with a fellow she has deemed agreeable, some hairy lumpen thing with all of the natural romance of a tree squirrel who, prone to either hunger or arousal, has been for the moment persuaded not to eat.

She'll touch him anywhere, and he'll groan with pleasure. Then she'll snicker and make—it's been my experience—some sort of deflating remark. In one sense, it's women who account for the thriving state of prostitution as men sometimes need a partner who'll take money not to laugh.

Lizzie, though, was all grinding kisses, pelvic thrusts and breathy moans, and I had cause to believe that we were on our way to the sort of union that I'd lately only hypothesized at home in my half bath about. Lizzie drew free from me to switch off a lamp and tune in her stereo to the station that I had to believe I'd awakened to on the rug back at the Duke. Baby, baby, baby. Baby, baby, baby, baby.

Then she mounted me after a fashion. We were still each of us dressed at the time, but Lizzie straddled me nonetheless, and she rocked and gyrated with her eyes shut and her hands uplifted, with her fingers in her hair. She quivered and quaked a little and loosed shortly the manner of moan that most men only hear after an hour of rigorous instruction, violent cowlick distress and temporary paralysis of the jaw.

She flopped down on top of me, quivering still, and nuzzled against my neck. We were quite plainly finished, and I had yet to emerge from my trousers which I was laboring to formulate a declaration about when Lizzie set in to complimenting me on my considerable prowess and applauded me for the pitch and quality of her orgasmic spasm which, as commentary goes, pretty much served to stave off talk from me. I'm far better suited to discussing the underlying mechanics of ion propulsion which I happen to know absolutely nothing about than engaging with a woman in intelligent talk on the topic of her sexual release. While I may have seen an actual photo of Lizzie's nether parts, I had reason to know that I was unfit to operate them.

So Lizzie lay heavily against me, dozing and apparently satisfied, and I chose to be convinced that I had pleased her without having gotten dislodged from my briefs. I realize now that the sex itself had been essentially cinematic—the low lighting, the sultry music and the economized climax with no lubricated plumbing exposed. She simply behaved as if we'd joined together in intimate union, as if there were a special tenderness between us and a bond that supplied her the authority to guide and to instruct me, served to make her interests mine and to make my interests hers.

"We've got to tell them," she said.

"What? Who?"

"The police. We'll go over first thing."

"I can't." I touched my puffy cheek for effect.

"You have to." She raised up and laid a finger to my lips. "First thing," she said and allowed for no objection.

Lizzie smiled and kissed me very nearly on the lips. We slept together chastely in our clothes.

6

They rolled slowly along the main street toward the station house as Carl gnawed a toothpick and circulated phlegm, as he vented a wholly unmuted eructation. It was nearly four, and they had passed the bulk of the afternoon eating lunch twice. Ray lay slouched against the door. He'd had the veal cutlet at Little Ruth's, the whipped potatoes, the three-bean salad. He'd had the biscuits and gravy, the butterscotch pie.

Then they'd answered a call from a woman well south of town off the Lynchburg pike, a frantic widow with wretched riffraff for neighbors. She'd been convinced they'd made off with her posthole diggers and had stolen her string trimmer, had confided in a whisper that they were a filthy and godless sort. Ray had located the string trimmer behind the furnace in her basement, and Carl had found the posthole diggers beneath the red-wood deck out back. There'd been nothing for it but a spot of tittering embarrassment and a plaintive offer of lunch, and Carl had shoved his feet beneath the table before Ray could draw breath to object.

More bean salad, cold chicken, red slaw and white bread along with some manner of cobbler with an Oleo-and-brown-sugar crust. They'd napped briefly on the roadside in their slot back in the bushes, and Carl had written a geezer from Boca Raton a citation for questionable tread.

Ray slapped himself awake as they drew up before the station house, and he noticed a spruce green Chevy Blazer slant-in before the building with the Park Service logo stenciled on the door panels.

Ray could hear the chief talking from his office as he stepped into the squad room. "Of course, we're happy to cooperate in any way we can. I was telling my deputies just this morning how I wish that—"

He slipped up alongside Ailene's desk. "Did you check with the state police?"

Ailene sifted through a stack of faxes on her desktop. "Just a couple of missing kids." She showed Ray a grainy reproduction of a snapshot of a pair of toddlers. "Looks like their daddy grabbed them."

"How about Lynchburg? Lexington?"

"I've got calls in all over."

"Ray? You out there?" the chief called from his office and stepped shortly through his doorway, turning to squire into the squad room a woman, a black woman in a crisp green Park Service uniform. She was tall and angular, handsome and with remarkable hazel eyes.

"Kit Carson," the chief said. "Ray Tatum. It's his case."

Ray offered his hand, and she took it and pumped his arm stoutly.

"Why don't you bring Miss Carson here up to speed."

"Yeah, sure. A couple of hikers found him off the trail. He was down below a—"

Kit waved a hand to stanch him. "Just show me the body."

"It's out in Carl's trunk."

"Excuse me?"

Ray gestured toward Carl who dropped onto his desk chair. "We've got him in a sack."

Carl eyed Kit bluffly along her entire length. He winked at her and grinned while relocating a dollop of saliva in a fashion that sounded distinctly lascivious.

Kit waited for Ray on the walk outside, was agitated, he could see that plainly enough, was unambiguously ill. Ray tried on her his toothsome smile, the one he had been assured was warm and beguiling by Karen, his ex, well back before the vitriol and the attorneys.

"Open the cocksucking trunk."

Ray eyed Kit over his shoulder as he stepped toward Carl's cruiser. "That's some mouth. Raised on a frigate?"

"What are you? A delicate flower?"

Ray depressed the catch on the trunk latch and lifted the lid. He swung his head from side to side as he swept his arm with a grand flourish. "The cocksucking trunk, she is open."

Kit eyed the black plastic leaf bag resting upon the spare tire and reached in to uncinch the neck of it, revealing the bones heaped and tumbled in together indiscriminately. She lifted out the skull and examined it. Lightly with her finger, she traced around the jagged edges of the twin fractures.

"ME's report?"

"Male. Maybe twenty to thirty. A previous leg fracture. A little run-of-the-mill dental work."

"Cause of death?"

"Blunt trauma to the head."

"Weapon?"

"The doc didn't have much to say on that, but I'm guessing a hatchet, a hammer maybe. They're two pretty regular holes."

"Any effects?"

Ray nodded and took up the brown clasp envelope from the trunk floor, which he handed to Kit. "A few buttons, a little pocket change, a comb and a ring."

As Ray spoke, Kit spilled the contents onto the flattened plastic sacking. She took up the afro pick and the double-banded ring and then laid her head back and moaned. "I come all the way to Crackerville to find this? A dead homeboy?"

"Funny, huh? Not known to be keen outdoorsmen."

"Well, shit." Kit dropped the ring and the pick back into the envelope and gave the leaf bag a jerk. "And nothing but bones?"

Ray nodded. "But you never know. We poke around a little, something might turn up."

"He probably came off the interstate and got dumped by his buddies. Some kind of drug shit. He could be from any damn where." Kit slammed the trunk lid shut.

"Well, I can take it from here if you don't want to bother. I mean, I'm sure you've got better things to do there at the Park Service than mess around with—"

"I'm paid to bother, Roy."

"It's Ray."

Kit checked her watch, gazed up and down the deserted main street of Hogarth. "But I'll bother tomorrow. Think you can point me to a motel? Some place to eat?"

"Sure." Ray fished a local map off the dashboard of Carl's cruiser and opened it on the roof.

"I guess you've already had lunch," Kit said, softening a little, Ray noticed, but only a little.

"Uh-huh," Ray told her. "Twice."

The room was paneled in knotty pine, and the carpet was a plush revolting amber. The dresser was low and contoured— late Eisenhower in blond maple veneer. The lamplight was excessively bright, and the bathroom stank of Lysol. As Kit reclined on the motel bed, she sank deeply into a mattress so soft as to be orthopedically criminal.

She wore a gray Camden PD T-shirt and Mighty Mouse panties, took up the telephone receiver and held it pensively for a moment before returning it to the cradle and switching on the television with the remote control which was fixed to a swivel bolted to the nightstand.

Headline News. Court TV. Fitness Beach. Cubic zirconium. The war in the Pacific. An Acadian remoulade in progress. Buffy and Jody. Fred and Lamont.

Kit snatched up the receiver again, with agitation now and

unguarded seething. She punched eight for a long-distance line, the area code, the exchange.

"Shit." She tossed the handset, sending it skipping and clattering across the nightstand, and then explored further along the dial. *Travelwise.* Line dancing. *Matlock. E! News.* A lanky model was sharing her dietary secrets—mineral water, clementines, salad greens, cigarettes, and by the looks of her, recreational heroin.

She was blond, Kit couldn't help but notice, mercilessly young and nearly six feet tall. Kit felt another relapse coming on, more of the feverish agitation and the mindless jealousy, the inexplicable regret. She fished up the telephone receiver, drawing it by the cord, and was rigorously peeved with herself before she had it well in hand.

He'd probably had his eye on the creature all along—that trashy paralegal with the cleavage and the black roots. With the tits, she'd told him, and the inseam. She should have known from the way he'd talked about her, always casually and dismissively but insistently. Kit imagined those two together, her boyfriend and his date, and it galled her—him quiveringly passionate, her entirely flabless and double-jointed.

On the E! channel, the lanky blond model complained of feeling homely on account of how her ears impressed her as a bit too big for her head.

The wife of the motel manager heard the racket from the office—the thump and rattle, the snap of shattering plastic. She stepped out into the breezeway and down the side stairs to the lot where she played her flashlight beam about and spied an item on the asphalt. Curiously, it was one of their ebony desk phones, but the thing had been violently disassembled by its impact with the pavement and was attached still to the jack and a sliver of knotty paneling that had broken away when the cord was jerked from the wall.

The wife of the motel manager approached the thing, creeping slowly, glancing uneasily about the lot. She nudged it with the toe of her shoe.

They knew him by name, immediately and without equivocation, had enjoyed together dealings with him before. I'll confess, I was a little surprised. I'd shown up harboring hopes that, in a city of 7 million, maybe even a massive Samoan enforcer could blend into the crowd.

Once Lizzie had squired me by the arm into the squad room and had led me through the mayhem and the stable reek to Vitale and Doogan's desks against the wall, I'd described him—at her prompting—about as sketchily as I could. Bald, I'd told them, oversized and, as a practical matter, neckless.

Nonetheless, they'd glanced straightaway at each other and had declared in unison, "Jumbo," and I could very nearly feel at that moment the bore of his pistol against my skull.

"Was Giles with him?" Doogan asked me, and I squinted and gazed toward the ceiling as if casting back to conjure the scene.

"Black guy." Vitale raised a hand earlobe-high. "About this big."

"Yeah," Lizzie told them.

"Figures." Doogan nodded and then went off to hunt us chairs which he snatched, once again, out from under perpetrators—an ashy black fellow in a knit cap and some manner of Latino who indulged together, at Doogan's expense, in a brace of colorful remarks.

"Word is he's pissed," Vitale said and looked to Doogan for confirmation.

"Pissed," Doogan confirmed as he buffed the chair seats with his dingy noserag.

"It seems him and the decedent had some kind of falling out," Vitale told us, ushering Lizzie to a chair and settling her onto it as he spoke. Doogan shoved the other one toward me with his foot.

"You guys know just everything, don't you," Lizzie cooed. She smiled at Vitale, tossing her hair, and I passed a moment in bilious hatred of the man.

"Your boy worked for Giles," Doogan told me. He sorted through a stack of folders on his desk, selected one and flipped it open to reveal an unflattering black-and-white photograph of Giles. A mug shot, it was, and he looked glum and irritated, appeared to be half awake.

"Doing what?"

"Glorified mule," Vitale declared, toward Lizzie chiefly. "Bag boy. Gopher."

"What exactly does Giles do?" I asked it of Vitale in a bid to draw him off Lizzie and gain his notice.

He glanced at me but spoke still to her, smiling, winking even. "Every damn thing. Real go-getter."

"Crack baby," Doogan told me, and he offered me another photo, this one stapled to a rap sheet. Giles was hardly recognizable in his puffy down jacket. He had two gold bicuspids, lint in his hair. He was sneering, wiry, fifteen maybe. "Started out up in Morningside Heights with the Dominicans. Rock and hash. Just street-corner bullshit. Moved on to heroin. Crystal meth. Coke. Small arms. Untaxed cigarettes. Bootleg videos. Knockoff couture." Doogan shrugged. "You name it."

"He seemed nice enough." I don't know why exactly I said it. It just came out. Giles had struck me, after all, as polite and well-spoken, stylish and tidy, which is rare enough anymore among ordinary lawful civilians and an authentic feat, I had to figure, for a former New York City street thug.

Doogan and Vitale exchanged snorts at my expense. "Yeah," Vitale told me, "a real prince. Word is your boy pinched a load from him. We're hearing a dozen keys."

Doogan considered my contusions, my stunningly bloodshot eye. "Did he get that looked at?" he asked Lizzie, who shook her head as she reached casually, familiarly, toward Vitale's breast pocket and helped herself to a cigarette from the pack there.

"What are we thinking here? Assault one?" Vitale watched Lizzie smoke as he talked. She was worth watching, inhaled with languid savor enough to make a cigarette seem unspeakably delectable.

"Jumbo maybe," Doogan allowed.

"Why not the both of them? That little shit hit you too, didn't he?"

"No, not him."

Vitale held out a flimsy tin ashtray on his palm for Lizzie to dip her ashes into. "Well," he said, "might as well snatch them up, see what happens."

Doogan groaned and stretched. "Might as well."

And, remarkably, that's exactly what they did, not Doogan and Vitale per se, but their contacts and emissaries, their fellow officers on the street. Somebody anyway reached into the boiling human chaos of metropolitan New York and succeeded in plucking Giles and Jumbo out. They were ensconced each in dingy little interview rooms not two hours later, and I cannot even so much as imagine how.

Occasionally, I'll see footage on the Roanoke news of some local fugitive who's been rounded up and fetched back in shackles. He was arrested, our spunky newsgirl of the moment will announce, in a Jersey City boardinghouse, in a Philadelphia apartment, in a Far Rockaway motel. Routinely, I can only bring myself to ask her back, "He was!?" as those stories are evermore ripe for me with prestidigitation.

I searched once for my eyeglass case in my front room for a week, so it struck me as purely miraculous to see Giles, to see Jumbo, through grimy sheets of one-way glass from a darkened observation room. Their attorney, a Mr. Kirkwell, swept into the squad room in the most beautiful cashmere topcoat I ever hope to see. He asked after Doogan's wife and Vitale's health, introduced himself with a courtly bow to Lizzie and offered me his hand as he considered my injuries.

"How unfortunate," he said. "A misunderstanding, I'm sure."

He had a meeting at two, he informed us, and he checked his dazzling gold watch. Mr. Kirkwell had a lovely manner about him, was pleasantly insistent and altogether irresistible, effortlessly charming. He made a chummy jab at Vitale's arm and smiled at Doogan, at Lizzie. He laid a finger to his lips as he lingered over her, as he considered and tried to place her.

"Haven't I seen you on—" He weighed his sundry options.

"Gravy lady," Lizzie told him. "You know"—in dumb show

she displayed an imaginary bottle—"rich and silky. Poultry or beef."

"Ah," he said, gratified and relieved. "Of course."

The interviews Vitale and Doogan conducted were brief and, ultimately, fruitless. Doogan did most of the talking while Vitale sat by chewing a drink straw, supplying the skepticism and the silent scorn. Lizzie and I watched from the darkened back room, concealed by the grimy sheets of one-way glass. She said little if anything to me and stood resolutely apart. We could easily have been abject strangers with no history of brief unsatisfying cinematic sex between us.

She was intent upon Giles, watched him and studied him. That was, I've come to believe, the purpose of the entire exercise as Lizzie wanted to see him up close, had need to gauge and to read him. I was simply the means she'd employed to draw him to her.

"What did you tell him," she asked me when at last she spoke, "about me?"

"I just said you were Troy's neighbor."

She stroked me after a fashion, lightly on the small of the back, in a show of praise and approval that would have been fitting for a hound. "Right," she said. "Good."

Giles and Jumbo, separated from each other by a dingy green interrogation room wall, told the same story down to the last identical detail. They held resolutely to it, no matter how Doogan blustered and lied. He claimed to have damning statements from the desk clerk at the Duke, from a maid, from a guest, from a uniformed patrolman who'd spied their sedan on the street.

"I was dining with an associate," Giles informed them, "in his home." He proved very nearly as pleasant as his attorney, was certainly as unflappable and even more impeccably dressed. "Please do call him." Giles drew a heavy ivory note card from the breastpocket of his jacket and, declining Doogan's offer of a ballpoint, jotted down a name and telephone number with his own gold-nibbed fountain pen.

"Now, if there's nothing else—" Giles rose and tugged at his shirt cuffs. Mr. Kirkwell stood as well, smiling.

"So tell me something." It was the first comment Vitale had ventured, not counting the theatrical snorts and the rolled eyes. "If you and Tonto didn't get to him, who did?"

"Hard to say." Giles shrugged. "Tough town."

They left us in that grimy little closet of a viewing room until Giles and Jumbo and the delightful Mr. Kirkwell could be shown out of the building. Since we had nothing to look at and nowhere to sit, we were obliged, in the end, to chat.

"When are you going back?" Lizzie asked me.

I glanced at my watch. "About an hour ago. Tomorrow, I guess. Want to get some lunch or something?" I recall sounding hopefully adolescent and chirpy, vaguely lovestruck.

Lizzie was wincing and shaking her head even before I'd finished speaking. "Can't. Audition."

"Maybe dinner?"

"Yeah," she said as Vitale opened the door to let us out. "Maybe. I'll call you."

Vitale insisted on walking Lizzie down to the street to put

her in a taxi while Doogan explained to me several of the niceties of New York state criminal law and local police procedure—the sorts of stipulations that forestalled Doogan and Vitale from doing anything much for me at all by way of protection.

"I'll have a radio car drive you to the airport," Doogan offered.

"I missed my flight."

"You'll get another one."

"But I've got plans for this evening." I was still sufficiently smitten to consider "Maybe. I'll call you" plans.

"You too, huh?"

Vitale strolled toward us across the squad room as he spoke. He winked and smirked, and naturally I couldn't help but picture Vitale and Lizzie sweaty and naked on Lizzie's hide-a-bed since Vitale didn't strike me as the sort likely to tolerate sex in his clothes.

"Mr. Tatum here's a little worried about Giles and whosie," Doogan said.

Vitale snorted dismissively and swatted.

"Want us to run you up to the Duke?" Doogan was reaching already for his coat as he spoke. "Remember that chicken place on sixth?" he asked Vitale. "With the slaw?"

"Which chicken place?"

"You know, with the slaw."

"You mean the one on Seventh?"

"Sixth. Up around Perry."

"With the waitress? The brunette?"

Doogan nodded.

"Seventh."

"Sixth. West side. Near corner." Doogan was reaching for his wallet as I crossed the squad room, as I headed alone for the door. "How much?"

"Money just don't mean shit to you, does it?"

"How much!"

The streets are unnumbered in lower Manhattan. As the island tapers, the avenues run at angles and intersect oddly, and I suspected after a block or two that I'd gone wrong somewhere, knew I was well overdue for straying across Canal Street with its unending tractor trailer traffic and triple-X video vendors. I wandered into a slovenly warehouse district where foot traffic was scanty and the sidewalks were frequently blocked by panel trucks, and I veered onto a fully cobbled side street and into a sort of square. The road widened anyway around a scraggly patch of ground fenced with iron palings. There was a bronze statue of a man in a waistcoat in among the dead vines and leaves gazing nobly toward a loading dock across the way.

That square was encircled by massive brick warehouses with truck platforms out front and tin signs attached to the awnings that identified each business as some manner of rustic enterprise: Sunny Glen Farms. Greendale Dairy. Wheyside Acres. The signs were painted with pictures of cows and chickens and untainted rolling countryside.

I crossed to the little weedy patch of park and sat on the only bench there with slats enough to support me from where I focused my attention on the likeness of a dappled painted cow across the way which was grazing in an expanse of emerald pasture. I was soothed somehow by the notion that, west across the Hudson and beyond the squalid clutter of metropolitan New

Jersey, there were woodlands and beanfields and livestock and yokels and battered half-ton pickups with rust-eaten fender wells.

It's just the sort of thing I indulge in occasionally in Roanoke, though there it tends to function in reverse. I'll spirit home about twice a month a magazine from reception, usually one of those glossies stuffed with subscription cards and samples of scent. I'll flip through it over dinner in my stunted bungalow atop my homely lot on my quiet Roanoke street, will soak in the fashion ads, the art-film reviews, the high-society gossip and exotic recipes as a means of shoring up and reaffirming my suspicion that there are places on this earth where it's possible still to lead a manner of life unilluminated by shabby price-club bright brass table lamps, unserenaded by mini-mall orchestrations of the collected hits of Sting and uncatered by that wretched pseudo-Italian franchise restaurant that tends to wash up on the verge of shopping plaza lots.

I'd had enough of the city, was actually looking forward to dropping through the clouds and taking in again the plush tree-napped contours of the Appalachians while the pilot informed us of wind conditions and our appalling lack of fuel. I'd settled, in fact, on just precisely what I intended to do by the time I heard the squeal of rubber sidewalls against the cement curbing.

They didn't crowd me. That, I'm sure, was Giles's doing as he proved to be blessed with the native decorum of an Edwardian valet. I looked up to find them across the square where Jumbo was still jockeying the sedan on account of how his talent for menace, apparently, outstripped his parking skills, and he eased the car up and down the gutter making lateral adjustments until either he'd grown satisfied that he was snug against the curbing or, more likely, Giles had instructed him, for the love of Christ, to stop.

I could make out the silhouette of Jumbo's bulk through the windshield, could see the rhythmic pulsing exhaust from the tailpipe, the brake-light glow from the weight of Jumbo's foot upon the pedal. He blinked the headlights at me—quickly, once. The rear door opened, shoved from within, and was left to stand wide by way of invitation.

I unburdened myself of a breath as I rose from my bench and fumbled idly with a topcoat button. It was a slow trip, excruciatingly so, and I stopped in the middle of the roadway twenty yards short of the sedan. I couldn't see Giles. With the glare on the windshield, I couldn't even see Jumbo, so I told the Town Car I hadn't intended to go to the police, told it Lizzie had insisted, had fairly herded me to the precinct house and had caused me to speak with the detectives who'd reasoned on their own just who to round up and bring in. I hadn't named names, I told the Town Car, had merely shown up with my bruises, and I informed that vehicle that I was sorry, slouched and grimaced in such a way as to exude, I hoped, regret.

The headlights flashed again—quickly, once. Condensation dripped from the tailpipe.

He was on the telephone, a dainty little cellular hardly bigger than an open book of matches. I had to bend to see him and had only barely set about with introductory whimpering when Giles raised an open hand to interrupt and silence me.

"Where was he?" I could hear the nasal chirp of a voice through the phone. "Uh-huh. No cash either?" Giles patted the vacant seat alongside him. He smiled and winked, beckoned to me, but I lingered on the cobbles and gazed a little forlornly about the square. I was feeling by then pretty sumptuously sorry for myself.

"Tell Spooky I need him awake. Inwood, right." Giles checked the time on his splendid gold watch. "Twenty minutes, depending on traffic. Yeah."

He switched off the phone and clapped it shut, slipped it into his jacket pocket. I set immediately into repeating talk I'd shared with the grille of his car.

"Paul," Giles said.

I revisited the salient features of my case, heaped blame upon Lizzie, upon Vitale and Doogan. I begged, I seem to recall, for my miserable tedious life in a fashion that Giles probably found unseemly.

"Paul," he said again, this time with volume and force enough to interrupt me. "Get in." He slapped at the tufted leather cushion, smiled and sidled a bit toward the far end of the seat. I took a last look at the mottled heifer across the way in its lush cow lot and then slid onto the car seat alongside Giles, who gave the slightest of nods toward Jumbo's reflection in the rearview mirror as he reached across me to draw shut the door. We rolled forward—barking a time or two against the curbing—and swung out onto Hudson against the light.

"I didn't want to tell them," I said. "I wasn't going to tell them, but she made me."

"The girl?"

I nodded, and Giles pinched his lips together in such a fashion as to suggest that he thought me ungentlemanly, foisting blame off on a girl. Somehow it stung, though I can't say why exactly. It was just that Giles's strain of disappointment had a magnitude to it, seemed uncommonly significant and leaden, and I felt as if I had failed him.

"I'm sorry," I said.

Giles smiled and patted me lightly on the forearm. "I know," he told me. "I know."

In hopes of redeeming myself a little, I set in on an explanation of just how Lizzie had come to sway me. I described for Giles her charms and her allurements, and I recounted for him in dignified and unoffending detail the history, such as it was, of our quasi-consummated romance.

"An actress, you say?"

I nodded. "Gravy lady. Silky and rich. Poultry or beef."

Giles, as it turned out, didn't watch television and appeared genuinely surprised to learn that someone had bothered to bottle gravy.

"Is it any good?" he asked me.

"Never had the gravy. Just the gravy lady."

He smiled, and I saw fit to feel slightly rehabilitated. "Just the gravy lady," Giles said toward the rearview mirror glass. Jumbo grunted and nodded, and I imagined his dingy jagged teeth out taking the air.

We turned left at Canal, worked slowly past the clotted Holland Tunnel entranceway and continued the few blocks to the northbound lanes of the West Side Highway where traffic was heavy and erratic and raced senselessly between lights. Jumbo shifted among lanes with ruthless indifference, never so much as glancing left or right. He only sneered at the drivers who pulled up alongside us to yell obscenities his way, was solidly unflappable, serene, armed.

Traffic thinned substantially along the upper reaches of the highway once we'd passed the boat basin at Ninety-sixth Street and had raced along the length of Riverside Park. Opposite the hilly side streets of Harlem, we came upon an actively inciner-ating Buick that sat burning on the far margin between the roadway and the river. Flames whipped and boiled out of the driver's-side window, and the vinyl roof smoldered lowly in ex-otic aquamarine.

The southbound motorists crawled past, eyeing the confla-gration and the quartet of cops who had arrived to eye it as well. They stood in the grass on the riverbank down near the water chatting among themselves while, behind them, that Buick was gaudily consumed unsupervised. We were just abreast of it when one of the overheated radials blew, and I was the only one of us who saw fit to convulse with alarm.

Giles took a call on his puny chirping phone as we passed be-neath the motorway of the George Washington Bridge. He lis-tened and looked out the windshield to reconnoiter. "Five minutes," he said and hinged the thing shut, returned it to his pocket.

"Where are we going?" I asked him. I think I even managed to sound passably calm and only casually interested in whatever Giles might see fit to tell me in reply.

"For a walk in the woods," Giles told me which Jumbo felt compelled to chuckle wickedly about.

I imagined my obituary in the *Roanoke Times and World News,* lower left beneath a quarter page devoted to some hard-driven executive with a coronary, below the assorted octogenarians of the day. My notice would be brief and businesslike, arid even. My middle name would probably be misspelled.

We took the ramp to Dyckman Street, just above the Cloisters,

which I had heard about and had always wanted to see, had read
that the structure, squat and medieval, is actually little more
than an ambitious souvenir. Most tourists might see fit to bring
back a plug of sod from Skara Brae or a weather-blasted scrap of
marble from the ruins at Thessalonika, but the Astor or Mellon or
Rockefeller—whoever it was—who made off with the Cloisters
had carried home portions of a half dozen monasteries instead.

I pointed toward a crenellated wall cap visible through the
leafless treetops. "I've always wanted to go there," I said.

"Well," Giles told me, glancing up the hillside, "we'll see
what we can do." And I was giddy, I recall, at the prospect of
having before me a future, regardless of how paltry and how
scant.

Jumbo let us out curbside once he'd grated another layer of
rubber off the tires, and he stayed with the car as I followed
Giles along a cinder path up a hardpan slope and into what I can
only call a forest. I know the place now for Inwood Hill Park
which is colored the same shade of green on the maps I've consulted as all of the other parks in the city. However, it's nothing
much like them as best as I can tell.

City trees are ordinarily runts, city woods glorified hedge-
rows, but that patch of forest in Inwood had a distinctly primeval
feel about it. The trees were towering and massive across their
girths—white oaks and maples, poplars and hickories. Their
roots ruptured the ground and lay unearthed all about the
forest floor. Their canopies, even in February, entwined in a
thickety tangle overhead and effectively blotted out the sky.

We passed a ragged hunk of cement with a bronze plaque
fixed to it which served to mark the spot where Peter Minuit

had purchased, for a handful of guilders and a few pestilential blankets, the island of Manhattan from the Algonquins.

Though the trail forked and splintered any number of times, Giles never hesitated, was plainly well acquainted with his route. I could hear the dull rhythmic whoosh of traffic on the Henry Hudson Parkway, car horns and tinny syncopated salsa from the streets of Washington Heights. I followed Giles down into a crease of terrain and up again onto a knoll that was bald and hard-packed and root-plagued and where a man waited for us, a Latino, who leaned against the barkless trunk of a massive tulip tree eating some manner of scarlet candy. Just above his head, a spot of graffiti was artfully painted onto the timber. *Okie Phou U!* I recognized the color from the Rustoleum palette, had sprayed, in fact, my lamppost by the drive the self-same shade.

The man nipped off a bit of his ropy length of candy and chewed it as he spoke to Giles. "Got him down at the creek."

"Spooky," Giles said, "watch my friend Paul for me, won't you?"

Spooky considered me along my length with grinding deliberation and a dash of sneering distaste. "Sure."

I looked on a little uneasily as Giles descended the tree-studded hillside and Spooky shoved toward me the cellophane packet that held his remaining scarlet candy. "Twizzler?" he asked me. It was more of a challenge really than a question.

I recall meaning just to shake my head and decline thereby in silence, but nerves induced me to prattle about the potential danger to my bridgework and the unsettling effect of processed sugar on my digestive tract which Spooky responded to by loosing a stream of gaudy pink spit. His hair was dark and thick and wavy and hung rather unbecomingly to his shoulders. His cheeks were acne-pocked, and his mustache was thin and unsuccessful. His eyes were black and quite conspicuously lifeless. Even I could sense that Spooky was immune to the usual restraints, was the sort who'd sit in dull silence through an installment of *Jonny Quest* with the same slackened expression he'd treat you to as he perforated your spleen.

Spooky meant to be well dressed, and I suspect he'd even convinced himself he was. He looked, however, like a central-casting mobster from one of those dreary made-for-TV movies but with a maladroit Caribbean twist—Rego Park by way of Hispaniola. His boot heels were a bit too high, and his indigo trousers were ivory-piped and shiny. The collar wings of his rayon shirt were nearly large enough for controlled flight. Spooky wore against the cold just an unlined jacket which was shiny and cow-grained and looked to be made from the family of materials that car dealers are fond of calling leatherette.

He hadn't even troubled himself to button the thing shut there in that shady wood in the breezy forty-degree weather. I could see, consequently, that he had a pistol shoved into his pants which, unlike Jumbo's model, was nickel-plated and fulsomely etched. He started in on another Twizzler, and I looked down the hillside to where Giles was approaching two men along the eroded bank of a sluggish little creek. I couldn't see them clearly as my view was a trifle obstructed by the pitch of the terrain, by intervening tree trunks and limbs, by a yellow shopping bag that had snagged on a branch and was whipping and rustling loudly in the breeze.

One of the men was bloody. I could see that much. He dabbed at his lip with his shirtsleeve, and his near eye was swollen like my own. He sat on a rock as Giles closed on him, but he didn't trouble himself to watch Giles come and didn't stand once he'd arrived. The other man spoke to Giles, a creature on the order of Spooky who held his own nickel-plated pistol in his hand. The mauled one on the rock ignored them, blotted at his lip and gazed about at the terrain—at the sluggish little creek and the bare treetops. He inspected his sleeve for blood.

They were soon having, as best I could tell, a conversation: Giles anyway was talking to the bloodied man on the rock, not with noticeable heat or agitation but calmly, genteelly, I felt sure. He paced as he spoke, wandered up the creek bank and probed at a root with the toe of his shoe. Giles had the look of a hobbyist out on a hike.

He asked, I have to think, a question that went unanswered, and his associate stepped in to deliver a precipitous blow with the side of his pistol, knocking the bloodied man over, sending him almost into the creek. He then snatched him up by his shirtfront and planted him again on his rock, where the man dabbed briefly at his lip with his bloody sleeve end and then cocked back his head and laughed. The sound was sharp and joyless and desperate, I have to think now, at its core.

I turned toward Spooky, who was working to free a scrap of Twizzler from between his teeth with his fingernail and hydraulic bursts of saliva. I was intending to ask after that fellow's offense, had even pointed down the hillside when I heard the first shot, and the sound of it broke upon me with a jolting crack that surged and echoed and ebbed. I think I leaped entirely off of the ground.

Spooky, for his part, snagged his wayward scrap of candy with his nail, examined it, and ate it in due time.

They lingered there by the creek, chatting—Giles, that is, and the fellow with the gun—but I couldn't find the bloodied one straightaway as he'd toppled into the creek bed and was hidden by the bank, so I shifted about and strayed for a better perspective. Spooky informed me significantly, "Hey!" and reached out to collect the scruff of my topcoat collar in his fist.

I spied the sole of a sneaker that had hooked on a root along the creek bank and watched Giles's associate shield himself from splatters with his open hand as he squeezed off another round. He then drew from his topcoat pocket a Polaroid camera, popped it open and framed the corpse with nearly artistic care. I could see the flash against the creek bank, hear the high-pitched mechanical whirr.

He handed the print to Giles, who fanned it casually to dry it as he and his associate departed from the creek. They fairly strolled through the swale of ground and up to the rooty hilltop where we stood. Giles smiled a little wanly as he slipped the photo into his jacket pocket, shook his head as if he'd just put down his favorite spaniel, as if life for him at that moment was a bit of a trial.

"Paul here didn't give you any trouble, did he?"

Spooky shook his head and shrugged, didn't seem the sort who would know from trouble.

Giles pressed a hand to my back and escorted me down the hillside. We paused to listen to the chatter of a tree squirrel. The woods were full of them, mink-black and raucous. Giles examined the blighted and ruptured bark of a maple tree, scraped with a twig a clump of mud from the sole of his shoe.

As we emerged from the woods on the knoll above the street with its sparse grass and its flinty hardpan, I managed to bring myself to ask of Giles, "What did he do?"

He glanced my way with lifted eyebrows and the merest hint of a smile and said to me blandly, harmlessly really, "Who?"

I think he liked the economy of it, the convenient marriage of business and pleasure. We had, after all, but to detour briefly along Riverside Drive where Jumbo let us out so we could climb, Giles and I, up a winding trail to the rocky perch of the Cloisters. I had thought we would flee instead, had assumed we would be racing by then south along the river, that I would be receiving pointed instruction in our alibi, but Giles hardly seemed to share in my respect for consequences and had decided that, since we were handy, we ought to take in a little art.

Giles studied the medieval tapestries, the Catalan sarcophagi, the Gothic choir stalls carved with scenes from the life of the Virgin. He marveled over an elaborately tooled crucifix of walrus ivory, delighted in the play of sunlight through the Austrian stained glass.

From the west terrace, we admired together the view of the Palisades across the river and the latticed towers of the George Washington Bridge. Standing in a turret at the head of the walkway, I could see our forest to the north with its massive hardwoods and its canopy of leafless limbs, with its cindered trails, I knew now, and its rooty hard-packed floor, with its ebony squirrels and its trash and its graffiti, with its doves and its pigeons and its mistletoe, I'd noticed, far up in the reaches of an oak, with its bloodied corpse oozing into its sluggish trickle of a creek.

I'm prone to think now it was chiefly the velocity that undid me, the Old Testament decisiveness of it all. I was accustomed to the resolution of disputes at all deliberate speed, with claimants and respondents jousting in triplicate over the thorny implications of insurance boilerplate. Here, suddenly, was another way to function and behave, without review, without appeal or reconsideration and everyone with terrible swift swords.

As we savored the vista like the other few tourists about us, I kept waiting for sirens, a swat team, the unspeakable wrath of God. I gazed up the Hudson between the headlands and toward the Tappan Zee Bridge. The husk of a man in the woods below me bled into a creek that fed into a river that sparkled gaily in the winter sun.

Giles joined me in the turret. Loudly and robustly, he filled his lungs as he soaked in the view. "Beautiful sight, isn't it?"

And I remember thinking that, yes, it was a beautiful sight, and I remember trying to smile, to breathe, to stand without clinging to the rough stone wall.

"Paul, Paul," Giles told me, speaking softly, almost in a whisper as he laid a hand to the back of my neck. He squeezed fondly, I remember, with compassion and what impressed me as tenderness and then took from his blazer pocket a fresh linen handkerchief that he put into my hand.

I troubled myself to thank him for it, as best I can recall. I remember that I blubbered like a child.

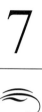

Downriver, they'd called in the divers by then, probably before Giles and I had even come out of the forest. That's how I heard it anyway from Doogan and Vitale once they'd troubled themselves to barge into my room back at the Duke. It seems that a pair of gentlemen had happened onto the grisly leavings.

"Some Adam," Doogan told me. "Some Steve."

Those fellows were out for a stroll on a West Side pier off Christopher Street. They were engaged, apparently, in a vigorous set-to, had only lately taken up together in a domestic sort of way and were hotly at odds over an item of décor.

The little one, Doogan informed me, with the peroxided hair and the multiriveted earlobes and the amber fun-fur jacket, had purchased without consultation a piece of statuary that his partner and helpmeet—who Vitale assured me was hulking and unappealing—had elected to air assorted incendiary objections about.

Doogan, for his part, roamed through the room, taking in the fixtures and furnishings. He picked up one of the sanitized glasses from the tray on my dressing table, and he considered the thing in a way that suggested it held distinct charm for him.

"Yeah," Doogan said, "had me a hell of a few weeks here." He settled the glass in its wax paper wrapper back again onto the tray. "Trouble at home," he added and set in wandering afresh.

They had yet to ask me where I'd been, had neither of them had word of me for a good twenty-four hours by then. We'd not spoken since back when they'd vowed expressly to keep me safe from harm, but even still, they didn't bother with any meaningful inquiries, didn't seem to notice that I was hardly the man who'd wandered out of the squad room the day before.

I'm not even talking necessarily about my creeping moral desolation. My suit was severely rumpled and grimy about the trouser hems. I'd dribbled a wine reduction down my shirt, and I was musty and cowlicked and slightly dazed still from my encounter with a woman, a stately creature of Giles's acquaintance with an agreeable disposition, something on the order of Ringling Brothers' flexibility and enough embedded silicone to grout a fleet of shower stalls.

The little blond one with the ear studs and the amber fun-fur jacket had purchased at a West Village gallery a piece of salacious sculpture, a plaster cast of male genitalia alert and at full salute that had served, after a fashion, to set his partner off.

According to Vitale, it wasn't so much the nature of the thing that disturbed him, and Vitale paused to allow that your Adams and your Steves had pricks around the house like probably most of the rest of us have coasters. The artist, however, had turned out to be the little blond one's former flame who'd made a plaster cast of his own privates, and the hulking boyfriend didn't want the thing around the house.

"Tell him about the dog," Doogan said from over by the nightstand where I watched him pocket a Duke Hotel ashtray and a jotting pad.

Vitale laughed, clapped me even on the back. "Dwayne!" he cackled and shook his head. "The fucking dog! Dwayne! Like a goddamn pork loin with legs. So they're fighting," Vitale said, "out on the pier. These two are way out at the end just going at it. The big one is yelling and screaming. The plaster dick goes or he goes. That kind of thing. And the little blond one, he gets hysterical."

"Born hysterical," Doogan volunteered. He was working with a pen knife on the minibar lock as I'd declined to pay the deposit for the key.

It seems that the little blond one with the ear studs and the amber fun-fur jacket had threatened to fling himself into the river. He had declared, apparently, that he could hardly see cause to go on living if he was expected to deny his past.

Now, to hear it from Doogan, that pier is just an old shipping platform, reinforced concrete with weeds sprouting in the seams, mooring cleats, no fences, no rails, an unhindered view of Hoboken across the river. It seems that the little blond one was teetering recklessly there on the edge of the pier and visiting the occasional lacerating remark upon his companion when he landed upon some species of insult that set his boyfriend off, prompted him anyway to favor that little blond fellow with a shove.

"Into the river?" I asked Vitale.

He gave a dire shake of his head. I had seen the river by then from the parapet of the Cloisters, had smelled the river through the Town Car air vents along the West Side Highway. It was remarkably fragrant even in the cold.

"Could he swim?"

Doogan had started in on the four-dollar carton of Cheez-Its. He nodded. "Sort of."

That fellow was fortunate, as it turned out, in his choice of leisurewear. His fun-fur jacket proved unusually buoyant, so he could primarily devote himself to shrieking as he bobbed on the chop and barked against the slimy barnacle-encrusted pilings.

The big hulking one with the hairless dog went looking for a rope or chain, anything to lower down and let the blond one cling to. He returned instead in the company of a tae bo instructor with little more than stirring abdominal definition, and together they watched that little blond fellow yell at them from the water until the wake of a Circle Line boat rolled in and washed him beneath the pier.

I groaned involuntarily with disgust.

"Yeah," Vitale said. "Under the damn thing."

Doogan popped the tab on a three-dollar can of club soda and set about washing down his Cheez-Its residue. "*Now* the guy's really sounding off," Doogan said. "And the girls come running from all over that damn pier. Nobody'll go in after him. They can't find a rope. The little blond one's about to have a stroke from all the trash and shit in the water. He's wailing down there, and him and his pallie are still at it. Sniping at each other, and all those other sweet things are chiming in and taking sides."

Doogan paused, partly for dramatic effect, I have to think, but partly as well to lavish his uncompromised powers of concentration upon the balky box end of a Toblerone.

"And that," Doogan told me as he went at the carton with his teeth, "is when he saw it."

"Saw what?"

"A hand," Vitale said from over by the bureau as he showed me one of his own by way of a visual aid. "Just floating around under the pier."

"A human hand?"

Doogan nipped off and worked over a lump of chocolate. He nodded and ran his index finger across the joint where his radius and carpal bones met. I glanced toward Vitale who had stepped into the bathroom and was checking himself in the mirror for unwanted nose hair, it appeared. He stood upright and stilled himself, holding his breath, listening. It was my neighbor—I could hear her myself—whimpering through the wall.

"Troy's hand?" I asked him.

Vitale considered his profile in the glass and dragged a palm across his face to gauge his whisker stubble. "Tell him," he said.

Doogan held up a finger to purchase himself a moment's delay and, with concentrated effort, loosed his chocolate from his molars and accumulated spit enough to sluice it down.

"One of them goes out to the West Side Highway and flags down a radio car. The cops call in a police boat. He gets the grapple out and snags the little asshole, fishes him out of the water and brings him on board. So he's going on about some poor hacked-up fucker under the pier, won't shut up about it until they call in the divers."

Doogan nipped off another piece of chocolate and became immediately preoccupied with it.

"What did they find?"

Vitale had stepped out of the bathroom by then. He paused before the bureau to yank open a drawer just to see, I guess, what he'd look like so employed in the bureau mirror.

"You put your clothes in here? Who the hell does that?"

"What did they find?"

"The hand," Vitale said. "It was just floating there. The rest of the stuff was down on the bottom in a pillowcase."

Doogan excavated a tooth gap with his fingernail, Spooky fashion. "The other hand," he told me. "Head. A couple of bloody rags. A hammer. A hacksaw."

"Brand-new," Vitale added."Home Depot out the Gowanus."

"Troy?"

They traded again in significant glances, and Doogan exhaled ponderously by way of preamble. "Hard to say. He got thumped pretty good. Not much face left."

"But you can get fingerprints, right?"

Doogan winced and shook his head. "They got kind of . . . rubbed away."

"Scraped," Vitale offered as an apt revision.

"Yeah," Doogan said. "Scraped."

"So now what?"

Doogan shrugged. He grinned with a trace of embarrassment, and I managed to take his meaning and retrieved my top-coat from the wardrobe, put it on, buttoned it, opened the door and stepped into the hall.

"You want to go now?" Doogan asked me. He cut his eyes a

little forlornly toward the minibar cabinet, with its sack of Old English Cheese Wafers, its packet of Milanos, its untouched tin of cocktail nuts.

I don't think I even noticed the smell on that visit or took any heed at all of the singing whine of the bone saws. They followed me along the corridor and into the chilly anteroom with its homely little settee and its wretched Parisian street scene. Before Vitale could stop me, I threw the toggle that swiveled open the blinds.

An orderly sat opposite the window with a bottle of Orangina in hand. Doogan rapped on the glass. "Get it," he said and then pointed to the decedent's father by way of clarification.

The head rested in the middle of a gurney upon a tray. The hands were situated just alongside it atop a green surgical towel, and the hammer and the hacksaw were each sealed up in plastic evidence bags.

Vitale troubled himself to lean in and tell me, "Take your time."

There was nothing really to consider and weigh, no examination to be made. The head was a pulpy mess, battered and fractured and effectively skinned by hammer blows, I had to think. The hands were bloated. The flesh had been gouged and, yes, scraped from the finger ends. The tag on the hacksaw handle read, "Your Price—$9.95."

The hair was all wrong—graying, coarse and thinning. The face was jowly, and the eyes were set too close. The jawline impressed me as weak and inordinately receding.

"Your son?" Doogan asked me.

I managed a shrug, a slight despairing shake of my head. "I didn't really know him," was all I could see fit to say.

Kit drove, had insisted on driving. Ray rode in silence beside her in her spruce green Blazer as she roared out of town past the branch bank and the crumbling rolling mill, roughly over the railroad siding and onto the Lynchburg pike.

"Wave to Grover." It was his opening bit of commentary.

Kit looked toward the margin of the roadway where Grover sat in his sagging lawn chair flailing his arms over his head, and only Ray threw up a hand. She turned off the pike at Ray's direction and onto the secondary blacktop where she accelerated upslope. The Blazer's suspension was rock-hard and unyielding, and they bounced and skittered through the switchbacks as they climbed toward the ridge. Ray clung to the armrest, to the frame of the wing window.

"Do you work out of D.C. pretty much all the time?"

Kit nodded. "We all work out of D.C. Precisely all the time."

"And go all over?"

"East Coast west to the divide."

"Are there all that many killings on federal land?"

They gained level ground and raced along the spine of the ridge. "Enough. Bears mostly." She glared pointedly at Ray. "Hillbilly trash sometimes."

Kit followed Ray down along the trail through the poplar grove, past the primitive log shelter and onto the springhead path. She only spoke along the way to ask after an insect that was sizable and gaudily speckled, armored and knobby-legged and sat upon a galax leaf.

"What in Christ is that?"

Ray examined it closely. "Some bug," he told her.

The grave site was as they'd left it—haphazardly excavated and carelessly disturbed, and what ground wasn't churned up had been trampled flat. Kit bent to pinch a cigarette butt between her fingers and rose to show it to Ray.

"The chief," he said.

She shook her head as if she harbored a distinct distaste for amateurs.

"His head was down this way," Ray told her, pointing. "His right-hand fingers were poking out of the ground."

Kit sifted through the loose dirt, and Ray squatted beside her, sitting on his haunches. "I pulled out everything that was in there."

Ray had hardly finished speaking when Kit reached to take his hand. She turned it up and dropped onto his palm the corroded tab of a trouser fly before standing to peer down the hillside toward a break in the trees.

"What's down there?"

"Pasture."

"Whose?"

Ray was still shrugging as she struck out down the slope. He followed at a trot, stumbling through the scrub and the rotting leaves, dodging the limbs that Kit loosed to fly his way. She and Ray eased through the upper strands of a barbed-wire fence at the edge of the tree line and stepped into a rocky highland pasture. A few dozen heifers loitered beneath a sycamore by the bank of a half-acre pond that was spring-fed and earth-dammed, hopelessly murky.

Kit pointed toward a gravel road on the far side of a fencerow. "Where does that go?"

Once Ray had shrugged, Kit waded through the fescue and the knotty tufts of weeds toward an orange pipe gate which she found latched by a simple hook and chain. She leaned against the gatepost and gazed back toward the tree line.

"Up from the bottom or down from the top?"

"I'm guessing up," Ray told her.

The cattle snorted and fussed at the pond bank. A lone raven lit on a limb of the sycamore tree.

"I didn't even see that trailhead. And this damn road." Kit glanced at the gravel track along the fencerow. "No telling where it comes from. Let's say it's dopers out of D.C. Hell, out of Richmond. How are they going to find this place unless they know where they're going?"

"Probably wouldn't."

"And with those guys it's usually tap, tap." She aimed her index finger at Ray. "No hatchets. No hammers."

Ray nodded. "So we look under *our* rocks."

The road descended in looping switchbacks to the river, which was shoaly and muddy, was lined with clammy locusts and littered with snags and stumps. A leathery old black man stood shin-deep in the scummy water fishing with a spool of twine and a bobber and wearing against the sun a yellowing paper hat folded from the *Richmond Times-Dispatch*.

The blacktop widened to accommodate a community of sorts along the trashy north bank of the river. It consisted of a dozen tar-papered houses with dirt yards, a country grocery, a beauty shop in an ambitious utility shed and a roadhouse, low and windowless, built of raw cinder block and knotty planking. The only door stood propped open, a staub shoved in at the hinges. A half dozen sedans—shiny, tricked out, late model—crowded the litter-strewn lot.

Kit wheeled in by an immaculate Eldorado and parked. She and Ray climbed out of the Blazer and stood gazing together at the squalid little building as music drifted out through the open doorway, sultry and boudoirish in the silky tradition of Barry White—a throbbing bass line with, by way of vocals, a deep, rutting moan.

The interior was lit by a lone shaft of sunlight through the doorway and a couple of neon beer signs. A half dozen black men sat at a wobbly table drinking tallboys from the can.

"Gentlemen," Ray said, smiling and making for them as he fished the pewter ring out of his pocket. "We're looking for a fellow." He tossed the ring onto the tabletop. "Would have worn this."

The men looked at the ring, at each other, all of them anyway but for one. He wore a brown velour jacket and a shiny rayon shirt with an oversize collar and gardenias in the pattern. He considered Kit a bit brazenly, winked at her and shoved the tip of his tongue between his teeth. The other five left off with the ring to watch him watch her.

"Fellows," Ray said as Kit circled the table, as Kit reached to take up a bit of that gentleman's lapel and test the nap of his velour between her fingers.

"Well, well," she told him, "if it isn't Superfly."

He cackled, and his buddies threw in to laugh with him.

"Uh, guys," Ray said as that gentleman in the jacket and the shirt reached out a hand of his own which he brought to rest lightly upon Kit's posterior, and Ray watched her take it up in what appeared a loving fashion even as she hinged it over and thereby prompted that gentleman to launch into a vigorous complaint.

"Owowowowowow." He sounded off like an agitated Chihuahua as Kit calmly and without any noticeable effort pressed his thumb against his wrist bone and held it there. He seemed to feel a sudden need to come out of his chair and drop to the gritty roadhouse floor, and he only managed to leave off wailing long enough tell Kit, "CleveCleveCleve."

A buddy of his worked an extrapolation, pointing indifferently toward the doorway. "Got a store up the road. Knows everybody."

"Fine. Good." Ray took up the ring from the table and was halfway to the door before he turned to summon Kit. "Grasshopper," he said.

He waited for her out in the trash-strewn lot, stood pitched against the Blazer. "What in the hell was that?" Ray asked her when she'd finally wandered out to join him.

"I took a class," Kit told him. "I excelled."

Ray offered his hand for the sake of demonstration, and Kit obliged him with a spot of agony that was blended somehow, Ray noticed, with unmistakable arousal. Ray intended to congratulate Kit on the remarkable leverage she could manage, the extraordinary discomfort she was inflicting, but instead he dropped his jaw and told her, "Owowowowow."

They walked to the grocery mart just down along the river, and Kit entered the shabby little store with Ray just behind her. The place was choked with merchandise—canned meats, cookies, sodas, and beer. A side of heavily peppered fatback hung from a nail in the ceiling. Two black children—a wiry little girl in a dirty pink jumper and a chalky shirtless boy—played a pinging electronic game in the front corner of the store.

The proprietor, an elderly black man in a suit coat and tie with hair the color of grate ash, sat behind the cluttered counter reading a *Trading Post.* He was without spectacles and had his nose pressed flush against the newsprint.

"Are you Cleve?" Ray asked him.

He lifted his head and considered Ray and Kit together. "Yes, sir."

"A fellow down at the bar said you might be able to help us."

Cleve folded his *Trading Post* and shoved it beneath the counter. He stood and smoothed his shirtfront. His suit coat was tailored and spotless, thirty years out of date.

Ray produced the ring from his pocket and offered it to him. "We're looking for a guy who used to wear this. Maybe you've seen him, might have been a couple of years ago."

Cleve took the ring and turned it in his fingers, considered it on his palm. "Didn't never know a Raj. I knew a Roger once, a Chambliss he was. Wouldn't wear mess like this." A thump and a spot of giggling from the front corner of the store set Cleve off. "Quit kicking that thing, or you're leaving here."

"Remember anybody passing through?" Kit asked him. "A couple of gold teeth. Flashy sort. Would have been twenty-five or so."

"The Gaither boys up the river, they used to run with a boy."

"Do you recall his name?" Kit asked.

Cleve shook his head. "Never knew it. Wouldn't even remember him but that he was a bad one for stealing. Chips and mess. Shoving them under his shirt. Had a little blue car. I remember that."

"Have you seen him lately?" Ray wanted to know.

"Not for a while."

"How about those Gaither boys?" Kit asked. "They still around?"

"Alton's over at the penitentiary in Bland. Franklin stays with his aunt just up the river. Blue house. Sticker bush in the yard. Big old Camaro. Can't miss it." Another thump and a spate of giggling. "Hey!" Cleve snorted and shook his head, working it deliberately, disgustedly, from side to side. "Stinking grandbabies," he muttered.

The house was puny and shabby, tumbledown. The sticker bush was a pyracantha, and the Camaro was yellow and brand-new. Kit parked in the ditch just opposite the drive and then hung back in the yard as Ray approached the front door, leaving her an unobstructed view of the side yard and a portion of the overgrown back lot.

Ray skirted the clutter on the porch planking—a rusted-out grill, a pair of dilapidated folding chairs, an unruly heap of yellowed and rain-puckered *TV Guides*. He tapped on the screen-door frame. The wire of it was bulged loose at the bottom and split wide at the top. Ray heard her coming well before he could see her as she worked her feet across the floor without troubling herself to lift them. She was a thick woman, deepest black, in a house dress and bedroom slippers. She wore a quartet of pink plastic curlers in her hair.

"I'm looking for a Franklin Gaither."

She gazed dully at Ray. "Booger B." She called it out loudly, watching Ray still. "POliceman here for you."

The sound Ray heard was hardly alarming, not remarkable in any way. It was a rustling, a scuttling from inside, like a man rising from a sofa, like a man retiring down a hallway. Ray considered the noise, weighed it, placed it at length.

"Back door!" he shouted as he entered the house, as he pushed past the woman and in through the dim musky front room and down the short dark hall. He saw only a scrap of T-shirt as Franklin Gaither charged through the kitchen, out the back doorway and down off the stoop to the yard. Franklin was scaling already a vine-covered fence at the bottom of the lot as Kit rounded the house at a run and charged across the yard, climbing over after him. Ray fought his way through the crowded kitchen, mastered the balky storm-door knob and stepped onto the back stoop where he found himself quite alone.

Kit could see Booger B. tiring already up ahead. He was short and a little jowly and left his scent in his wake—stale Kools, dried sweat, and the sweet vegetable reek of hash. He struggled for breath as she closed and dodged right, crossing the road to run along the bank of the muddy river. Kit gained on him sufficiently to grab his shirt, and, ducking his flailing arms, she wrapped him up at the thighs and brought him heavily to the ground.

He thrashed with his legs and caught her with the heel of his sneaker on the bridge of her nose, blinding her, enraging her. Kit punched at him and grappled with him as he kicked and squirmed, as he slipped from her grip and climbed stumbling to his feet, lurching directly into Ray, who grabbed expressly onto Booger B.'s thumb, who torqued it back and forced it as best he was able toward Booger B.'s wrist bone.

"I don't know nothing about them cigarettes," Booger B. blurted out. "I ain't even seen that truck."

He glanced at Kit who sat pinching the bridge of her nose

between her fingers, at Ray who labored over Booger B.'s thumb with his tongue poking out of the corner of his mouth, wrenched it as if he hoped to snap it off.

"Hey!" Booger B. told Ray, jerking his hand free and plunging it into his pocket. "Quit it."

Ray had invited her over impetuously, had expected her to decline. There on the sidewalk before the station house as they were leaving for the evening to let Booger B. stew in his puny cell with its wafer-thin mattress and its stainless steel toilet, Ray had treated Kit to one of his toothy grins. "How about dinner?" he'd asked with more treble in his voice than he'd hoped for or intended. "I'm cooking," he'd added, even though he never cooked.

She'd surprised him, had huffed out a breath and told him, "Why the fuck not?"

Ray's lasagna noodles clung and tore as he scraped them off the pot bottom and then, in disgust, pitched the pot into the sink where it demolished a tumbler and cracked a coffee saucer. Monroe sat placidly on the linoleum, watching. She grumbled, lowly, deep in her throat.

"I don't want to hear shit out of you," Ray informed her and went back to concocting his entree.

He had scorched his tomato sauce and incinerated his sausage, had skinned and barked three of his knuckles on his rusty box grater, had tasted already the evening's wine which was sour and metallic.

Ray's oven pan was encrusted and unsightly, badly dinged, warped and misshapen. Ray built his lasagna with the rattiest noodles on the bottom, spooned on his black-flecked sauce and crusty nuggets of sausage which were followed by a sprinkling of cheese and more tattered noodles.

"Tatum. You in there?"

Kit stood at the front-door screen, her hands cupped to her eyes, and peered in through the wire at the shabby interior, getting for her trouble a snoutful of unsavory must bouquet.

"Come on back."

She drew open the door screen and stepped into the dingy foyer. Kit had taken in already the weedy front yard, the rickety porch steps, the fungus-stained clapboards, and she tolerated with a sour sneer the stale dusty air in the front hallway. She peeked into the parlor at the homely camelbacked sofa, at the fuel-oil furnace on the hearth, the ungodly eyesore of a chifforobe. Monroe approached to sniff Kit's legs, bare below the hem of her dress, as she negotiated the brief back hallway and arrived in the kitchen.

"You clean up nice." Ray looked her over a little more thoroughly than he'd intended.

"Some place you've got here."

"It's about equal parts mildew and field mice, but we like it."

Kit sniffed the air with an expression of rancid disapproval. "What the hell are you making?"

"Lasagna. My mom's recipe."

"Your mom's not Italian, is she?" Kit pointed toward the dog who was sniffing her left pump.

"Monroe," Ray told her.

"Funny name for a dog."

"Funny dog."

Kit took up Ray's open bottle of wine from the countertop.

She read the label and passed the uncorked throat beneath her nose, failing to stifle an involuntary shiver.

"I wouldn't drink that if I were you," Ray suggested.

"Inedible food. Unpotable wine. Quite the host." Kit reached into her shoulder bag and pulled out a fifth of Scotch. "Think you can manage a little ice?"

Ray glanced forlornly toward the drainer by his sink where his lone blue plastic ice tray dried upended.

Once they'd sat down to dinner, Kit drummed her block of lasagna with the back of her fork. She stabbed at it a time or two with her knife and shoved it clattering around her plate by way of recreation. She offered it to Monroe, who refused to so much as lick it. Kit cracked open the Scotch, and Ray joined her. They drank from Ray's lone matched pair of disreputable coffee mugs, took the stuff neat and unchilled, fairly sluiced it down as if in competition. The two of them were telling each other soon enough the untempered ill-considered truth.

"Who the fuck is this?" Kit asked, gesturing vaguely with her mug toward Ray's tape player.

"Lester Young."

Ray had selected with care his favorite cuts to play through dinner, and this was the first notice she'd taken. With her fork, Kit beat a tattoo on the crusty top of her square of lasagna out of all pace and rhythm with the tune.

"Let me get this straight." Kit set her fork aside and leaned forward, planting her elbows on the dinette. "You burned the sauce."

Ray nodded.

"You burned the sausage."

Ray nodded.

"You burned the noodles."

Ray nodded.

"Then you put them all together in a pan and burned them again."

Ray nodded and shoved at Kit his empty mug.

"It does sort of look like lasagna," Kit allowed.

"You ought to try the version out at Little Ruth's. Comes with gravy. Awful proud of their gravy out there."

Kit laughed, swinging her head from side to side. "Jesus, Tatum, how'd you end up here in Mayberry? You just don't strike me as the type."

"We've all got to wash up some place. What about you? You don't exactly say Park Service to me."

"What does?"

"You know." Ray lounged back in his chair. "Forestry geeks. Highway patrol washouts. That ilk."

"A girlfriend from the academy had gone over. She sold me on it."

"So what do you do exactly?"

"Lie on my back in the bullshit and try to float."

"You live right in D.C.?"

Kit nodded and sipped.

"Married? Boyfriend?"

Kit glared at Ray.

"So I'm nosy."

"There's sort of a guy. Just some prick I know."

Ray brightened. "Oh. Like me."

"What's your story anyway? I'm guessing some girl had her

hooks in you, but it didn't work out." Kit studied Ray, sizing him up. "You married your high school sweetheart. She got dumpy. You grew apart."

"I got dumpy. We grew apart."

"Any kids?"

Ray drew a breath, deeply, slowly. He nodded. "Yeah."

Kit followed Ray's glance to a framed photograph on a corner shelf at the end of a row of cupboards. A little girl in a sandbox played with her toes. Kit rose and stepped over to fetch it.

"She's beautiful."

Ray's smile was wan and halfhearted.

"You must be crazy about her."

As Kit set the photo on the tabletop, Ray took it up and ran a finger across the glass.

"Yeah," he said. "I was."

Kit studied Ray as he handled the frame, as he gazed out the back window toward the far tree line.

"A custody thing?"

Ray shook his head.

"Dead?"

He nodded.

"What happened?"

"It's an ugly little story."

Kit said nothing, watched Ray as he lingered over the photograph.

"Karen," he said presently, "my ex. I met her at a church supper."

"You? A church supper?"

"I was casting around back then, figured I'd give the Baptists a crack. Me and Karen really hit it off. We dated a couple of months. Got married. Bought a house down near Charlotte. I was on the force there, making pretty good money."

Ray turned to peer again out the back window toward the hedgerow by the pasture. "Karen wanted the baby. I wasn't so sure. Molly, we named her, after Karen's mother."

"Did she get sick?"

Ray shook his head. "It got to where me and Karen used to fight all the time. Nothing big really. We'd just bicker and chafe about everything, and one day she was on me about something. I'd put a red in with the whites. Hadn't used a coaster. Hadn't rinsed a dish. Who the hell knows? But we were going at it pretty good." Ray fingered his mug, spinning it slowly on the tabletop. "One minute we could see Molly out the window, and then the next minute she was just gone."

Ray drew an appreciable breath, tipped up his mug, and drained off the contents. "We had this weedy little pond down at the bottom of the lot. We'd told her a blue million times not to go down there." Ray paused. He shrugged. "It took a while to find her. I pulled her out and tried to bring her around, but—" Ray favored Kit with a wan little smile.

"Oh, Ray."

"It's funny," Ray said. "You always hear how grief binds people together, but me and Karen, we couldn't stand the sight of each other after that. I took a job down near Bristol. Memphis. Jackson. Tampa. Mobile. Here." Ray reached toward Kit's plate with her crusty untouched square of lasagna upon it. "I guess you're through with this."

He pushed back his chair and stood. Kit rose alongside him and laid a palm to Ray's cheek in a simple gesture of compassion.

"I'm so sorry," she told him.

He placed his free hand on hers, and there was even a moment when he did nothing further, before the slow advance, deliberate and glacial even, before their lips touched, chastely at first, before her hand slid behind his head and she drew him to her, before the anger percolated up at men as a breed, at Ray as a man who had moved her and had grown to seem worth comforting, even a little worth having. Kit shifted about to lay her palm against Ray's chest. She pushed him, but lightly and without force, without resolve. He kissed her still against, she wanted to think, her wishes, in spite, she chose to believe, of her adamant signal that he stop.

Ray yelped as she drove a knee into his groin. He dropped her plate to the floor where it shattered on the linoleum.

"Goddamn men! Everything's a fucking line."

Kit snatched up her bag and stalked out of the kitchen and up the hallway before Ray could stifle his agony sufficiently to speak. He heard the screen door slap shut, the thump of her feet on the porch planking, the roar of her engine in the driveway. Gravel clattered off her fender wells as she backed into the road.

Ray was still gathering up pieces of her plate, her square of perfectly uncompromised lasagna, as the whine of her engine died down to idle somewhere up the street. She sat in the road just shy of the junction, just short of the blacktop, her face illuminated by the pale green dashboard lights. A mottled cow scratched herself against a fencepost in the adjacent pasture. A man stood in the road ditch calling to his dog. Kit knocked her forehead against the steering wheel, shoved the shifter into reverse and fairly stood on the accelerator.

Ray was kneeling on the kitchen floor picking up the last of the splintered crockery as he heard the whine of the engine, the crunch of the tires on the pea gravel in his drive, the thud of feet on the porch planking, the slap of the screen door. Ray set the broken plate on the countertop and shielded his crotch with both hands together. He was backing toward the corner beyond the dinette as Kit entered from the hall, as she closed on him, as she opened his shirt with a tug.

"Goddamn you," she said but with tenderness, Ray was prepared to believe, with a detectable trace of affection.

Monroe watched. She sat on the braided oval throw rug at the foot of the bed and looked on studiously as shoes were loosed to drop to the floor, as Ray's trousers sailed through the air, his clasp and fly chattering against the bureau mirror.

Kit's dress caught on the arm of the shabby upholstered side chair, and her bra hung up on the windowsill by the underwire. A pair of fuzzy *E.T.* underpants with exhausted elastic landed close enough to Monroe for a casual sniff. Kit kissed Ray forcefully, almost violently, and then rolled on top of him to grip him by the chin. "What the hell are you doing?"

Ray showed her both of his hands. "Nothing."

"I don't need this. I'm just getting rid of one fool. Had to tell your sad little story, didn't you?"

"You asked me."

Kit kissed Ray's neck, his chest. As she slid down his torso, Ray groaned so suddenly and loudly that Monroe felt obliged to bark.

"Get that mutt out of here."

Monroe rose to all fours and grumbled, lowly, deep in her throat.

"You shouldn't have said that. She's a little sensitive."

Monroe barked at Kit, bouncing on her front feet. She persisted at it while Ray moaned, while Kit moaned, while they bucked and moaned together. She kept up with the barking until Kit had flopped onto her back with abandon and force enough to cause the steel bedframe to pop and clang, alarming Monroe into silence.

Ray worked an arm around Kit in a bid to draw her to him, in an attempt to hold her and lie with her that way couples will, but she wriggled free and climbed from the bed, set about gathering her clothes. Ray watched as Kit slipped her dress over her head.

"What's your hurry?"

"Like you're going to reload."

She hunted for her shoes by the unsightly side chair and beneath the bureau.

"You could stay here if you wanted. It's got to be better than the motor inn."

Kit snorted as she glanced about the room. Fully dressed now, she perched on the edge of the bed.

"Listen, Ray." Ray could tell by her tone what was coming, and he was sighing already and rolling away from her as she began to speak. "You're a sweet guy, and you tell a sad story, but this has got to be a one-time thing."

"That bad?"

Kit shrugged. "You knew where everything went, but we're working together. I'm a long way from home. I guess you're a long way from home too. So maybe we both needed that, but now let's forget about it."

"Just like that?"

Kit nodded. "No crazy needy guy shit, right?"

"I'm not the crazy needy type."

Ray flung back the sheet and moved to climb from the bed. "Don't get up," Kit told him. "I'm good."

She managed a slight smile, a curt wave as she left the house. Ray listened, following the sound of her footsteps across the planking and down the steps, through the yard to the gravel drive. She revved the Blazer engine mercilessly as she backed through the autumn olive and out into the road.

Ray lay on the bed pitched against the iron headboard. He heard the dying roar of the Blazer engine as Kit gained the junction at the blacktop and turned east toward town. Monroe leaped onto the mattress and stood for a moment watching Ray before she nosed him in the thigh, poking him firmly once.

"Back at you," he said.

8

We never actually saw those police boats congregated at that pier since we swung east across town upriver, a little north of Chelsea. I was pretty well myself again by the time the elevated lanes gave out, had pocketed, at Giles's insistence, his crumpled handkerchief, and, as he was fairly steadily occupied with business on the phone, I was largely free to gaze idly out the window.

I was prepared still to believe that they would drop me at the Duke, that we would swing south on Fifth Avenue where Jumbo would aggravate drivers and menace pedestrians clear down to Washington Square Park. I would hop out there by the awning, I guessed, and take my leave of Giles, would favor him with some manner of wholly unsuitable nicety.

"Appreciate the lift," I'd tell him. Or, "Thanks again for the lovely afternoon."

Then I'd enter past the sullen desk clerk behind his Plexiglas, board the elevator for the halting glacial excursion four floors up to my room where I'd hang my suit jacket, empty my pockets and stack my change by denomination on the dresser lid. I'd flop onto the bed to sprawl and twitch, to listen to my neighbor through the wall.

It seems a ridiculous notion to me now, the very idea that Giles would loose me, armed with what I'd seen, to mull and stew and fuel perhaps sufficient moral indignation to tempt me to lead Vitale and Doogan up past the George Washington Bridge to that sluggish little trickle of a creek back in the forest. I know now, of course, that Giles was not remotely finished with me, but the fact I'd decided he was serves as tribute to his manner as he'd charmed me by then and had won me, had put me at ease to a degree that even his oversight of an open-air murder couldn't entirely undo.

As we sailed east through the junction at Fifth, as we failed to make the turn, Giles switched off and hinged shut his dainty little phone. "Paul," he said to me, "I've got some business out in Queens. Could I trouble you to ride along?"

I smiled back, for godsakes, and told him, "I don't think I've ever been to Queens."

"Fly into LaGuardia?"

I nodded.

"Queens," he said.

He slapped me on the knee. It was all very convivial and jolly, so I hardly had cause to feel confined or suspect myself abducted, which impresses me now as the chief and prevailing beauty of Giles's technique—the pseudo-democracy of it, the apparent complicity.

Jumbo followed a harem-scarem route on an erratic south-easterly bearing toward the Lower East Side of Manhattan. In between phone calls, Giles pointed out the occasional landmark to me, even had Jumbo stop in traffic in the middle of an avenue in such a way as to frame to Giles's liking a view of the Wool-worth Building which Giles calmly recited, while cars piled up behind us, salient facts about.

Giles was like that—engaged and informed, eager after a fashion. He all but physically shifted me about to join with him in a view of the Manhattan skyline as we rattled across the East River on the Williamsburg Bridge. The sight of the city in jagged profile seemed to thrill and recharge him a little there in the middle of what must have been for him an uncommonly hectic day, moving like it had from a hostile police interroga-tion uptown to a tour of the Cloisters and a bucolic homicide.

I don't know where we went exactly once we left the bridge as there were precious few landmarks to speak of. Queens seemed to consist chiefly of squat unsightly buildings, gaudy billboards and unending gritty squalor. I only know we trav-eled briefly north along the Brooklyn-Queens Expressway and then exited by a cemetery and took a divided boulevard through a slovenly commercial district where the roadway was lined with furniture outlets, franchise restaurants, grocery marts, nail salons and laundries, seedy little storefronts in the business of check cashing for a fee. There was a regular wealth as well of brightly painted auto shops that seemed invariably to specialize in either window-glass replacement or the cut-rate installation of subwoofers and alarms.

I know we traveled through distinct cities and townships because there were signs along the street that told me as much, though I surely wouldn't have suspected it otherwise. Elmhurst gave way to Corona which yielded to Rego Park, but the clutter and sprawl remained uniform and unebbing. Every now and then the pedestrians would undergo a change of hue—from white to black to dusky Latino and then back to white again. Otherwise, the municipal boundaries seemed but a postal service conceit.

Even Giles, who was interested in everything, wasn't interested in Queens. He consulted with associates on the telephone all the way out to Jamaica, I believe, where we turned onto a side street and parked beneath a billboard that advertised a libation called Powerhouse—a sparkling blend of fortified wine and beer with some manner of ferocious livestock on the bottle label. A goat, I think, possessed somehow of the coiled horns of a ram and the bleary saffron eyes of an overindulgent conventioneer.

The street was lined with warehouses, a few of them abandoned and dilapidating, but the one opposite Giles's Town Car was buttoned-up and tidy. I followed Giles across the walk to a gray steel door where he tapped twice with his knuckles and raised a man who unbolted it from inside. He was thick and lumbering, was built on the order of Jumbo, and I couldn't help but picture the two of them tossing phone poles back and forth in a jolly recreational sort of way.

Though the warehouse floor was rather gloomy, I could see

that it was stacked thickly with merchandise which was sealed up in boxes and settled onto pallets. A lean and stunted gentleman, Rudy as it turned out, came scuttling toward us from an illuminated office attached to the back wall. He was in shirtsleeves, was bespeckled and ink-stained, and I felt an immediate kinship to him, recognized him instinctively for a bean-counting middle-management type much like myself.

As he approached, he waved at Giles a tissuey bill of lading. "These fucking guys," he said. "They ain't going to make it right. Put it all on us."

"Rudy," Giles told him with his usual unhurried calm, "this is my friend Paul."

Rudy twitched his head my way. "How ya doing."

"Have you found the order?" Giles asked.

"She's still looking for it." Rudy glanced toward the office where I could see a matronly woman through the lone window who was sifting through papers in a file drawer until the telephone interrupted her. A bell attached to the outer office wall clanged like a fire alarm.

"Where are they?" Giles turned to peer about the warehouse floor.

"I've got one in the office." Rudy led us across the cement warehouse floor and into the office proper.

The place was surprisingly well appointed for a boxy cubicle attached to a warehouse wall. There was a handsome fringed rug on the parquet floor, a stylish Chesterfield couch and matching bronze floor lamps on either side of the bolsters. The pictures hung about the beadboard walls were tastefully matted and framed, prints of foxhounds and thoroughbreds, scarlet-coated horsemen, an etching of a bull moose beset by a pack of wolves.

On a shelf between the windows that gave onto the warehouse floor, three pieces of salt-glazed crockery were tastefully illuminated by spotlights recessed in an ornate punched-tin ceiling.

That room was stylish in the manner of a Tidewater attorney's office, but the effect had been spoiled a little by the employees. Rudy's desk was an unambiguous eyesore, a sort of paperwork thicket set against the back wall of the room while his associate had gone in for a spot of counter-decorating.

Marie, her name was. Giles took occasion, naturally, to make the introduction as soon as she had gotten off the phone. She was a heavy woman in a shapeless print frock and a wig, I have to think, since the thing was blond with a pinkish tinge and looked to be extruded. Marie offered me a cup of the coffee she had made, and the stuff proved woefully thin and tasted of hand lotion.

She had ornamented her corner of the office with family photographs, some of them framed and settled on her desktop but the majority of them taped to her lampshade and pushpinned to the wall. Apparently, Marie had a daughter she couldn't do without the sight of, and she'd put a dozen or so snapshots of her on display along with a couple of photos of an ancient corgi mutt which was bloated and rheumy-eyed, with teeth so yellow I could almost smell its breath. I noticed in a hideous plate frame a picture of a woman I took to be Marie back when she was still content with her natural head of hair along with two photographs of a man I chose to think her husband who was young and fit in one and wore his air corps uniform while in the other he was slouched in a housecoat breathing oxygen through a tube.

Rudy scrabbled about in a pasteboard carton just alongside

his cluttered desk and produced from it a handsome lady's handbag. The thing was brown leather, or maybe leatherette, with sandy highlights and a design embossed upon it. Rudy indicated to Giles a bit of tooling along the top before he groaned rather stagily and threw up his hands.

Giles turned toward me and offered the handbag. "What do you think?"

There was a pleasing heft to the thing, and it was well stitched and comely. I unzipped it and poked aimlessly through the tissuey wadding inside. "Nice," I said.

"See it?" Giles asked me as he tapped with his finger on a band beneath the zipper along the top where the brand name had been worked into the leather. I was rather slow to recognize the problem, so Giles pointed out that the manufacturer had spelled *Vuitton* with but one *t*.

"Can't move them in the city."

"How about out on the island?" Rudy offered.

I shifted the thing about to examine it further. "It's just a knockoff, right?" I asked Giles, and I can only say that he shot me a look in return, a glare really, grim and flinty.

"*My* knockoff," he told me, and then he summoned me to him, fluttering his fingers. "Walk with me, Paul," he said.

I followed Giles onto the warehouse floor where he gripped me by the elbow and steered me into the gloom, squiring me back among the pallets of merchandise as he favored me with a lecture on cachet. He had perfume, scarves and deerskin gloves, wallets and purses, ladies' blouses, pseudo-Tiffany bracelets, British cigarettes, Cuban cigars, compact discs and videotapes, logo-infested leisurewear.

But for the smokes, which were merely untaxed and smuggled, the stuff was all pirated and phony—well pirated, however, and not conspicuously phony which apparently meant quite a lot to Giles. He considered himself, he told me, a merchant of prestige at a discount, spoke as he slit open a box with a penknife and produced from it a lovely scarf, maroon with an overlaid pattern of golden yellows and blues.

"Ferragamo?" he asked me.

I scanned the thing for its maker's mark, imprinted along an edge. "That's what it says."

"But is it?"

"Well—" I made a point of peering about at the pallet of boxes. "I guess not."

"Draped about a woman's neck? In passing? On the street? Ferragamo?"

I studied the scarf which was plainly what he wanted me to do, rubbed the cloth between my fingers, and made to savor the sensation. I shrugged, nodded.

"Context, Paul."

Giles relieved me of that item and returned it to its carton. He laid an arm about my shoulder and walked me toward an open loading bay, out of the murky gloom of the warehouse and into the flat afternoon light. "Context. Everything in its place."

Giles spoke to me at passionate length about the curious habits of consumers and the senseless tyranny of brand names, had plainly given the topic appreciable thought. "What makes a Gucci? The quality of the materials? The workmanship? The genius of the design?"

He ushered me down the cement steps at the head of the loading platform and into a grubby street that ran along the side of the warehouse. The roadway was wide and trash-strewn, comprehensively salted with grit. The warehouse standing opposite was abandoned, was shabby and dilapidated.

"Of course not. It's the label. The name."

"Yes," he allowed me. "Right."

"The trouble with most knockoffs," Giles informed me as we walked together along the street, "is that they're not convincing."

There was no sidewalk but no traffic either, so we walked out in the roadway followed by Jumbo at what, for a normal-sized human, would have been a discreet distance.

"Have you seen the guys with the watches?" Giles asked me.

I had, in fact, seen one of the guys with the watches. He'd been displaying them on Fifth Avenue in an open briefcase just up from my hotel, and he'd caught my eye when I'd glanced at him, had said to me in a lilting central African accent, "Hey, mister."

He'd had silver watches, theoretically. Gold watches, ostensibly. They were laid out on black velour, were tinny-looking with a cheap surface shine.

"Yeah," I said. "I saw one."

"Obvious trash. A bad buy even at fifteen a throw. But my stuff—"

Once we'd reached the end of the block, Giles looked left and then right along another litter-strewn roadway bordered by more abandoned warehouses. We lingered together alongside a jagged rupture in the asphalt.

"I treat my merchandise like currency. A phony twenty still has to look like cash to pass. Am I right?"

I made an effort to appear enlightened and edified as I nodded.

He then rattled off a few more scraps of his mercantile philosophy, and I noticed that Giles's line of reasoning was terribly
conventional and ordinary at bottom, tedious really, and that's
coming from an actuary. We could have been a couple of J. C.
Penney vice presidents out taking the winter air. What's more,
he kept at it as we wandered back toward his warehouse, acquainted me with various of his commercial strategies and indulged in a disquisition on his marketing and pricing. He was
engaged and wholly enthusiastic, had gone to the bother to de-
velop a detailed five-year plan.

I'm given to thinking anymore that quality bootlegging
tapped into Giles's skills in a way that his illicit narcotics business never could. The drug trade, while surely more profitable,
was appreciably less stimulating, since the market was ready-
made after all, and the customers were ravenous. To succeed, a
fellow like Giles just needed chiefly to stay alive, so there wasn't
anything to engage him really, little strategy to discuss. Giles
could have talked about his ladies' accessories probably all the
day, but I never heard him say a thing about his dope.

I knew virtually nothing about the narcotics trade before I
went to New York and met up with Giles. Like everybody else,
I'd seen the occasional shrill reports on the national news, and
I'd sat through—I'm sorry to confess—sufficient episodes of
Cops to have realized that there's a fair percentage of the popula-
tion at large who routinely smokes crack cocaine, permits their
toddlers to run naked, and prefers—when settling disputes—
serrated knives to reasoned dialectic.

Beyond that, I had nothing to call on really, and, in fact, there
was precious little to learn. As it turned out, Giles and I had

been flung together by a gym duffel full of heroin, and I still re-member the homely sight of the stuff when at last I saw it. Bagged and wrapped, bundled and taped, it looked very much like a dozen bricks of silt and hardly struck me as the sort of thing that someone might slaughter to steal, might stalk and murder simply to retrieve.

Giles's tiny phone chirped from his jacket pocket, and he ex-cused himself before he answered it, always troubled to do so. Giles was beautifully consistent in his manners.

As I stepped away to afford Giles what privacy I could, Jumbo watched me closely, even followed me after a fashion with a lurching stride or two until Giles had snapped his fingers to gain my attention, to summon me back his way. He pointed toward the billboard above the warehouse roofline, a sparkling blend of fortified wine and beer, and he swung his head from side to side and smiled in such a way as to enlist me to marvel with him over the things some people will see fit to pour down their throats.

"Put the word out," I heard him say. "I want him to know his dad's with me."

He winked at me and clapped shut his tiny telephone, re-turned it to his pocket and then laid a hand to my shoulder and steered me along the street back toward his warehouse. With his free hand, Giles pointed toward the Powerhouse bottle label.

"What is that?" he asked me, and I managed to tell him I thought it was a goat.

Franklin "Booger B." Gaither sat in a straight-backed metal chair at a narrow table in a cluttered interrogation room with the black lawn and leaf bag from Carl's trunk resting at his feet. Franklin had been permitted to light up a Kool and dipped his ashes into a jar lid.

"I told you. Them boys give me a ride. I didn't know nothing about them cigarettes. I was just sitting in the car."

"What boys?" Ray roamed as he talked. Kit leaned against the shut door, her arms crossed over her chest.

Franklin shrugged. "Some fellows."

"*What* fellows?"

"Hell, man, I don't know. I run up on 'em at D. W.'s. We was all pretty lit. They said they was going down to Roanoke. I figured, what the hell."

"So you were just sitting in the car?"

Franklin nodded. "That's me. Just sitting."

Ray drew an item from his pocket and tossed it onto the table where it clattered and skidded across the tabletop, coming to rest against Franklin's forearm. "Was one of them wearing that?"

Franklin Gaither picked up the ring and had grunted once with surprise before he caught himself, before he slouched again and merely smoked. "This ain't even about them cigarettes, is it?"

"You tell us," Kit said, leaning still against the door.

"Whatever he's into, I don't know nothing about it."

Ray stopped hard beside Franklin to speak. "He who?"

Franklin pointed with the leavings of his Kool toward the ring across the tabletop.

"His name."

"Raj, man. I ain't even seen him in—shit, I don't know— years."

"Name."

"Tony. Antony Smalls. But he ain't been around, and whatever shit he's into, I ain't got no part in it. That motherfucker's crazy."

"How do you know him?" Kit closed on Franklin as she spoke.

Franklin ground out his cigarette. "We cousins. But I'm telling you, whatever he did, I ain't got nothing to do with it. Goddamn crackhead motherfucker."

"You boys have a falling-out?" Ray asked.

"He's just crazy, man."

"Are we talking about the same guy?" Kit said. "Twenty-five maybe? All sparked out?"

Franklin nodded. "But I don't know where that nigger's at."

Ray reached into the plastic sack at Franklin's feet and drew out the skull which he slid along the tabletop toward Franklin who retreated up his chair back.

"So?" Ray gave the skull a nudge. "Know him?"

"His teeth maybe."

"Want to tell us what happened?" Kit's tone was soothing, forgiving and almost collegial in the what's-a-homicide-between-friends vein.

"I ain't fucking Quincy. I don't know."

"You fell out over money," Kit offered. "Maybe Tony smoked all your reefer."

"We ain't never fell out! I told you, I ain't seen him till now. I don't know what went with him."

"Think back," Ray said. "What were you doing the last time you saw him? Where were you?"

Franklin lit another Kool. He ruminated and smoked. "Over at Junie's, I guess."

"Your aunt's?"

Franklin nodded. "Seems like we was watching the series. The Braves and somebody. I don't know, three or four years ago. That cluckhead Tony, he was flying. Couldn't sit still. He was up for some kind of mess. But shit, man, the Braves was on."

"So?"

"So he left," Franklin said.

"Where'd he go?" Ray asked him.

"Man, I don't know. But he was zipping, just looking for shit to get into."

"Who with?"

"Hell, anybody. Said something about going up to the grave-yard and messing around. Tony had a thing about them boys, especially when he was high, and hell, he was always high."

"What boys?" Ray asked him.

"Them soldiers. You know, back in the corner. Them rebels. They set Tony off. And he took my fucking hammer, man. I've been needing that damn thing."

"Walking? Driving? What?" Kit asked.

"Took his car. Didn't never come back."

"So you didn't hear from him anymore," Kit said, "and that didn't bother you?"

"He stayed down in Lynchburg. I figured that's where he went. And anyway, I didn't want to hear from him. Crazy bastard. The hell with him. He just up and went off. Didn't *never* come back."

Franklin looked toward the skull on the tabletop with its twin symmetrical fractures, its glittering smile.

"Well," he allowed, grinned even. "Till now."

———

Ray directed Kit off the main road and onto a side street. They passed the branch bank, the vacant warehouse, the dilapidating Sunoco station, rolled over the ancient iron bridge with its scaling boltheads and turnbuckles, its clattering plank roadbed, and plunged into the shade of the luxurious canopy of massive white oaks lining the roadside.

Kit eased to the curb before the ornate cemetery gates. She and Ray climbed out of the Blazer and let themselves into the graveyard which was gently rolling and shady, mossy and undeniably serene. Just inside the gate, flanked by two cedars of Lebanon, they came across the Hogarth family plot—five grave sites in rank with each stone smaller than the last. Kit paused before the colonel's marble marker which was elegantly carved with the family crest and name.

"Founding father?" she asked.

Ray nodded, moving down the line of headstones, pointing at each in turn. "Founding mother. Founding daughter. Founding son." He paused somberly before the final stone. It was the smallest of all, largely unornamented and less finely wrought, was engraved with the name "Silas." "Founding blind three-legged muskrat," Ray said and left Kit to follow him up the hillside.

They were at work in the far corner, were scrubbing stones and manicuring about them. Four ladies, Ray counted, each silver-haired beneath her sensible straw sunbonnet. Kit joined Ray on the hilltop by a perilously listing and frost-blasted headstone that was capped with a weathered lamb of Christ.

The ladies left off with their labors to watch them come—the new deputy fresh from Mobile and the black forest ranger with the temper and the gutter mouth. They had heard all about them by then, had traded with each other actual news of them seasoned with idle speculation and flavored with abject concoction.

"Hello, ladies. Lovely spot you've got here."

Evelyn McClendon watched Ray closely, gauged and ranked him, found him more handsome than Carl and Walter and hardly so ruthlessly grim as Larry.

"You must be Mr. Tatum. And Miss Carson"—she smiled at Kit—"from the Park Service."

"Yes, ma'am," Ray said. Kit didn't offer to speak. She had decided already she didn't care for the woman's tone, nice-nasty with a distinct hint of treacly venom.

"Evelyn McClendon. Brady's aunt."

Ray couldn't place a Brady and stood squinting at Evelyn.

"The chief," Evelyn told him.

"Oh, right. Brady."

Ray uncorked one of his dopey counterfeit chortles and could feel Kit glaring at him.

"I hope this is a social call," Evelyn McClendon said gaily as she pocketed her clippers in her gardening apron.

"Yes, ma'am, pretty much. Do you and your friends here maintain this place?"

"Where are my manners?" Evelyn indicated the ladies each in turn. "Iris, Frances, Clair, this is Deputy Tatum and Miss Carson." Evelyn leaned toward Kit and spoke lowly, discreetly, to her. "I'm sorry, sugar, but what do you go by?"

"Kit."

"Kit? Carson?"

Kit nodded.

"Isn't that the cutest thing."

Ray noticed Kit's upper lip twitching, curdling into a sneer. He hurried to speak.

"Tell me, Ms. McClendon—"

"Evelyn."

"Evelyn. . . . Do you and your friends here keep up the whole cemetery?"

"Just this end."

She strolled between two rows of scrubbed granite markers and beckoned for Ray to follow her. She paused before a weathered obelisk, oddly ornate among the modest granite markers—a colonel, Ray noticed.

"We've got veterans here from Sharpsburg, Harpers Ferry, Malvern Hill, Chickamauga, Fredericksburg, Chancellorsville. It's hallowed ground. We're proud to tend it."

Left on her own, Kit approached the statue of the Confederate soldier on its massive stone pedestal. The rock was smooth and polished but for a bit of pocking about the inscription. The damage had been patched roughly, with little craft, and Kit rubbed her palm across the fills, along the engraving: *For when he dieth he shall carry nothing away: his glory shall not descend after him.*

"Miss Carson."

Kit scratched at a plug of patching with her fingernail. It was gritty and brittle, cement, she decided. Kit turned to find Evelyn McClendon watching her, smiling still.

"Despite the filth you might have heard on public TV, these were honorable men." Evelyn McClendon swept an arm to take in the scrubbed markers at her feet. "They were simply defending their homes and did not traffic in neegras."

"Right," Kit said. "The war of northern aggression and all that."

"Precisely." Evelyn McClendon's smile tightened further still as Kit joined them by strolling across a lieutenant.

"Evelyn, has there been any vandalism in here to speak of?" Ray asked. "Say in the past two or three years?"

"We have a little trouble every now and again. Mostly beer drinking and . . . I'll call it romancing." Evelyn smiled. She shook her head. "These girls today," she said. "They are awfully forthcoming."

"But they don't tear the place up, right?"

"No. Just litter and sacrilege."

"How about damage to the markers and headstones?" Kit asked. "Anything like that?"

"We had an incident a few years back."

"What sort of incident?"

Ray left off even attempting to speak once he got a whiff of the sulphurous animosity passing between Kit and Evelyn which impressed him as simultaneously female and racial, pointed and estrogen-rich. Ray retreated a few paces and stood, he noticed at length, squarely upon a cavalry corporal.

"Some boys came through one night. They'd decided they were Nazis."

"What boys?"

"Cousins, I believe, from up toward Flat Rock." Evelyn turned toward her lady friends. "Who were those boys? The ones with the paint?"

"Gentrys," she was told by all three of them harmoniously together.

"Right. Gentrys. They came in here and painted up Mr. Feldman's headstone." Evelyn McClendon pointed toward a sizable granite marker up the rise in the heart of the cemetery. It was boxy and ornate, with scrollwork and baroque relief.

"Painted what?" Kit asked.

"You know." Evelyn traced out a swastika in the air. "And 'kike,' I think it was." She glanced at her lady friends who nodded, who smiled. "Of course, the Feldmans are all Presbyterians. Used to be anyway, anymore they're heathen trash."

"And those Gentrys?"

Evelyn placed a finger to her chin, reflected for a moment in silence. "Methodists, I believe."

"No," Kit said. "What became of them?"

"Brady tracked them down. I think they got a couple of months, and they helped clean up the place. Cut limbs. Raked leaves. They didn't turn out to be such bad sorts. Just thick."

"Any other trouble?"

Evelyn glanced again at her lady friends, who merely gazed back.

"How about here at your end?"

"Kit, sugar, these are veterans." Evelyn grinned carnivorously as she spoke, clear back to her eyeteeth. "There's some things even rabble won't do."

9

We sat for maybe a quarter hour before we climbed out of the Town Car. Jumbo had eased, I'll call it, to the curb at the south end of Lizzie's block, and he rigorously scanned the sidewalk and the street, studied the individual doorways. Giles watched him with scrupulous attention, saying nothing until Jumbo had completed his survey.

"So?"

Jumbo shook his head, and Giles smiled and reached across the seatback to give him a chummy squeeze at the base of his neck. "Jumbo here has a nose for the constabulary," Giles told me.

The super let us in once Giles had shown him a fifty-dollar bill through the doorlight, and Jumbo led the way up the stairwell, testing the air as he went for even the feeblest whiff, I have to guess, of law-enforcement bouquet.

"You're not going to hurt her, right?" I asked Giles.

"Why would I do that, Paul?" His smile was disarming, nearly narcotic.

We'd run into a snarl in Brooklyn, I think. It was late by the time we'd left Giles's warehouse, crowding evening really, and we'd gotten hung up in rush-hour traffic on some thruway that had been choked with cars and panel trucks and semis, all of them creeping forward and darting laterally.

Jumbo had done his bit, juking us from lane to lane and generating what animosity he could manage, while Giles took a few calls on his dainty little phone, but they had come sparsely and sporadically as if your drug runners and knockoff merchants were all actually nine-to-fivers at heart.

He'd tended to ignore me when I'd asked him about Troy, would point out a model of vehicle he admired, direct me to a vista I should see, ply me with whatever question had popped into his head.

"Have you ever had *uni,* Paul?" he'd asked me. "That senator of yours with the white hair, what's that idiot's name?" "Did you know that the tidal surge in the Hudson often runs twenty miles upriver?"

"How do you know he's not dead?" I'd kept after him, filling the chinks and the lulls with questions of my own. "Just tell me that."

"Ear to the ground, Paul."

"What exactly did Troy do?"

Giles had shifted slightly and peered out the side glass. "I wouldn't have a Lexus," he'd said. "Such a poor value."

"Please."

He had laid a hand to my knee and had squeezed with light pressure. "He disappointed me," Giles had said and had considered me in such a way as to cause me to know that we were, for the moment, finished talking.

The door to Troy's apartment sat ajar. The glossy yellow police tape had been stripped from the jamb and unshaded bulbs were burning inside. We paused by the doorway, and Giles consulted Jumbo with a glance, Jumbo who applied his special faculty and confirmed with a nod that no officers were present. Giles gave the door a shove to swing it open.

There was a man inside in painter's whites, perched upon a stepladder and slopping a second coat of stark white latex on the back wall. He said something to us in Polish, I believe.

The wood flooring was puckered and buckled from the blood. The stain on the wall by the door had leached already through the paint, and the place stank like a slaughterhouse. Giles reached in and, with an affable wink, drew shut the door.

She thought we were Vitale, was expecting Vitale, and Lizzie answered Giles's knock with a gay smile and the first burblings of a spot of girlish prattle, but the sight of Giles upon her threshold corked her up precipitously.

"I don't believe we've been properly introduced." Giles stepped into Lizzie's apartment as he spoke.

"I'll scream," she said.

Giles ignored her as he surveyed her furnishings and possessions. Jumbo followed us inside and shut the door.

"My friends call me Giles." He offered his hand, and Lizzie, as it turned out, required but the scantest of moments to adjust and temper her role, managed in short order a wholesale transformation from date to damsel.

She took Giles's hand. "Lizzie," she told him, haltingly and quivering a little.

"Odd that we've never met, what with you and Troy being so close." Giles favored Lizzie with the manner of bland and benign expression I'd seen previously as we'd emerged from the woods up past the Cloisters.

"Just neighbors," Lizzie said.

Giles wandered about the tiny apartment, considered the head shots of Lizzie lining the walls, seemed to study the variations in eyeshadow and the evolving hairstyles. Giles paused before the artful black-and-white photograph of Lizzie posed upon a rock and engaged in a leisurely survey of her anatomy. "Of course, you know Paul," he said as he contemplated, it appeared to me, her vulva.

Lizzie eyed me briefly with a pinched smile and nodded before conspicuously checking her watch. "I'm expecting someone."

"Oh?" I couldn't help myself, and my tone had that nasty sneering edge to it that rarely comes off well out loud. Giles took occasion to consider me at some length as he was a helplessly devoted student of human frailty. I just stood there by Lizzie's sofa and fumed.

"Anyone we know?" Giles asked.

"Lieutenant Vitale, as a matter of fact." Again she lifted her arm to look at her watch. "He'll be here any minute."

"Vitale." Giles muttered the name with corrosive contempt. "He's never been on time in his life." Giles replaced a photo he'd lifted from Lizzie's bookshelf, took pains to reposition it precisely. "And he'll never make lieutenant."

"Yeah, well, he was supposed to be here nearly twenty—"

"Cut!" Giles barked at her. He knew a performance when he saw one. Lizzie made a splendid job of looking fearful and pathetic as Giles approached her, closing in until he was snug before her. "I had a chat earlier," he said, "with Mr. Ramirez."

Giles reached into the inner pocket of his blazer and withdrew from it the Polaroid his associate had taken in the woods. Giles held the photo up in such a way as to display for me the image—Mr. Ramirez, perforated and bloody, sprawled in that trickle of a creek. "Didn't I, Paul?"

I nodded, and Giles turned toward me, prodding me with a glance. "Yes," I said. "You did."

"It was most productive. I came away—" Giles paused in a self-conscious and actorly fashion, entirely suitable for Lizzie. "Wiser," he announced. "Naturally," he added, "sadder too."

"I don't know any Ramirez," Lizzie assured him. She elevated her nose and twitched her head as she spoke, and her voice was tinged with a strain of soap-opera indignation as if she were insisting she had no feelings whatsoever for the handsome young cardiologist recently come to Bay Side from Harbor View.

"Odd. He knows you." Giles offered Lizzie the photo, pressed it upon her really. "Knew you."

When she declined to clutch it on her own, Giles took her by the wrist and placed the picture upon her palm. She glanced at it and flung the thing onto the floor. Jumbo lumbered over to pick it up with a groan and wiped it on his pant leg prior to returning it to Giles.

"As you can imagine," Giles declared, "I'd very much like to chat with Troy as well."

"Troy's dead."

"After a fashion." Giles smiled as he removed from the side pocket of his suit coat a small brass case. He opened it and took from it what looked like a business card, creamy white and stout, imprinted with a telephone number alone.

"This," he said, raising the card, its corner pinched between his thumb and forefinger, "is an opportunity."

He stepped over to a bookcase by the wall and stood the card up, leaning it against the framed photo of a wizened white-haired woman. Lizzie's mother, I decided. Giles winked. "Don't waste it."

He didn't wait for a reply, made plain with his bearing that he was hardly keen to entertain a reaction but turned pretty much on heel and crossed toward the door. Giles stepped into the hallway, where he waited for me to join him, and I remember still the sight of Lizzie—thespianically defiant—glaring at me as Jumbo shoved me out before him and shut the door behind us.

We lingered at the head of the block in Giles's sedan, were probably a good twenty minutes or so waiting for Vitale who climbed finally out of a taxi and paused at the curb to render adjustments to his shirttail and pick lint from his trousers. He was openly savoring his reflection in the doorlight as Lizzie buzzed him in.

I'd reasoned already she'd probably see clear to retain him through the night, for security's sake, unofficial police protection. Accordingly, as we pulled off, I set about detesting him for it, and I seem to recall that I succeeded at detesting her a little as well.

"Hungry, Paul?" Giles asked as we rounded a corner onto Sixth Avenue. I'd had an icebox waffle and coffee at Lizzie's what seemed to me, by that time, years ago.

"I know a place," Giles said, and he told me what must have been the name of it—something brief and phlegmy with a French r.

Jumbo grunted and bobbed his massive head. He turned onto a cobbled side street and jostled us along its length until it gave out at the West Side Highway where he veered north and made of himself straightaway a vehicular irritant.

"She's a pretty one all right," Giles said, suddenly and without incentive or preamble. "I mean, in a way. A little long in the tooth for an actress these days."

I'd been thinking independently about Lizzie myself, naked, of course, and entwined with Vitale on her fold-a-bed. "She told me she's thirty-two," I said.

Giles laughed as he glanced out toward the Hudson where a ferry, its windows illuminated in the darkness, warped away from a Jersey pier into the river proper.

"She knows where he is, doesn't she?

Giles watched the progress of the ferry as it chugged Manhattan-bound in the light chop. He glanced my way. He nodded. And it struck me that I was privileged, in a fashion, to see a competent detective at work, particularly after the hapless comedy of Doogan and Vitale. Giles was everything they weren't—keenly observant, canny and incisive, devoted—was merely conducting, after all, his own investigation, in his own way and with his own resources, in pursuit of his own manner of justice.

Giles could enjoy, of course, the luxury of single-mindedness since he had no one but Troy to concern him and ample lingering disappointment to provoke and to fuel him. With Doogan and with Vitale there was scaled city pay and the distraction of other civilians getting robbed and beaten and dead. Even if Troy's case had served as Doogan and Vitale's lone concern, there would still have been the coffee and confections, the idle barbed chatter and senseless debates, the bureaucratic fruitlessness of it all.

We traveled but briefly on the highway before Jumbo fairly swooped into a darkened side street lined with low brick buildings, ancient and unsightly. They housed meatpacking concerns: Stavritz & Sons. Colossi Brothers. Little Flower Poultry and Fowl. Regina Prime. The cobbled street was greasy and deserted, and there was the distinct smell of suet in the air.

Halfway along a darkened block, Jumbo slowed and double-parked before an awninged entranceway. As business concerns go, that restaurant was terribly discreet, retiring even. I never once saw the name of it printed anywhere. It wasn't stenciled on the front glass or the lip of the awning. I couldn't find it on the menus or the matchbooks. The business card I eventually picked up from the hostess's lectern had but a few graphic scratchings on it and, beneath them, a phone number punctuated with periods in the continental fashion.

We entered through a brief foyer and between plush draperies hung against the draft to find a gentleman sniping at the hostess who was wondrously lanky, was Asian, and carelessly beautiful in a way that would have sent Lowell into authentic raptures.

"Do we or do we not have a reservation?" That gentleman was scarlet and irate. His wife alongside him had dressed with all of the tasteful reserve of a show pony.

"You certainly do, sir." The hostess smiled ever so slightly as she consulted the massive ledger book laid open on the lectern before her. "It'll be thirty to forty minutes for your table, if you'd care to wait at the bar."

"Eight-fifteen, right?" He tried to show her his watch face, but she wouldn't deign to look at it and instead caught sight of Giles and rushed to greet him.

"So nice to see you again," she said, offering her hand, and Giles pressed the knuckles to his lips. He made his usual species of introduction while the gentleman with the watch and the reservation and the brassy wife openly seethed at us.

"Can you fit us in?" Giles asked her.

"Certainly." She motioned for us to follow her into the dining room.

"Pardon us," Giles said, waiting for that gentleman to ease out of the way.

He glared at Giles. At me. I do believe he was in the vicinity of an unsavory remark when Jumbo swept open the draperies and stepped inside. It would be difficult, I imagine, to improve upon a three-hundred-pound Samoan for social lubrication, and that gentleman saw clear to retreat without comment, snatched his wife to safety as well. Giles and I eased past and followed that lanky hostess while Jumbo parked himself at the bar where he could watch us while he ate mixed nuts and drank what looked to be ginger ales.

We were given the best table, a manner of banquette actually and the only vacant spot in the place. It would likely have accommodated five in a pinch, but the hostess deftly whisked away the superfluous silver and invited us to settle in opposite each other. There rested between us a delicate vase with flowers and ferny greenery in it. Giles glanced at the thing, and his expression soured slightly.

"I don't care for violets," he said, and they were snatched away as well, gone with the extra napkins and the bread plates, the stemware and the unneeded cutlery.

I could see the faces turned our way in the candlelight. The scrutiny was very nearly palpable. The patrons were talking about us—I could feel it. They had all gotten a whiff of Giles as he passed and had sensed, I guess, his native star quality and unassailable self-assurance, much in the way that Jumbo sniffed out cops. They were trying, I had to imagine, to figure out precisely who he was, what he did, why they should know of him. They were obliged as well to attempt to settle to their satisfaction just what in the name of the great Lord and Maker he was doing in the company of a dowdy and half-throttled sort like me.

Giles summoned the captain with eye contact alone. As Giles ordered wine, I took occasion to consider the other diners who were a handsome lot and well dressed in, what I had to suppose, was a tony and up-to-the-minute sort of way. I had never before imagined black could come in so many hues—flat deep black, middling black, faded black, glossy black, sheer black tinted by fleshtone peeking through from underneath.

That room was also rich with remarkable haircuts, no few of them drastic and alarming. I saw a man against the far wall with a strip of scalp above one ear who looked as if he'd come away from the hospital for dinner in the immediate wake of a cranial procedure, and I got the distinct impression from the diners about that what time they hadn't squandered on their clothes and their coiffures, they'd probably spent selecting eyeglass frames.

"Bordeaux?" Giles asked me.

I nodded again, even though I didn't know from Bordeaux as my preference is for bourbon in modest quantities. What wine I buy tends to hail from well west of France.

The captain approved of the choice with an enthusiasm that suggested it was pricey, and he returned shortly with our bottle and some manner of elaborate rig that permitted him to decant the wine over a candle into a carafe. He splashed a bit into Giles's glass which Giles sniffed and sipped like a man who often sniffs and sips such wine. He then allowed the captain a taste and had a stem sent to the chef.

We toasted, Giles and I, tapping our glasses together. "Health," he told me.

I smiled as best I was able. "Health," I said.

We shared something raw to begin, though I can't say what precisely. It was pinkish and tissuey thin and napped with a satiny sauce. Giles ate but little of it and enjoyed his wine in measured sips as he was one of those rare people who, when he said he wanted only a taste, actually wanted only a taste in fact. For my part, I left some gauzy pink meat and a ribbon of sauce on the plate strictly because that's what I'd been raised to do.

I had the duck which was presented to me in a confounding architectural heap, a pillar really of kale and glazed onions and roasted fingerlings with a seared breast balanced upon it beneath a mound of lacy salad. The whole thing was capped off by some manner of crisp root-vegetable chip, and that had been planted by its pointy end and was standing fully upright.

I was obliged to sit and contemplate the strain of engineering I'd have to undertake to get anything in my mouth. Giles noticed me, I guess, studying my entree and distilled from my expression my trouble, so he reached across the table and, with the back of his fork, delivered a blow to my dinner that served to fairly demolish my pillar of food.

"Eat," he told me.

And I did. Everything tasted, as I recall it, predominantly of salt.

The chef stopped by as we were finishing up, got to us eventually anyway once he'd paraded through the restaurant and had paused at various tables to accept the praise of his patrons. I noticed that he appeared a little too gratified by the attention, and he was openly preening by the time he'd drawn up before us.

Giles made straightaway his customary gracious introduction, and I was given out to the chef as his good friend Paul. The chef shook my hand, and he was the first person I'd come across all day who didn't betray any sign of noticing my bruises and contusions, didn't appear the least bit tempted to inquire after my puffy lip.

As it turned out, he wasn't the observant sort, or rather, he was accustomed to paying measurable heed only to those details that bore upon him most directly. He was handsome in a way and very probably telegenic. He hosted, I gathered from hearing him talk, some manner of cooking show, and when he finally inquired of me how I'd enjoyed my dinner, he didn't trouble himself with listening to what little I had to say back.

"I could use some air," Giles announced, dispatching the chef with a wink, and then slipped out from the banquette and smoothed his jacket front.

We crossed the dining room toward the doorway as the chef retired to the kitchen, and I noticed that the patrons weren't torn and weren't conflicted. It was Giles they elected to watch go, Giles who paused to buss the hostesses on the cheek, who left Jumbo a lump of cash with which to settle up the bill.

I had given up by then even idly wondering when they might carry me back to the Duke. Giles grabbed the front seatback and drew himself forward to offer Jumbo instruction, and we lurched out of the gutter and yawled along the cobbled street. We headed south toward the World Trade Center and the narrow neck of lower Manhattan which we crossed along a deserted side street east past City Hall and up a sweeping accessway onto the span of the Brooklyn Bridge.

Even I could recognize the stone towers, the drooping cables studded with lights. The span was thick with traffic, and the lanes were terribly narrow. Jumbo was feeling, I have to think, particularly devilish, and by the time we'd exited on the Brooklyn end, he'd left appreciable vitriol in his wake.

We shortly barked against the curbing before a brownstone on a quiet residential street. Giles tugged at his shirt cuffs and shoved open his door. "Walk with me, Paul," he said.

Giles waited to allow me to draw abreast of him. Jumbo followed us at a seemly distance as we strolled along the tree-lined street and turned down a brick-paved walkway to an esplanade above the harbor with a view of the illuminated office towers of lower Manhattan that was little short of spectacular.

I followed Giles to the iron railing at the far edge of the promenade where he pointed out to me the sights. He said nothing, merely drew them to my attention—the Woolworth spire, the Statue of Liberty, a Staten Island ferry, schoolbus yellow and brilliantly illuminated, nosing into its slip. A roadway ran just beneath us, and we were treated with some frequency to sooty plumes of rising tractor-trailer exhaust.

Giles tugged me away from the railing by my coat sleeve, and together we walked south down the esplanade which was over-hung with trees on the back verges and bordered by the rear fa-cades of brownstones, was lined along its length with benches, nearly all of them vacant in the cold night air. We passed the oc-casional civilian with a dog and a couple necking heavily canted up against the fence. We were just coming upon a trio of youths, I guess I'll call them, as Giles's dainty telephone chirped in his coat pocket.

Giles reached in after it and had but hinged it open and spo-ken into it once when the music started from a boom box on the bench among those boys. They were black, the three of them, like Giles, but they were not like Giles at all. They wore puffy down jackets and voluminous jeans, and one of them appeared to sport a scrap of pantyhose for a cap. They drank from a com-mon bottle that they passed among them which they had left in its brown paper bag. A sparkling blend, I decided, of fortified wine and beer.

Giles shot a look their way to size them up, I have to think. "Hold on," he said into his dainty cellular phone. Then he turned and caught Jumbo's eye, pointed with the pitch of his head, and Jumbo straightaway approached those youths so as to enter into consultation.

I think anyway that he might have asked them to switch their boom box off. His back was to me, though, so I couldn't really see him, and I certainly couldn't hear him over the musical selection which sounded like a heated domestic dispute with a bass line and a drum.

The next thing I knew, Jumbo had that boom box over his head which was no mean feat since the thing had the heft and girth of a length of tree trunk. The young man with the panty-hose on his head shouted, "Yo yo yo yo yo!" as Jumbo flung that contraption down and broke it into assorted pieces which put an end to the music as chunks of plastic skidded about the brick.

At first those boys seemed afflicted with some strain of hip-hop shock. They looked at each other, at Jumbo. "Damn, man," one of them managed to say.

For my part, I'll confess I was a little thrilled since I had, af-ter all, just witnessed a middle-aged white man's wet dream; Jumbo had up and done the sort of thing that my ilk only has ulcers and strokes about. Giles, for his part, merely proceeded with his telephone conversation. "Go ahead," he said, and I could hear the tinny warble of a voice through the receiver.

I don't think those boys had even noticed Giles until then, and the sight of him made a distinct impression upon them. They seemed, the three of them, to recognize him, but not like the patrons back in the restaurant since these fellows appeared to know exactly who he was and just what his capabilities might be, and somehow, without speaking, they agreed among them to engage in a retreat.

The one in the stocking cap raised his hands to show Jumbo his bare palms. "Yo, man," he said. "Yo." And he stepped back-ward with what slink and style he could muster under the circumstances. His colleagues had headed already down the promenade at a trot, and he walked after them until he had thought better of it and set up a jog himself.

"Yeah," Giles said into his puny phone and turned to look my way. "He's right here. But if he doesn't care, then he doesn't care. Right. Yeah." He hinged shut the dainty contraption and shoved it into his pocket. Only then did it occur to me precisely what Giles was up to, the course of action he'd elected to pursue.

"It won't matter to him," I said. "Why would it?"

"You are his father."

It was touching after a fashion—Giles's faith, that is, in the strength of the blood bond, in the helpless potency of the family attachment. He'd reasoned somehow that the standard allegiances and currents of feeling would pertain for even a son like Troy toward even a father like me.

"So now what?" I asked him.

Giles displayed for me the sour little smile he reserved for distasteful enterprises. A jogger wheezed by us, a portly gentleman in a shiny running suit that sang rhythmically as his thighs glanced in passing. "My business is like anybody else's," Giles told me. "Things have to be done a certain way."

"How much did he take? I don't have a lot of money, but maybe I can come up with—"

"You can't," Giles assured me. "You shouldn't. I have my rules, Paul."

Giles paused to soak in the view. We could see clear up to the Chrysler Building to the north, to the strung lights of the Verrazano to the south. "Almost looks civilized from here, doesn't it?"

"But he's my boy," I told him.

"No, Paul. He's my boy."

Giles struck back out the way we'd come, but I didn't follow him straightaway, lingered instead at the railing which left Jumbo in an awkward predicament since he didn't seem to know exactly who to lurk behind and watch. Giles paused some thirty yards along the esplanade and tugged at his shirt cuffs.

"Walk with me, Paul," he said and thereby clarified matters for Jumbo who drove me ahead of him until I'd drawn up alongside Giles proper.

He smiled, Giles did, and drew a hardy breath. "Nice night," he declared.

The television played in Kit's motel room as Kit lay sprawled listlessly on the bed with her trousers unfastened and her twill shirt unbuttoned, with a crumpled huffy note from the motel manager in her hand. It seems they didn't much approve at that motor inn of their telephones getting pitched into the lot.

She kicked off her shoes onto the hideous deep-pile carpet and gazed at the ceiling, a field of twelve-inch acoustical tiles that were mildewed and water-stained, laughably outdated. Kit reached blindly toward the nightstand to change the channel, jabbing at the remote fixed fast to its bolted swivel.

Market Wrap. The Equalizer. News Chat. Entertainment Tonight.

Kit paused in her tour up the dial, watching the ceiling still, and she decided that she detected a pattern in a blotch of mildew above the window. She could make out a face with heavy-lidded eyes and a cleft chin—young Bill Holden.

"I fell in love with the script," a starlet said on the television.

Kit raised onto an elbow in time to see a movie clip of a

tanker truck exploding behind a willowy brunette who trotted just ahead of the flames and the shrapnel, braless, in heels, with a gun.

Kit changed the channel. A Nasdaq update. Weather patterns on the Iberian Peninsula. Swing mechanics. *Spenser: For Hire.*

She switched off the set and rose from the bed, crossing to the window to peer out through the blinds at the asphalt lot with its weedy border, at the murky neglected swimming pool, at the car dealership on the opposite side of the bypass with its plastic scarlet pinions rustling and popping in the breeze.

"No," she said, once and firmly, even as if she meant it. "No," she repeated, more this time in the way of a plaintive whine.

He was listening to Lester, beautiful silky Lester, was sitting with his feet on the porch rail and his backside punching through the rotten chair caning. Ray sipped at a beer and shifted ever so cautiously, had gotten skewered earlier by a chair-seat splinter, and the sensation remained vivid to him. Monroe lay stretched out on the planking by Ray's chair where she fluttered and twitched as she dreamed. Lyle had ventured from his house up the road to shout into the woods.

"Queenie!" he called. "Come on here, Queenie girl!"

Ray heard the tires on gravel, the puttering hum of the engine, and he anticipated that it would likely be his neighbor down the way, the fellow with the blue Dodge pickup with the whitewalls and camper top who usually had a frank glare for Ray as he rolled past. Instead Kit's Blazer whipped in through the autumn olive and stopped with a jerk in the yard. Ray dropped his feet from the porch rail and permitted his mouth to sag open until the view from his adenoids was fairly panoramic. Ray had grown, with good reason, wholly unaccustomed to blessings and granted wishes.

"Well, well," he said, watching Kit climb from her four-by-four and mount the porch stairs. Monroe stirred from her sleep and rolled onto her belly to blink at Kit as she gained the planking. "Color me surprised."

"Nothing else to do in this sumphole."

"Nice to see you too."

"Got another one of those?"

Ray stood and offered Kit his chair with the rotted punched-out seat, but she lowered herself onto the planking instead, dropping down alongside Monroe who shoved her snout at Kit, poking her in the thigh.

"Hey yourself."

When Ray returned with her beer, he sat alongside Kit and tried to make chat, indulged, that is, in the occasional idle inquiry, immediately regretted it and then embarked upon another—equally idle and inevitably regrettable. Kit asked after a bird down by the roadcut whose song Ray couldn't identify, a spindly plant in the yard that Ray was unable to name.

"What is it with you and this music, Tatum?" she inquired of him at length.

"You don't like it?"

"No, I like it fine, but look at you. You ought to be listening to that country fool in the big black hat. What's the story?"

Drawing on his beer, Ray paused to cast back and recall the details, to pin down the particulars.

"I came across Lester in Jackson, Mississippi, of all places. I used to pull speed-trap duty on the Vicksburg road. When there wasn't much business, I'd tune in the radio. A little college down there had a station. They'd play crap all day and jazz at night, and one night there he was. I'd never heard anything quite like it. Sad, you know, but beautiful."

Kit considered Ray with a sneer. "That's some kind of line, right?"

"Queenie!" Lyle shouted from the ditch on the opposite side of the road. "Queenie girl!"

"Who is that? He was out there last night."

"Lyle. He lives up the street."

"What did he lose?"

"His dog."

"What kind of dog?"

"A dead one."

Kit watched Ray rise from the planking and enter the house. He returned with a snapshot which he handed to her, a picture of a man on a settee with a scruffy mutt in his arms.

"Turn it over," Ray said, and Kit flipped the photo.

"Queenie! Queenie girl!" Lyle's voice was anxious and a little forlorn in the twilight.

"Sad," Kit said, "but beautiful."

She set her beer can on the porch step, stood up and descended into the yard where she paused and turned toward Ray. "You coming?"

Lyle proved exceedingly grateful for the help, suspected his Queenie was nearby, up a hollow probably after a rabbit or a deer. They chatted as they roamed the road cut with Kit quizzing Lyle about the particulars of his life. He owned up to a late wife, a wayward son, a thirty-year career at the pulp mill out between the airfield and the quarry.

Lyle showed Kit a scar on his shin from a wound he'd received near Pusan, on the Yalu River. He intoned with ceremony and conspicuous affection a scrap of his late father's tinhorn philosophy. Lyle allowed that he quite possibly loved his dog unduly.

"Queenie!" they shouted up the road cut and into the woods. "Queenie girl!"

It wasn't the sex Ray had ached for, quick again and spasmodic, with a canine audience of one, but the aftermath, the languid surrender, her hand upon his chest, her cheek upon his arm, the easy complicit silence, the night.

"Cool tonight," he said and drew up the spread about them.

She crowded against him, nuzzling and fitting close. She had brought in her grip from the Blazer, had set it on the floor beside Ray's closet, decisively and without commentary. The clothes she'd shed were folded neatly on the dresser top.

Ray's arm grew numb from the weight of Kit's head upon it. His feet were tangled hopelessly in the sheet. His skin was stuck to Kit's everywhere they touched, and his itches were all far-flung and unreachable, but Ray lay on his back smiling, possessed by a strange sensation. He suspected it might pass for contentment, imagined it was something like peace.

I can't name the hotel, though I know it was located somewhere up by Central Park. I had a partial view of an ice-skating rink from the windows of my suite, had a living room with a marble-faced fireplace, had a wet bar and a kitchenette, a rosewood baby grand piano.

Giles took me up himself, leaving Jumbo in the car, and Spooky was there to meet us with a Twizzler hanging limply from his mouth. He'd opened the TV cupboard and watched wrestling as Giles toured me through the suite, from the common rooms to the bedroom to the dressing room to the elaborate bath with its European fixtures.

"Of course, if you like," he told me, "I'll have Jumbo drop you at the Duke."

And maybe he even would have, but I allowed it probably wasn't necessary. Giles switched off the television on his way past the cupboard and pointed out to Spooky a chair that he could carry into the hall.

"Enjoy," Giles said as he followed Spooky out and shut the door.

She must have been downstairs already having a drink in the lounge, I imagine, since I recall that she tasted faintly of gin. I was still in my jacket and topcoat, was lingering by the window looking out over the park, over the city, when Spooky swung open the door to admit her.

"Paul?" she said.

She dropped her shoulder bag onto a chair seat. As her coat was only draped about her arms, with a graceful shiver she shrugged her way from it and let it fall onto the couch.

"I'm Rachel."

She looked, from where I stood, flawless, was tall and lean, and her hair was the color of burnished copper. As she crossed to join me at the window, she reached back to remove a clasp and shook her head to loose the tresses to fall about her shoulders. Rachel offered me her hand and pressed close against me, encouraging me to put my arm about her. She adjusted the lay of my hair with a light touch of her fingerends.

"Some view," she said.

And as I looked toward her to make reply, she kissed me. Not lewdly, though, not one of those grinding syrupy kisses that is the clinical specialty anymore of the cinema screen. She merely touched her lips to mine, gently and tenderly, and then blotted with her fingerend her lipstick from my face.

"That Giles thinks of everything, doesn't he?"

Rachel smiled. It was as far as she would go toward thwarting the illusion and dispelling the romance. She helped me out of my topcoat and my jacket.

"How about a drink? I make a wicked gimlet."

"Right," I told her. "Yeah. Sure. A drink."

It is my personal custom to speak to beautiful women in the lilting tones of a startled primate since I know a superior being when I see one, and I hadn't by then entirely adjusted to the notion that Rachel was a creature for hire. She was lovely after all and seemed to be well-spoken. I observed her as she traveled to the wet bar, and she moved with an easy grace, was statuesque and voluptuous both at the same time, had a runway model's build with an appreciable silicone assist.

She did make a wicked gimlet, tart and liberating. Rachel adjusted the lighting in the room, switching off the overheads and dimming down from Spooky's hospital-corridor ambience, and then perched beside me on the couch, kicking off her shoes and hooking a leg beneath her.

Rachel interviewed me after a fashion, asked after my interests and my profession. I owned up to being a neural surgeon with a passion for downhill skiing, and, well into my second gimlet, I disclosed that my friends called me Tod. We never had the conversation that I'd suspected we would have, the little chat Rachel probably endures almost nightly. I didn't press her, that is, to account for her curious choice of careers. With her beauty and her bearing, Rachel was plainly a woman who must have had options, was hardly like that female with the tarpaulin wig working the West Side avenues who'd seemed entirely suited for the service industry.

I'd figured I would scold and redirect her, do what I could to set her on a respectable career path, but then she retired to the bedroom where she lingered for a time before she called out to invite me to join her, and I entered to find Rachel in the sort of scant inventive underwear that I'd only previously seen in catalogs. That was the moment I decided that her given occupation was, in fact, an authentic option too.

She helped me out of my clothing, and I was keen to help her from hers, but, being a man, I was incompetent to operate her catches. So I stood there quite naked while, covered still, she enthused over my assets.

"Oh, Tod," she told me in a breathy whisper and with a fond tug, "you're so big."

She shoved me onto the bed as she'd reasoned, I guess, that I was the sort who might thrill to a bit of shoving, and then she shucked for me—with agonizing deliberation—her delicate underthings.

What ensued was a theatrical experience for me, a performance on Rachel's part of the highest thespianic order. I merely provided the implement while she manufactured all of the friction, and when at last she quivered and wailed and thrashed, she seemed awfully much like a woman who'd been driven to it by glorious congress with the likes of me. As counterfeit orgasms go, Rachel's put Lizzie's spasms to shame.

She'd been paid, apparently, to stay the night. Rachel nuzzled against me and, in the way of a polite consideration, she remained awake long enough to allow me occasion to recover and have at her once again, but I only held her instead until my arm went numb when I worked myself free and rose from the bed to enjoy my own strain of satisfaction. I gathered, that is to say, Rachel's underthings off the floor, collected her stockings and her dress off a chair seat, and I folded them all and placed them neatly in a bureau drawer.

10

Ray tapped on the chief's doorjamb, and, with the phone receiver to his ear, the chief motioned for Ray and Kit to step inside.

"Now hold on here, Mrs. Crowder. We can't be running out there every time she breaks a plate." The chief plucked a file out of the clutter on his desktop and handed it to Ray.

Ray flipped open the folder which proved to contain Antony Smalls's yellow sheet. It was extensive, four pages of arrests for assorted misdemeanors and felonies, grand theft, assault, battery, possession, larceny, manslaughter.

"I can't haul off the woman for being loud. I just can't do it. I'd have my wife's sister under the jail by now if all you had to be was loud."

Ray showed Kit a printout from the DMV. "Blue Toyota," he said as he handed the folder over to her.

"Well, you do that if you feel like you have to. I'm sure the governor'll be delighted to hear from you. All right then." The chief cradled the receiver with a toss.

"What about those cigarettes?" Kit asked. "Where's Booger B.?"

"State police came for him. It was a giveaway. The driver handed over his rig at the rest stop out by Raphine. He turned up in Wheeling at his girlfriend's. They picked up Booger B.'s buddies on the Jersey Turnpike with the truck." The chief dropped heavily into his desk chair. "So. Where are you with the cousin?"

"We went and talked to your aunt," Ray said. "Out at the graveyard."

"What for?"

"Franklin told us Smalls might have gone there."

"Gone there for what?"

"Had it in for the Confederacy," Ray told him. "Especially when he was good and cracked up."

"Booger B. said he carried a hammer," Kit told the chief. "And the base of that statue looked like it had taken a beating."

Ray drew the gritty plug of cement from his trouser pocket and offered it to the chief who took it and examined it between his thumb and forefinger.

"We asked your aunt about it," Ray said. "She told us ice had seeped in and busted up the stone."

"Then that's what it was." The chief closed the cement plug in his palm. "Anything else?"

Ray gestured toward the folder in Kit's hand. "We'll get on

this. See if we can track down his car. That might take us somewhere."

"Sounds like a plan. Try the salvage yard out past the quarry."

"Line two," Ailene shouted from the squad room. "Somebody
from the governor's office."

"Sweet Lord and Maker," the chief groaned as he reached for
the handset.

They stopped at a service station and a produce stand for directions and were finally put on the proper route by a Nicara-
guan they came across along the edge of a nectarine orchard. His
face was wrapped in a bandanna, and he wore coveralls and a
plug-chew hat, reeked of insecticide and fertilizer.

"Sabe molto coches junko?" Ray asked him and attempted
with his hands the universal symbol for junkyard.

"Yeah, sure," the fellow said and pointed back the way they'd
come.

The place was squalid and weedy, flyblown and overrun with
groundhogs. Rusting cars and tractors were littered down a hillside into a ravine, and a Norfolk-Southern coal car lay upended
on the slope. It was wheelless, and assorted squares of sheet steel
had been raggedly torched away from its side panels.

The proprietor emerged from his office as Kit and Ray pulled
up—stepped, that is, from a salvaged utility shed. He reamed an
ear canal with his pinkie, dredged mucus and spat, displayed his
scant remaining teeth as he informed the pair of them, "Hey here."

Leading them into the bowels of his junkyard, he shoved his
fingers beneath the band of his meshweave cap and clawed at his
scalp. "TOY-yota," he said. "TOY-yota." He swung his head from
side to side, considering the rusting carcasses.

"Don't you keep records of what moves in and out?" Kit asked him.

He shook his head and winked. "Cash business, little missy."

He took up a rusting steel slat from a leaf spring and thrashed at the grass with it, killing a baby copperhead which he flicked onto the roof of a sky-blue Ford Falcon to roast in the sun.

"What's that?" Ray pointed toward a hatchback that sat perched on top of an International state body truck which was resting upon a crushed Dodge half-ton.

Kit eyed the vehicle. "Worth a look."

For a moment, neither Ray nor Kit offered to move. The proprietor watched them watch each other as he ran his tongue along the rim of his mouth. "So?" he said.

Kit smiled sweetly at Ray as he unhooked his utility belt, offered to hold it for him and encouraged him as he ascended, rooted him on as he caught and ripped his trousers on the crumpled half-ton bumper, as he pierced his palm on a jagged chunk of International mirror glass. Ray gained the blue subcompact and clung to the door handle. Spelled in pitted chrome along the quarter panel was the word *Kadet*.

"Opal." Ray pulled himself up toward the open side window and peered into the car to find the steering wheel engulfed in a papery nest, the interior alive with hornets.

He came without warning really, and they could only step aside as he dropped, as he landed briefly on his feet atop a patch of hardpan before pitching over and rolling down the hillside, through the weeds past an Allis-Chalmers tractor, toward the upended wheelless coal car down the slope.

The proprietor spat and snatched off his meshweave cap to

get at a nagging itch on his topknot. "I guess that's one way to do it."

He stood briefly alone in the cemetery, his palm on the cool stone of the pedestal, before he crossed toward his aunt's house and mounted her porch steps. The chief called to her through the doorscreen, and she came clacking at him in her low heels along the hall. Surprised, delighted, she offered him her cheek across the threshold.

"He seemed quite charming," Evelyn declared, settling before the chief a lunch plate of leftovers—dessicated pork, stewed turnips, slices of beefsteak tomato, a Parkerhouse roll. Evelyn McClendon plucked a paper napkin from between her vinegar cruet and her jar of sourwood honey, shook it open and spread it on the chief's lap.

"Scoot up," she told him, and he inched forward until his belly pressed against the edge of the kitchen dinette.

"I think he's probably a very sweet young man, but that girl from the Park Service—" Evelyn paused to spoon sugar into the chief's tumbler of iced tea. "Give them a uniform, and you know how they get."

The chief ate with a bravura show of savor and relish. He hummed as he chewed, his habit since childhood.

"I've got ice milk," she told him. "Butter pecan."

The chief grunted and smiled.

"Did you hear about Bessie? Cancer. And that Clayton woman across the road had the very same thing. I'm wondering if it might be in the water."

"Or in the Tareytons." The chief shoved his plate away. "Water's tested every month."

Evelyn patted the chief's forearm and smiled. "You're such a comfort to me."

The chief fished a toothpick from the unstoppered pill jar on the table as his aunt whisked away his plate.

"You know, Ray—" he began.

"Sweet young man. Very polite."

The chief nodded. "Him and that Carson girl have been tracking down this fellow we found in the woods."

"Terrible thing. Such meanness about."

The chief nodded, felt professionally obliged to nod, even though he wasn't so sure about meanness anymore. He saw regular displays of mendacity certainly, stupidity and blind criminal self-interest, but most of it was detached and passionless these days. He had long since reasoned he would likely prefer authentic enthusiastic meanness.

"Anyway, they've been running down who he was and what he was up to. That sort of thing. Seems like he was maybe out here at the graveyard before he died."

"Oh?"

Brady nodded. "That cousin of his puts him here."

"It is a peaceful spot. I'd bet even a scoundrel could see that."

"He might have had a hammer. Might have been beating out there on something, say that statue of yours."

"I'd think I'd know about that."

"I'd think so too."

Evelyn placed a mug before the chief. The water in it was tepid, the Sanka thinly measured and weak.

"Sugar? Cream?"

The chief shook his head and sipped, flinched reflexively. "I took a look out there. Ray says you told him ice."

"Where we patched?"

The chief nodded.

"*Was* ice. Remember that storm? February? Four years ago? The lights were out for three days?"

"Yeah."

"Water got into the rock right there where it's engraved. I told you all about it. I think I even showed it to you."

"It just doesn't look much like ice. That's all."

"I can't help that."

The chief nodded. He paused. "You know—" he said and then left off.

"What?"

"Two or three years ago, Uncle Royce would have still been around. It'd make sense if, say, some fellow showed up where he didn't belong, doing what he ought not to be doing. And maybe Royce went out and—"

"Brady!"

"I mean if it was something like that, and things just got out of hand, then probably we could—"

"Well, it wasn't something like that! It wasn't anything like that at all! It was ice, just like I told you!"

"Yes, ma'am. Ice. I'll let Ray know." He pushed back from the table. "I guess I ought to get back."

"I guess maybe you ought to."

Evelyn followed him up the dim back hallway, through the formal dining room and into the elegant front parlor with its heavy draperies of lush maroon brocade, its Queen Anne side chairs and massive quartersawn secretary, its wine-red hand-knotted rug, its plaster cornices, its shrine to the Confederacy.

The chief stepped onto the front porch, and his aunt permitted the screen door to slap shut with no upturned cheek to peck, only the tight frown and the frosty glare.

They sat opposite each other in a booth by the window at Little Ruth's on the bypass where they drank iced tea out of oversize red plastic glasses and idly shifted their silverware about the tabletop while they waited for their food.

The dining room was homely and largely unadorned. The shiny beadboard paneling was hung with a framed and lacquered jigsaw puzzle of the Blue Ridge in autumn's glory, an orange Heimlich maneuver instructional chart above the register at the door. The waitresses all wore pink cotton uniforms. The patrons, exclusively male and white but for Kit, had largely neglected to remove their caps. There was scant ambient conversation, just the clatter of flatware and the rattle of ice on plastic.

"How's your ass?"

Ray winced slightly as he shifted on the banquette. "Padded, fortunately. We're probably wasting our time looking for that stinking car." Ray tore open a pack of fractured saltines and scattered crumbs across the tabletop. Kit blew them all back his way.

"Any ideas?"

Kit shook her head. "Hard to get too worked up over this guy. You saw his sheet. It had to take a little wind out of you."

"So he wasn't a model citizen."

"Hell, nobody even reported the asshole missing."

"Somebody beat him to death. I'd kind of like to know who."

Kit flopped back against the banquette. Ray snorted and opened his mouth but failed to speak.

"What?" Kit asked him.

He waved her off.

"What!?"

"I just thought you'd feel a little differently. That's all."

"Why?"

"You know. He was one of yours."

Kit stiffened and sat forward. "One of mine?"

Ray smiled a little helplessly, purely awash already in regret. "I just meant that—"

"And here I'd been giving you credit." Kit snarled. "Tell me something, all this yokel trash around here, are they yours? Are you boys just one big cracker brotherhood?"

"Come on, that's not what I—"

"But us black folk, *we're* all in it together."

Their waitress arrived with their orders preceded by a blast of her scent—Jungle Gardenia and Aqua Net. She set a plate in front of Kit. "Turkey club." She set a plate in front of Ray. "Veal cutlet." But for the shape of the lumps beneath the gravy, the dishes were identical.

"Christ!" Kit shoved her drowned sandwich across the tabletop and slid out of the booth. She charged out of the restaurant and into the lot, and Ray was waiting still for change at the front counter when the radio on his utility belt came alive with a staticky crackle.

Kit refused to speak to him and drove even more heedlessly than normal, out the bypass and back along a swooping asphalt road. The surface was all ungainly pitches, humps and seams, jarring depressions, and Ray bounced about the cab as they raced along the blacktop.

They came onto a finger of the local reservoir, shallow and swampy and grass-choked near the shore, passed a man fishing from the roadside, sitting in the dirt with his pole on the ground hard by him. He was pouring a pint of Ancient Age into a Pepsi bottle as they rolled by.

A clapboard shack of a bait shop sat opposite the lakeshore with a bin of live crickets by the block stoop out front. The property was littered with upended flatboats and discarded canoes, algae-stained motor launches. Cars and pickups were nosed in before the shop, and a crowd of men had collected at a corner of the building, silent and sullen onlookers.

Kit wheeled off the road and stopped in the hardpan lot. She took in the shack of a bait shop, the boats, the weed-trapped rubbish at the roadside, the clutch of patrons—backwoodsmen mostly, grubby hilltoppers in coveralls and brogans.

"A regular white-trash wonderland," she said.

They could hear Carl as soon as they'd left the Blazer, well before they'd seen him.

"Didn't I tell you to shut up?"

Ray parted the onlookers, pushing his way through with Kit just behind him.

"I don't want to hear another goddamn word out of either one of you!"

Carl stood along the side wall of the bait shop, just where the gutter had given way and the clapboards were water-stained and puckered. He had two men in hand, each grasped firmly by the collar. They were foul and greasy and incensed with each other, and Carl kept them apart by main force and liberal threats.

"Shut up!" he yelled, preemptively.

"Are you all right?" Ray stepped up beside Carl. "Ailene called me. Thought you could use some help."

"Naw. I've got it now."

Kit joined them and immediately became an object of general scrutiny.

"What's going on?" Ray asked.

"This one"—Carl jerked the fellow in his right hand, shaking him by the collar—"he figures Ricky Rudd is leading Dale Earnhardt in the points race by two thirty-seven." Carl gave a jerk to the fellow on his left. "This one, he's sure it's two forty-five."

The fellow on Carl's left ventured a comment. "Two forty-six," he said.

"Shut up!" Carl jostled him extensively.

"Hey."

Ray turned toward the onlookers.

"Hey." It was a man at the front of the crowd in a blaze orange Homelite cap. "Whose nigger?" He grinned, showing off gums and stumps and unopposed incisors littered with shredded plug chew.

Ray failed to trouble himself to so much as glance Kit's way. "Do you personally know a doctor, or maybe a competent veterinarian?"

The man spat disdainfully in a vile stream. Kit permitted him to swab his lips dry with his shirtsleeve before she drew back an arm and shattered his nose with a festive *Pop!*, managed it by spirited application of the heel of her hand in advance of sweeping his legs from beneath him and dumping him onto the ground.

"Great Christ, she kung-fued him!" Carl shouted and cackled, shaking the men he had in hand who threw in to laugh with him.

"Move!" Kit snapped, and a corridor opened before her.

She stalked toward the Blazer as Ray and Carl watched, as the two men in Carl's grasp watched, as the clump of onlookers watched, as the hilltopper in the Homelite hat moaned congestively from the ground and dripped blood mixed with tobacco juice onto the hardpan and the gravel.

Spooky drove me down to the Duke come morning, him and the other one to whom I'd not been properly introduced—the one with the camera and the hand upraised to shield himself from splatters who rode with me in the back. Apparently, Spooky didn't consider Twizzlers proper breakfast food as he was instead drinking a Yoo-Hoo and eating a Butternut bar. The one alongside me was gouging at his toothgaps with his Visa card and chewing loudly on the leavings he unsnagged and set adrift.

We hit a particularly dramatic dip in the roadway along about Thirty-fourth Street, and that fellow beside me, in getting flung about, was gouged by his pistol bore sufficiently to prompt him to yank his gun from his trousers and rest it on his lap, pointing it indifferently toward me.

I hardly paid any notice to the thing which I recognized even at the time was peculiar since I'd been raised by my father to a respect for guns that verged on abject terror. He'd been afraid his whole life of firearms himself and had passed the fear on to me, that along with an unreasonably poor opinion of carriage bolts. A friend of my father's had been run over and crushed under the wheels of his tractor because, as it turned out, a carriage bolt had failed.

The sight, however, of Giles's associate's semiautomatic on his lap didn't seem to have any detectable effect upon me. Even with the bore aimed my way, I didn't pay much attention to the thing which was partly, I imagine, due to my recent exposure to weaponry, but I'm convinced these days it was more on account of Giles's approach to his problems.

Giles's employees, it had come to my notice, acted strictly on Giles's instructions, and Giles was reliably guided by his unflagging sense of righteousness, was scrupulously consistent, and his retribution was considered. Riding down Fifth Avenue in Spooky's secondhand Ford, I simply believed I had cause to be at ease, had decided I'd be spared because I didn't have it coming.

"Hey," I said to that gentleman beside me and then pointed to his pistol and asked him if I could hold it without troubling myself to tell him I was working at the moment through tenacious psychological misgivings about guns.

He removed his credit card from his mouth and informed me, in ordinately colorful language, no.

They dropped me off at the Duke—put me out actually; shoved me, that is to say, from the sedan—and roared away, which marked the end, I have to think now, of Giles's experiment in family values. He had decided by then, it seems, to bank entirely on betrayal.

The day clerk was Windexing his Plexiglas as I entered, and he hunched down to speak through his cluster of bored holes. "You checking out, or what?"

"Yeah," I said. "I guess I am."

And, in fact, I intended to pack, meant to gather up my things and arrange for a ticket, planned to take a cab to La-Guardia to wait for the next available flight to Roanoke. I was ready by then to go home and try to forget I'd ever come, and I was fishing for my door key when I heard her—my neighbor.

Her television was playing loudly, was tuned to some manner of late-morning gabfest, and I could hear a man and a woman, hillbillies by the sound of them, discussing their marital problems in a fashion that was lively and profane. What with all of the unseemly expletives bleeped out, it sounded as if they were communicating primarily in Morse code.

As best I could determine, she was unhappy with him because he was a hound and a feverish womanizer, and he was unhappy with her because she'd taken up with the driver of their fuel-oil truck. I could hear the audience members breathing through their mouths even from out in the hall, could hear the creak of the hotel bedsprings, could hear my neighbor weeping. I crooked a knuckle and, without having decided to really, I knocked.

She was Korean, I think, slight and fifty maybe. She spoke no English, and she was desperately upset. She explained to me why precisely, but I didn't understand a word of what she said, and then she laid her face against my jacket and blotted her eyes dry on my lapel, but the smell had reached me by then, and I was actively retreating.

Kimchi, I think it was, both the rank cabbagy aroma of the uneaten product and the potent vapors of digested and discharged kimchi exhaust. Furthermore, the room was an absolute mess, was strewn with clothes and copies, for some reason, of *People* magazine and *Movieline.* As the fuel-oil truck driver stepped onto the stage and was wrestled to the floor by the husband, I suspected my neighbor had come with her fermented cabbage and her dreams to discover that America was something appreciably less than she had hoped for.

I pried myself from her, drew shut her door and hurriedly unbolted mine. I'd barely had time to bring my grip from the closet and open it on the bed when Doogan and Vitale, without bothering to knock, simply stepped into my room.

They had a hell of a tale for me, Vitale allowed. "Tell him about those boys," he instructed Doogan as he crossed the rug to admire himself in the bureau mirror.

Doogan laughed and swung his head from side to side. "Some Adam," he informed me. "Some Steve."

11

Her husband believed she carried a girlfriend with her mornings to the carpet-backing plant. Veronica, she had told him, from out past Guthrie which was why she dressed and left so early—not merely in Guthrie but past it.

"I'm gone," she called to him weekday mornings through the bathroom door.

"Yeah," he evermore told her, parked on the toilet, always only "Yeah."

She drove even toward Guthrie at first, sort of and for a while, before she turned west off of the Lynchburg pike and wound back into a hollow. The road was gravel and followed the bed of a stream which was muddy and deep and poured at length into the murky flow of the James River. The roadway ascended onto a spur of the bordering ridge where she slowed and turned off along a track into the woods. She could see that he had come before her, was waiting already, and she fairly thrilled at the sight of his tread marks in the soft ground.

She pulled into a clearing, their clearing, where he was standing on the verge of the bluff looking down through the woods at the flowing water. Hearing her, he turned and smiled. He always smiled, unlike her husband who had grown to prefer glaring, who slept with his mouth open and his breath popping moistly in his throat, who burped unapologetically at the dinner table.

He wore the black shirt she'd given him with the pleats and the ivory piping, his ancient jeans, his oil-stained Wellingtons, his bulging hand-tooled wallet chained to his belt loop and wedged into his back pocket. She joined him at their rock and touched his hair which was fine and straw-colored and hung to his shoulders. He draped his arm about her, and they kissed, always a little clumsily at first, still with embarrassment somehow.

"Hey," he told her.

She pressed her face to his shirtfront and absorbed his scent, straightened the lay of his pocket flap. She giggled a little girlishly and said to him softly, "Hey."

"Cold?"

"A little," she allowed.

She shivered as he squired her to his car, a Shelby Mustang—metallic blue and regally chrome-encrusted. He started the engine, and it roared to life and idled with a brawny chug. He switched on the heat and the tape player, keyed up, as always, to the Judds. They kissed across the shifter between the bucket seats until he drew away and moped, until he complained that he was edgy and tense.

"Oh, baby," she told him, just as she always did.

She kissed his neck, his chest, dropped south along his shirt flap and worked at his riveted trouser catch, tugging down his zipper. He pitched back against the car seat and moaned.

"Yeah," he said, but with passion, she could tell, and genuine affection, not at all like her husband at home on the toilet muttering between discharges.

He shouted and squirmed, panted and groaned, flailed with his arms and his legs and inadvertently manipulated the shifter as the earth began to move. The Mustang rolled forward, creeping at first but gathering speed. It crossed the clearing, passing their rock, and nosed down into the woods just as she raised up anxiously and peered through the windshield.

She screamed, but he was far too spent and drained straightaway to bring himself to brake and steer. Branches slapped against the windshield and scarred the paint. The Mustang glanced off a hickory tree and plunged into the stream where the current shoved it sideways, and it lodged against a rock as it began to sink. She heard water rushing into the trunk, the swampy chug of the engine, the anxious hurried breath of her boyfriend, the Judds.

I actually sat with her briefly alongside Vitale's desk. She was in shock, I have to think now, and a touch disoriented, and I recall that, every few minutes, she'd ask me for the time. Her name was Emily, she told me. Shackleton. "Like the polar explorer," she said.

Her husband had gone missing from his midtown hotel. A desk clerk had pulled his registration card and had called her, looking for him. She'd been home at the time in Columbus where she was busy shelling peas. His name was Dennis Shackleton. "Like the polar explorer," she said once she'd wondered of me if she could possibly trouble me for the time.

He sold pharmaceuticals, most particularly some manner of miraculous bunion salve. He was kind, she said, and thoughtful, walked with a slight limp. He'd had a beauty mark, she called it as she tapped upon my rib cage, shaped exactly like a lima bean. I told her I had been to Columbus once and had found it exceedingly lovely, even though I hadn't and I don't suspect it is. I made out to be acquainted with her husband's pharmaceutical concern, and I allowed that I had recently lost my son. I even briefly held Emily Shackleton's hand to comfort and to soothe her. Her hair was sandy and streaked with highlights. Her eyes were red-rimmed, and she had dressed, I guess, for travel the way people used to, wore a blue wool suit, stockings, heels, a brooch the size of an ashtray.

She clutched in her far hand a handkerchief that looked to have been white once, and I knew it straightaway for Doogan's nose-rag which I relieved her of as I offered her a fresh one from my pocket—pressed linen, lightly starched. I didn't suppose Giles would much mind if I passed the thing along, and, I'll confess, there was something about the tidy symmetry that pleased me.

"I don't know what I'll tell our girls," she said.

I could only wince and nod sympathetically by way of reply, could only cock my arm and apprise her once more of the time.

Vitale walked me to the squad room door. With a detective from missing persons, they'd essentially pieced it all together by then. "Go on home," he told me. "We'll take it from here," and I was halfway down the stairs before he called out behind me,

"This doesn't look too good for your boy." I dropped Doogan's foul rag in a trash barrel once I'd finally gained the street.

And I even believe, initially, I was intending to go home. I followed the proper course this time north across Canal and considered that I was heading for the Duke to finish packing until I found myself on Thompson Street opposite Lizzie's building where I paused to lurk, I have to call it, by the ramp to the parking garage. I'd been vaguely aware all morning of an impulse to warn Lizzie, of an obligation to tell her that she was deeply mired in trouble with precisely the sort of man her brand of acting wouldn't sway.

I was loitering still when she stepped out of her building onto the walk, but instead of speaking to her, I saw fit to follow her, trailed her left onto Spring Street west to the head of the block where she crossed the road and disappeared down the stairs of a subway station. Up to that time, I had assiduously avoided the New York City subway. Down in the hinterlands, where our nightly news of the nation at large consists chiefly of breathless reports of senseless tragedies, I had met with cause to believe that New York subway motormen routinely ran over more people than they hauled.

I stowed, however, my misgivings as best I could and went down into that station, climbed over the turnstile in the manner of a gentleman ahead of me, and slipped into the car behind Lizzie's as the doors were sliding shut.

"What happened?" Ray asked.

Carl turned and pointed up the rise behind him. "They come

down through the woods. Him and her. Says his car broke down, and she stopped to help him."

"Help him what?"

Carl grinned at Ray. Larry shook his head. Tight-lipped, angry, he spat into the water. "Goddamn women!" Larry stalked in a rage along the shoreline, pausing to kick at a stump.

"Don't mind him," Carl told Kit. "His wife left him. He's got this thing."

"So I hear." Kit watched Larry charge down the stream bank. "And nobody to lick it."

Carl wheezed with laughter and smacked Ray on the back. "And kung fu too."

The car was invisible beneath the silty water. Randy, the tow-truck driver from the Sinclair, shifted a lever to play out more cable while Dale, his assistant, drew a breath and disappeared beneath the surface. He shortly popped back up, sputtering. "Yank her," he said.

Randy engaged the winch which strained against the weight of the car and the force of the current. Slowly it reeled the Mustang shoreward, but the vehicle was invisible still even inches from the murky surface. Ray looked on as the trunk lid breached, then the louvered back window and the metallic blue roof. He shifted about to peer significantly at Kit, gazed in fact steadily upon her until she noticed him, until she asked him finally with her arms outflung and her palms upraised, "What!?"

Ray studied the county map spread out across his lap. "Left up here," he told Kit, and she wheeled off one gravel road onto another. They climbed past woodlands and pastureland, the occasional house, the odd barn and trailer home. "Right here."

Kit turned, and they rolled along beside a fencerow that separated them from a cow lot. Woodlands bordered the back pasture edge, a dense forest that ascended to the ridge toward the
springhead and the poplar grove with its primitive sleeping
shelter. Ray spied the orange pipe gate. "This has got to be it."

They walked across the pasture toward the muddy watering
pond. A half-dozen heifers watched them from the shade of a locust tree where they ground cud and lazily twitched away flies.
The pond edge was soft and generously perforated with hoof-
prints, each full of stagnant iridescent water. Ray hunted up a
handful of stones and sailed one into the pond, rippling the
placid surface and shattering the glare.

Kit stood watching as Ray circulated slowly about the water's
edge, pausing to pitch rocks until his supply was exhausted
when he gathered a fresh handful and continued. Ray had
gained the far side of the bank by the time he stopped and lingered. He tossed a stone into the water, a second, a third, and
then removed his utility belt and dropped it onto the ground.

Ray waded into the pond, sinking knee-deep, thigh-deep. He
pushed out farther, until the water had reached his waist when
he stopped and set to feeling about the surface.

"What is it?" Kit shouted.

Thigh-deep, knee-deep, calf-deep, Ray steadied himself as he
climbed from the trunk up the back windshield. Shin-deep, he
turned to wave to Kit from the roof of a blue Toyota.

"Hell, it ain't like I'm dry yet."

Dale, his coveralls dark and damp still from the collar down, hoisted the stout steel hook to his shoulder and marched into the pond. The winch whined as it fed out the braided cable, and Ray and Kit, the chief and Carl, looked on from the pond bank.

The silty water boiled and surged as the car was dragged across the pond bottom and up the near shoreline, as the blue trunk lid emerged from the water, dingy and mud-stained. Randy manipulated his levers and eased the vehicle backward, fully onto the muddy bank. The side panels were scum-fouled and algae-stained, and murky pond water drained through the door seams. A fingerling bream arced out through the open driver's window and plunged neatly into a swampy hoof depression.

"Got that VIN, Ray?" the chief asked.

"Right here." Ray pulled a folded sheet of paper from his pocket and cleared a palm's width of pond mud from the windshield. He wiped clean the tin dashboard plate and compared the numbers. "It's his."

"Pop it," the chief told Carl, who applied the tip of a lock punch to the latch on the trunk. He shoved the cylinder clean through, and the trunk lid hinged open with a rusty squeak.

The compartment was awash in mud and cloudy fetid water. Carl poked through the contents with the handle of the punch and turned up an aluminum ball bat, a rusted and sawed-off twenty-gauge shotgun, a set of battery cables, a corroded length of chain, a surplus munitions box, its latches rusted and seized fast. Carl battered them loose and flipped open the lid. He pulled out a fistful of decaying shotgun shells along with a freezer bag freighted with vials of what looked to be rock cocaine and a .9 mm Ruger.

"Well, well," he said. "A regular rolling indictment."

"See a hammer in there?" Kit stepped toward the back bumper and peered into the trunk. "What's that?" She pointed to a mud-bathed item on the trunk floor.

Carl pried it loose. "Tire iron."

Ray tugged open the passenger door to find the floorboards silted up, four inches deep. He leaned in to peer under the driver's seat, scratched with a stick on the back floorboard at a lump in the mud, the rusted head of a sixteen-ounce clawhammer skewered through with a scrap of rotted ash handle. He wiped it clean with his fingers and showed it to Kit.

"Any idea who owns this land?" Kit asked generally of Carl and the chief.

"It's that Glenn boy's, isn't it?" Carl said, eyeing the chief who shook his head, who pointed toward a far hedgerow.

"His property gives out down there." The chief swept his arm to take in the pasture and a surrounding swath of forest. "This is all Jimmy Lund's."

"Know him?" Ray asked.

"Cousin of mine." The chief shot a stream of saliva into the pond. "Yes, sir," he declared, lowly and largely to himself, "I guess I do."

I could see her through the doorlights where the cars joined as we clattered through the tunnel, watched her remove what looked to me a script from her shoulder bag, studied her as she ran through her lines. We traveled uptown, a half dozen stops or so. Lizzie rose from her seat as we rolled into the Fiftieth Street station where I loitered behind the other riders who waited at the doors, and I was still on the platform as Lizzie mounted the stairs and climbed to the street. I couldn't find her on Sixth Avenue, looked west along Fiftieth and then hustled down to Forty-ninth and caught sight of her entering a deli.

I was half persuaded she was probably on her way to an audition, wanted somehow to believe that Giles, after all, had been mistaken about Lizzie, that she was guilty of theatrics but not necessarily deceit. I tried on knit caps at a stall next door to the deli, tried on gloves and mittens, inspected a pseudo-Prada knapsack made from cheesy vinyl. I stole peeks at Lizzie through the deli window where I saw her buy a sandwich on a seeded roll along with a bag of chips and a soda, some manner of packaged cake, and then she came out onto the walk and continued west, leisurely, along Forty-ninth.

Lizzie walked two long blocks to Eighth Avenue where she turned and headed south as far as Forty-seventh before turning again west and traveling nearly to Tenth. The area was semi-seedy and strictly nonresidential. There were warehouses about, no few of them vacant and passably tumbledown, a couple of car repair shops, a few self-storage concerns, no foot traffic much except for a man in crusty clothes who veered off the walk to enter an alley and burrow in a Dumpster.

At the far end of the block, Lizzie stopped before a particularly scruffy-looking warehouse. Its windows were caked with soot, and there was trash strewn about the entranceway. Lizzie glanced toward an upper floor and then approached the front wall of the building as if to hide herself from view. She dug around in her shoulder bag and came out at length with a telephone which was hardly so compact and handsome as Giles's dainty model. The card she produced from her coat pocket was creamy ivory and stout. She consulted it as she punched in the number. Her chat was remarkably brief.

Lizzie entered the warehouse through a steel door at the head of the littered front landing, unlocked it with a key she produced from her coat pocket and then kept it from latching shut with a scrap of wood across the sill. She was standing with her back to me waiting for the freight elevator as I slipped up upon her. That car was rattling and groaning so in descending from an upper floor that she didn't even know I was there until I touched her, until I spoke.

"So," I said, had hoped for something pithier and a bit more triumphant, but, in casting around, all I'd come up with was "So."

I can't say that she seemed to me truly surprised. "You don't want to be here," she told me.

"He's coming, isn't he?"

She said nothing, looked elsewhere.

"You called him. I saw you."

"Yeah. He's coming."

"Then you don't want to be here either."

She laughed, snorted really, in a way that was haughty and dismissive as if she were mildly amused by how dull and wholly unpenetrating I could be. The elevator hit bottom with a thud, and the cable twanged and chattered. The steel latticework door had to be wrestled open by hand. I entered the car just behind her, and we started our ascent with a shudder and a merciless jolt.

I pointed toward the white paper sack in Lizzie's hand, the end of a drink straw protruding from the neck. "Nice touch," I told her.

She shook her head and sneered my way. "Wait till you see him. Just wait. He's not worth saving anymore."

He was singing, humming actually. I could hear him as we lifted between floors. The building was vacant but for the clutter, the rats, the pigeons nesting in the rafters, and he had the entire upper story to himself. Sunlight passed feebly through the sooty windows. There was rubbish about and disheveled stacks of planking, soggy vermin-chewed packing boxes on poplar pallets.

We stopped very nearly at floor level, and I grappled open the gate, but I couldn't find him at first in the gloom. The sound of his voice ebbed and echoed. He was everywhere, nowhere. Lizzie pointed him out where he lay upon a cot in the far corner. He pitched about, rolling uneasily back and forth as he hummed what turned out to be the snappy theme from *Entertainment Tonight.* He must have heard the elevator, must have known that she was there, but he just tossed and rolled on his cot, just hummed until we were almost upon him.

"About fucking time," he said as he sat upright and shifted his feet to the floor. He wore just socks and sweatpants, a T-shirt from a Soho bar. His blanket lay in a heap on the floor even though it was damp in there and frigid. He looked awful, drawn and filthy.

"Troy?" I said.

"For shit's sake, what's he doing here?"

Troy glared at me. Once Lizzie had ventured near enough to him, he snatched the deli bag from her hand. "He ain't our fucking buyer, I know that." Troy tore the wrapping from his sandwich and gnawed at it, looking me up and down. "Who beat the shit out of you?"

"*You* did it?"

Troy wiped his mouth with the back of his hand and looked dully at me.

"You butchered that man?"

"Who?" he asked me.

"Cut off his head?"

"Oh, that fucking guy." Troy glared at Lizzie. "Goddamn geezer." It had the sound of an accusation and a curse.

"Shut up," Lizzie told him.

Troy cackled. "Thought she'd snare us some beefcake, figured she still had the goods." He leaked mustard and tomato pulp as he spoke. "How many bars did you have to go to?"

"Shut up!" Lizzie turned away.

"And all she can get is him. Shit. He didn't look a thing like me. Did you see him?"

"Yeah," I said. "I saw him."

And I couldn't help but imagine how it must have gone with Lizzie in her cluttered apartment building corridor leading by the hand her trophy with his flat feet, his erection, his jacket pockets stuffed with sample tubes of miraculous bunion salve. She probably tossed her head and laughed by way of a signal, that gay little chirp she was capable of at the least of provocations, so Troy could be ready in his darkened apartment with his hammer and his spanking new hacksaw—Your Price $9.95.

There were deli sacks and potato chip bags strewn about the warehouse floor, countless drink straws and dozens of paper napkins, and Lizzie set about collecting them as if she meant just to tidy up.

"You're going to bring rats," she said.

"I don't want to hear about no goddamn rats. Where's our fucking money guy? That's what I want to know."

"I told you, I'm working on it."

"She's working on it." Troy glanced my way, shaking his head at me, grinning as if we were maybe chums.

"Money? That's what this is all about? Just money? What the hell is wrong with you? That man had a wife. That man had children."

"Ah!" Troy jerked his head from side to side and swatted away my objections. "We've all got our stories," I heard my son tell me.

Lizzie gathered her trash into a hefty bundle as she carried it toward the fire door in the adjacent corner where she leaned against the push bar, shoved the door open, and dropped her ball of litter, I have to guess now, onto the sill. I noticed, once she'd joined us again, the fresh streak of sunlight on the filthy warehouse floor.

There was a corroded steel drum at the head of Troy's cot that he was using for a table. It had a camping lamp on it, a couple of hypodermic needles, a soup spoon, a propane torch, a half-expended brick of heroin and a gun—a stubby little revolver that, given the pistols I'd lately seen, looked quaint and rather antiquated to me. I reached for it and held the thing in my hand, found it to be heavier than I'd expected, colder than I'd supposed.

I pointed it toward the ratty gym bag on the warehouse floor. "All of this for that?" I asked Troy, who wiped potato chip grease on his pants, who smiled.

I didn't hear them enter from the stairwell. Troy and Lizzie plainly didn't either, and we none of us even saw them, in fact, until Giles had already spoken.

"So," he said, "here you are."

He was flanked by Jumbo and Spooky, each with an arm upraised, each with a pistol in hand. Only once Troy had glanced frantically toward the barrel lid did I show him his puny revolver on my palm.

"You've caused me a lot of trouble," Giles told Troy. "And no little pain," he confessed, shaking his head, looking lacerated and authentically disappointed.

"Pop," Troy said to me, whispering. "Dad." With his eyes alone, which he widened and shifted, he endeavored to instruct me how to save him, but Giles was drawing by then alongside me. I could hear his shoes upon the gritty floor.

We passed a moment untroubled by talk as we considered together my boy. "This," Giles told me by way of introduction, "is Troy." He was wretched, filthy, narcotic-glazed and doomed, I was prepared to allow.

"I never really knew him," I saw fit to declare as I settled the revolver on Giles's palm.

"Why don't you go with Spooky. You've got a plane to catch."

"Right," I managed. "Spooky."

Troy leered at me from his cot in his nasty corner. His laugh, when it came, was sharp and bilious, a little mad in fact, and he gave it over shortly to hum again the lively theme from *Entertainment Tonight.*

I truly don't believe that Lizzie so much as suspected her run was up until Jumbo refused to let her pass, to let her join me and Spooky in the elevator car. Jumbo grabbed her arm and held her. He smiled, I could see him. He showed to Lizzie his dingy jagged teeth.

I heard her attempting with Giles a strain of actorly indignation which she supplemented with a manner of stagy ire. I saw her touch his arm and make a moist appeal to Giles's humanity, but he merely reached into his jacket pocket and offered her a handkerchief which was pressed and neatly creased, was sparkling white.

We heard two shots from between floors. We heard two more from the street.

12

They eased to a stop before the ornate cemetery gates, passed in among the civilians, crested the rise and descended into the Confederate quarter of the cemetery. Ray drew out his jackknife as he approached the infantryman on his polished marble pedestal. With the tip of the blade, he picked at the patching, popping out chunks of cement and revealing assorted dings and pocks in the stone. He laid the muddy hammer poll cleanly into one of the hollows.

"So what are we thinking here?" Ray asked.

"Are there sons?"

Ray shook his head.

"How about the husbands?" Kit glanced about at the surrounding houses.

"Just McClendon. The rest of them would have been dead already."

"Not much of a career move, hanging this on your boss's dead uncle?"

"Makes sense, though. Let's say this Smalls came around all cracked up and was out here beating this thing to pieces. You've got to figure they all heard the racket." Ray swept his arm to take in the houses bordering the cemetery. "The uncle comes out here to stop him. They fight. Smalls gets the short end."

"Why drag him into the woods and bury him? Why not tell the nephew? Even if it only smells a *little* like self-defense, he can make it all go away."

"Wouldn't be seemly, you know?" Ray said. "How would it look for decent people to be up to such as that?"

"Couldn't have been just him, though," Kit said. "Digging a grave. Sinking the car. Busy busy."

Kit considered the surrounding houses, the four tidy, stately structures with their lavishly planted and immaculately manicured lawns. She paused, gazing toward the lone shabby property. Paint flaked from the clapboards. The yard was weedy and overgrown. A window screen lay on the roof.

"Whose place is that?"

"Some Yankee woman."

Kit was walking already, moving among the Confederates across the cemetery toward the gate. "Even a carpetbagger's got ears," she said.

The lawn was even more disreputable up close, all clover and chickweed, dandelions and purslane. The lone speck of color was provided by the blossom of a thistle that grew through a crack in the sidewalk. An iron sculpture rusted in the yard, a thin rectangle plunged into the earth at one corner. Serpentine slivers had been cut from it with an arc welder, and flaking rust had rained thickly onto the ground, killing even the weeds about the base. Silently, Ray named it as he passed: *Tetanus One.*

They mounted the porch, which was crowded with stacks of rumpled magazines and yellowed newspapers—*The Nation, Mother Jones, The New York Times, The Weekly World News.* The front door stood open, and the aluminum storm door had lost its glass panel and its screen, was just a rickety empty frame. They heard a voice from inside, a man's voice, crisply British and recorded.

"Dusk fell, hiding the first body of the dead man, which had been left lying with arms outstretched as if nailed to the ground, and then the revolving sphere of the night rolled smoothly over Patusan and came to a rest, showering the glitter of countless worlds upon the earth."

Kit knocked on the aluminum door rail, causing the frame to clatter and rattle. "Hello," she called into the foyer.

"Again, in the exposed part of the town big fires blazed along the only street, revealing from distance to distance upon their glares—"

"Anybody home!?"

"—the falling straight lines of roofs—" With a metallic click, the voice was suddenly silenced.

"Hold on a damn minute! I'm coming."

The floorboards creaked and popped as Mrs. Sizemore approached along the foyer. She was a big woman, not just doughy and broad but tall too. She wore a paint-spattered muumuu, and her gray hair was piled carelessly on top of her head. She held in one hand a paintbrush, in the other a tumbler full of watery gin with a slice of dill pickle floating among the melting ice cubes.

"Ah," she said, shoving open the storm-door frame and smiling pleasantly, "callers." She added nothing further, simply shifted her bulk about and returned along the foyer, leaving Kit and Ray to follow as they wished.

She was dabbing at a canvas by the time they found her again, in a back room off the hallway that was vacant but for her easel and a small table by the window, several dozen canvases leaning against the walls.

"Sizemore, right?" Ray asked.

She nodded, dabbing paint upon some sort of still life, Ray noticed.

"We're investigating a spot of vandalism that took place in the cemetery a few years back," Ray said. "Three, maybe four years ago. Were you in this house at that time?"

"Seventeen years."

"And Mr. Sizemore?" Kit asked.

She got a sidelong glare in return. "He was down in Biloxi with his"—here Mrs. Sizemore troubled herself to make quotation marks with her fingers—"clerical assistant. Found he preferred her metabolism." She gestured to take in her own considerable girth. "I don't suppose you'd like a drink." Mrs. Sizemore looked from Kit to Ray. "There's gin, and then there's gin."

"The cemetery," Ray said again by way of a prompt.

"Oh, right. Those Nazis."

"Not them," Ray told her. "We're thinking that maybe a few years back somebody went at that Confederate statue with a hammer. We were hoping you might have heard something."

Mrs. Sizemore laughed and then coughed violently. "Business must be way off." She produced from a pocket a box of English Ovals and lit one. "I listen to my books at night." Mrs. Sizemore raised her glass as if in a toast. "I take my consolation."

Ray wandered across the room, studying the paintings leaning against the far wall. Each was nearly identical to the next—a blue background, flat brown terrain, and, resting upon it, what looked to Ray like wrinkled rocks. "Boulders?" Ray asked.

"Not much of a detective, are you?" Mrs. Sizemore pointed toward a shriveled and richly sprouted potato on the tabletop before the window. "It's a series," she informed him. "A study in decay and degradation." She threw back another swig of gin, clamped her teeth onto the pickle slice and savored it. " 'Russet,' I called it."

Ray considered the canvas underway on the easel. It featured the same spud, comprehensively wrinkled.

"So, aside from the Nazis, you don't really—" Kit pointed vaguely toward the cemetery.

Mrs. Sizemore set her glass aside and toked deeply on her cigarette. "You've come to the wrong place. You need to talk to Evelyn. That's her little fiefdom over there. She can hear a weed sprout."

Mrs. Sizemore returned to her canvas, scraping paint away with her pallet knife. She glared at Ray. "You're in my light."

"So she watches the place pretty closely?" Kit asked her.

"Her and the daughters of the lost cause. I offered to help them once. Thought the air would do me good, but Evelyn let me know it wouldn't be right." Mrs. Sizemore tapped her chest with her finger end. "Norwalk, born and raised."

"I guess you knew her husband," Ray said.

"Royce? Sure."

"We hear he had a temper."

Mrs. Sizemore drained the last of her gin. She ground out her cigarette and smiled slyly, looked from Kit to Ray, gave her head a shake. "Her," she said.

Spooky had packed my bag himself, I have to think, since my clothes were balled up and crammed inside, and the zipper was sticky with candy residue. I rode in the back with my grip alongside me as Spooky negotiated traffic along Thirty-fourth Street. He lacked Jumbo's impatience and seemed to enjoy getting stopped at lights which permitted him to tune the radio without distraction and unwrap whatever manner of confection had come to hand.

With crisp new bills Spooky bought me a ticket on the first available flight out of LaGuardia. It wasn't direct and nonstop. I had to change planes in Baltimore which meant double the takeoffs and double the landings—twice the mortification. I made a bid to object, but Spooky ignored me in order to flirt with the ticket agent which, as those things go, was relatively painful to watch.

She was polite to him in an officious sort of way as he slouched upon her counter to make indelicate chat and pepper her with charmless inquiries. He leered at her as he talked, winked a time or two. I could hear him circulating his pink spit.

We sat at the gate for three hours or more. Spooky parked us before a TV on its bracket between two windows that gave onto a view of the taxi way and Flushing Bay beyond it. He watched the same news loop twice with wholly uneroded attention and sat riveted through the show business report on both occasions it ran. Spooky was particularly taken with a raven-haired starlet who'd sat for an interview wearing a sheer blouse that proved, in the camera lights, rather gauzy and revealing. He shared with me his wholly unsavory intentions for that creature twice.

I waited for the woman at the microphone to call my actual row before I took up my grip and set out for the gangway. Spooky insisted on walking with me clear to the lectern by the door, and he was standing there still, inflicting some hapless female with his palaver, when I rounded the corner and stepped onto the plane.

We sat at the gate, sat on the tarmac, crept along in a queue at the head of the runway. By the time we lifted off, it was growing dusky out, and the sun was half hidden by the marshy squalor of metropolitan New Jersey. Our route carried us northeast briefly over the Long Island Sound, and then we banked back to the south at a pitch I found disturbing. We picked up the Hudson at the Palisades and were following the course of it toward the harbor when the pilot came on with an alarming crackle over the cabin speakers.

"Evening, folks. We've got us a balky landing gear and a fuel-line leak. Winds out of the south-southwest at eight to ten knots. A bit of galloping carriage bolt fatigue."

My seatmate, a troublemaker, stood up to fetch a pillow before the seat-belt light had gone off and the dinger had dinged. He took a basting from two stewardesses at either end of the fuselage and retreated with just a linty blanket and a magazine.

"Beautiful view of the New York skyline for you folks on the left." I looked out my window where the view, in fact, was daz-zling. "It almost," I heard the pilot add, "looks civilized from here."

Descending over the Chesapeake, I found Troy's picture in my topcoat pocket, toothless, grimy, perched on a curbstone in his scarlet shirt and boots. I crammed it in the seat pouch with the in-flight magazine, the laminated airplane diagram, the flat-tened vomit bag.

They proved an attraction at the fish house, more engaging even than the scampi and the captain's platter. Diners watched them indelicately and with transparent disapproval, a white man and a black woman and her uppity on top of it—eating, for godsakes, her fish broiled.

Ray watched Kit shove a desiccated and paprika-stained lobe of flounder around her plate. "How is it?"

"How does it look?"

"Want some shrimp?"

"Any good?"

Ray shook his head. "But there's an awful lot of it." He gazed out the window past the fishing nets and the cork buoys, toward the sparkling lights of the Shenandoah Valley well below. "You've got to admit, it's a hell of a view."

"Yeah," Kit said, pushing her plate away and flinging her napkin on top of it. "Nothing like seafood in the mountains."

The hood of Ray's Grand Marquis was still warm from the drive home as they lay upon it, their backs against the wind-shield, and studied the clear night sky.

"There goes one." Ray pointed, following the arc of a shooting star.

Monroe toured the lawn, her nose to the turf. She examined with near clinical attention a bewitching clump of clover and then moved on to a ratty hyssop bush and the ragged fronds of a lily.

"Jupiter," Ray said, raising an arm and pointing westward.

Kit indicated a light to the east. "Jupiter," she assured him.

They listened to the jarflies, to the frogs, to the cattle across the way. They could hear jagged little shards of canned laughter from Lyle's TV up the road.

"So what are we going to do, Raymond?"

Ray cocked an arm under his head. "I don't know. Go through the car, I guess. See what we can turn up."

"Maybe we should just ask her if she did it, or he did it, or if they both did it together." Kit pointed toward the northern horizon. "Draco," she said.

"Yeah, maybe." Ray indicated a light to the east. "Jupiter," he assured her.

She laughed, kissed him.

"You know, it's not actually Raymond."

"Oh?"

"Delray."

Kit raised up on an elbow. "You're kidding."

"I came a couple of weeks early. My folks were on vacation in Florida."

"Delray!?"

"It could have been worse. They stayed in Smyrna the night before."

―――――――

The mud on the floorboards had hardened and crusted, was puckered and cracked. Kit kneeled by the driver's door of the blue Toyota and removed chunks of brittle silt, grinding them in her hands to glittering powder that she let sift between her fingers. Ray scratched through the muck in the trunk, hauled out the spare tire and the carpet. He poked with a length of hickory into the recesses beneath the back window well.

Alongside them in the Sunoco lot, the boy with the flyaway straw-colored hair worked on his Mustang, changed out the plugs, drained the gas tank, fretted over the scarred and dented door panel. He was stripped to the waist, wore just his grubby jeans, his chained wallet and his greasy boots. His torso was bony and peppered with moles, and he had a tattoo on his back just below his left shoulder joint, a grinning death's head wreathed in roses. The lettering was artful and gothic: **Fucking A.**

He pumped the accelerator and turned the key. The engine grated and chugged, caught and sputtered, smoothed out at last and rumbled lowly. The Judds warbled, moistly and at half speed. He shut the hood and the trunk lid and slipped on his shirt, black with white piping, before approaching Ray and Kit at the Toyota. His remarks were addressed primarily to the near rear fender well.

"Me and her," he said, "we was just visiting."

Kit drew away from the car, grinding a lump of silt between her hands. Ray raised up from the trunk and peered around the uplifted lid.

"Yeah," Kit told him. "That's what we hear. Isn't it?"

Ray nodded, and the boy with the wispy blond hair spit once, punctuationally, before he returned to his dented Mustang, which he wheeled gingerly across the lot.

Kit thought it at first a rock, just another rounded pond stone, but as she crumbled the silt and let it drop away through her fingers, she felt the hardware, the setting. She cleaned it with spit. The stone was an opal, in brass, and the mechanism was balky at first, but as Kit worked it with her fingers, she managed to free it up.

"Ray," she said.

"I'm getting nothing here." He scraped about in the trunk muck with his hickory staub.

"Ray," she said in such a way as to tempt him to peer around the upraised trunk lid.

She displayed it on her palm, a screwback earring. Just the sort of thing, Ray couldn't help but think, his mother used to wear.

The spot was of the chief's choosing, away from the station house and well out of town at an overlook on the Parkway. Ray anticipated the junctions and pointed out the turnings to Kit until they had eased into the elliptical lot which was crowded at the near end with cars and vans. Tourists posed for pictures by the fieldstone retaining wall with the Shenandoah Valley bathed in sunlight behind them. An elderly gentleman smoking a pipe walked a steel-gray cat in the grassy margin by the roadway. He used for a leash a length of ruby yarn.

The chief's low-slung Country Squire wagon sat apart from the other vehicles at the bottom of the lot where overhanging tree limbs blocked the view. The chief was out of his car waiting as they rolled up beside him, was admiring what little he could

see of the valley through the limbs of a hawthorn tree, was finishing off one of Walter's Pall Malls.

"Hell of a day, isn't it?" he said as they joined him by the rock
wall. He meant the cloudless sky, the bright sunlight, the dry
mountain air.

"Yes, sir," Ray said. "So far."

"Chief."

"Right. Chief."

The chief considered Ray. He shifted slightly and glanced at
Kit. "So?"

"We've got a theory here, Chief," Ray said. "Don't imagine
you'll like it much."

The chief loosed a breath. "Who? Uncle Royce?"

"No, sir, not entirely," Kit told him.

"Chief," he insisted.

Kit looked toward Ray who dug into his pocket after the earring which he displayed on the palm of his hand. Kit pointed
in the fashion of Carl, with her nose and the pitch of her head,
and the chief reached to take that item up between his thumb
and forefinger to examine it.

"How exactly?"

"We know that Smalls boy went there stoned, looking to
make trouble," Ray said. "We're thinking that, some way or another, he got more than he could handle."

"Who from? My people? Are you telling me they killed a
man?"

"No, not exactly," Ray allowed. "We're telling you they
might have. We're telling you that maybe they did."

"Did you talk to Evelyn?"

"We thought you'd want to," Kit said. "She might own up to it with you, or at least some part in it."

The chief turned again toward the fieldstone wall and gazed out over what he could see of the valley. "Own up to it." He snorted and shook his head. "You're not from around here, are you?"

"But you'll talk to her, right?" Ray said.

"Can't make any of this work at the courthouse, can you?"

"No," Kit said. "Probably not even a stone cold murder. Something else. Something in between."

"So," the chief said, "what are we up to here?"

Kit shrugged, consulted Ray with a glance. "We've got to bury those bones somewhere."

The chief gazed out through the tree limbs toward the sun-drenched valley, smiling, swinging his head heavily from side to side. "Why, Miss Carson," he said. "Ouch."

He visited the cemetery in the dusky twilight, had ample family there—his mother and father, his brother dead in infancy, his eldest sister's child killed with a girlfriend in a collision. The chief paused before his grandfather's simple weathered headstone. A fluted iron vase was overturned in the grass by the base of the marker, was empty and rusted through, and the grave site was sunken and weedy, undermined and overrun with red ants.

Only presently and at length did the chief make his way into the Confederate quarter of the cemetery where he lingered briefly before the statue of the rebel foot soldier—the jaw set, the gaze leveled south—before continuing on to the spot that Ray and Kit had selected, a gap just beyond the unknowns, not in with the rebels exactly but near enough to matter, near enough to make for an incessant antagonism.

His aunt's handsome bronze coachlights were lit already as the chief passed through the cemetery gateway and crossed the street. He gained her clefted slate walk and stopped to admire the aging blossoms on her peonies which were the size of cabbage heads. Her coral bells, he noticed, were ragged and stunted, had been feasted on by rabbits.

The chief knew already just how it would go. He would hear through the front door the television she insisted she never watched, would ring the chime, and she'd switch off the set and roll it back against the wall. She'd offer him her cheek across the threshold, would claim to have been reading, would even have a book in hand, something ponderous and flattering to her intellect. She would pat his paunch, would tell him he looked thin.

They would retire together to the kitchen where she'd pour him a glass of her weak tea, where she would set him a place at the table. The bowls would come out of the icebox—the reused coleslaw containers, the shortlegs knotted up in packets of foil. He would approach the topic obliquely and haltingly, steering her along, laying it out in morsels, bit by bit and fact by fact, until it was sturdy and damning, until it was frankly an accusation and bluntly a charge.

And even then she would only smile, would only laugh in that flinty mirthless way of hers. "Oh," she'd tell him, "Brady." And she would proceed to thwart him entirely by *believing* he was mistaken, by exercising her steadfast gift for groundless conviction, by withdrawing altogether into her fictions and her lies where battle was evermore glorious and romantic, where she was impeccably decent and God-fearing.

She would lay a hand to the base of his neck and give him a fond squeeze. He knew this. She would answer him by saying merely, "Eat."

Kit had prepared the meal without Ray's assistance, without even Ray's attendance in the kitchen. On the front porch Ray had entertained Lyle, their guest for dinner, had discussed with him the weather, the embattled local landfill, a shortcut through Tidewater out to Richmond. When called, they had arrived to find the kitchen transformed. The harsh overhead light had been switched off, and candles burned on the dinette. Kit carved a pork loin and directed Lyle to the chair beside the window, the only one with all four of its skids.

Ray sampled the pork, the potatoes, the sugar snaps, the salad. All delicious, he decided, but for the salt. He elected to smile and nod his head, to register uncritical approval with an enthusiastic necknoise. Lyle asked leave to feed Monroe and showed Ray a scrap of fat and gristle before he tossed it onto the linoleum where Monroe shoved it about listlessly with her nose.

"That Queenie," Lyle said, "she used to love a pork chop." He wagged his head from side to side and, smiling wistfully, unfreighted himself of a ponderous breath.

"You know," Ray told him, without proper planning really and due consideration, "I couldn't help but notice that the picture you gave me of Queenie had a date on the back."

It was a dull pain, the grinding of a heel into the top of his foot. Ray paused to glance at Kit, and she favored him with a pinched and significant expression, was still glaring pointedly at Ray as she spoke. "More potatoes, Lyle?"

"Naw. Too damn salty."

The muscles in Kit's face untautened, and her shoe heel lifted from Ray's foot.

"Nineteen seventy-something, wasn't it?" Ray said. "That dog would be awfully old by now."

"I guess," Lyle allowed. Kit watched Lyle shove uneaten sugar snaps about his plate.

"I mean, come on, Lyle," Ray said. "Queenie's probably passed on, don't you think?"

Lyle pierced a scrap of potato with his fork strictly by way of recreation. "Yeah," he allowed. "Maybe."

"I've been thinking," Ray told him. This was a wholesale fabrication as Ray had not been thinking and was acting strictly upon an impulse in the wake of two beers, a glass of wine and an inordinate dose of salt. "You know that boy we found up in the woods a few days back?"

Lyle nodded.

"We're going to be laying him to rest tomorrow."

"I hear he was a rascal," Lyle said.

"Seems so, but I was thinking that you might like to come out to the cemetery. What with Queenie probably being dead and all, maybe it could help. The service, you know." Ray paused, and Kit watched him, her mouth open and her adenoids on display.

"For . . . closure," Ray added, tossing it out and then regretting it before it was even well beyond his lips.

Lyle shoved a scrap of pork about his plate, considering a response, while Ray set about mounting the defense he would visit upon Kit. He reasoned he could insist he'd been poisoned by television and contaminated at the cineplex where life's miseries are evermore routed by melodrama, the healing saccharine gesture, and the plucky quip.

Lyle laid his fork on his plate rim, dragged his palm across his face as he considered Ray's offer. He spoke only eventually and at length. "Why in the hell would I want to do that?"

13

So I waited while making to seem as if I weren't, was careful to lead my usual unexceptional existence. I failed to tell Lowell about Troy or Lizzie, Giles or Jumbo or Spooky, only shared with him news of Rachel, who I claimed to have met in a bar, who I allowed that I'd wooed with my gift for desolation. Lowell, for his part, confessed that he'd been thwarted by his waitress, the one with the shorts and the boots and the gauzy tank top out in the ersatz saloon. It seems she'd tolerated his overtures more poorly than he'd hoped for, almost as badly, in fact, as had Lowell's wife, Erlene.

"I had the stuffed chilies," Lowell told me a little sadly, marking the occasion by the food that he'd ingested. "I had the taco salad and the black bean soup. They didn't any of them like me back."

Ronald had changed colognes in my absence as there'd been out at the superstore a British Sterling price hike, touched off, Ronald told me, by a grievous trade imbalance that the nightly news anchor had reported direly enough to persuade him—as a matter of fiscal patriotism—to buy American instead.

"British Sterling is actually British?" I asked him.

Ronald nodded resolutely. "I don't know," he said.

His new scent was, very possibly, sweeter and less subtle, with musky undertones to it and cloying hints of citrus and of lilac, a distinctive note of talcum and the suggestion of hard candy. The stuff smelled to me like the misbegotten marriage of Hai Karate and Canoe.

Ronald, in fact, was sitting in my office blinding me with his scent and visiting upon me another of his carpal tunnel questions when the boy with the mail cart stopped by and dropped off my correspondence in such a way as to reveal the corner of an ivory envelope. It was heavy bond and addressed, I discovered, in a calligraphic hand, and the postmark was three days old from Chelsea Station. I'd been back little more than a week and a half by then.

I ripped the thing open aggressively enough to attract even Ronald's notice. The envelope contained a lone Polaroid, a picture of my house. My Cavalier sat in the driveway. My front lights were burning. Windfall limbs were scattered through the yard.

"Your place?" Ronald asked me.

I nodded.

"Funny," he said.

"Yeah," I told him. "Funny."

As threats go, it was notable for its elegant simplicity. Of course, I'd never for even a passing moment doubted Giles's reach.

So I waited still and improved my time rehearsing my grim expression, and I noticed I'd grown less particular than previously I'd been, permitted my end tables to drift entirely out of true, let my book spines go unregulated and my coasters lie unstacked. I had lampshade seams at every point of the compass through the house.

Doubtless, then, I was slipping already before I had occasion to see her. I was parked, I remember, on my settee, watching a drama on the Lynchburg station, that show about the team of malpractice attorneys who, week in and week out, move heaven and earth to save doctors from themselves. It's hardly the sort of thing I'd ordinarily watch, but I'd been induced to pause along the dial by the sight of a lawyer speaking with high emotion to a jury in defense of his narcoleptic client, a neural surgeon named Tod.

I hadn't yet brought myself to change the channel when the commercial break set in, so I saw the tidy suburban house, the kids, the husband and the terrier, the wife in a quandary over what manner of dinner she should serve. She was a professional woman with a briefcase and a career who hardly had time to cook, she confessed, in the fashion she would like which was why she considered bottled gravy a blessing. Her family refused to believe it was store-bought until she'd actually shown them the jar.

"Rich and silky," she told them. "Poultry or beef."

I wandered out into the yard, my remote still in hand, and gazed up through my splintered dying treetops toward the stars. I might even have known a moment there of grim and desperate reflection if Luther hadn't gotten wind of me and chased me back into the house.

They were dead six weeks before anybody found them. He was a copper scrounger who'd broken in to plunder the place of wiring and pipe, and he was pillaging a lower floor when he noticed the smell. He reported the bodies out of a misdirected sense of civic duty, was waiting as the radio car pulled up with his grocery cart full of plunder, was expecting to receive some manner of cash reward.

Strangely enough, I was perched again on Lowell's credenza by his window, could see once more that girl from reception down in the water garden. She'd gone to a pageboy even though she was hardly suited for bangs, and I watched her flick her butt in with the koi.

"Mr. Paul Tatum?" He stood in the doorway speaking generally into the room, not Officer Hayes this time but a colleague of his ilk who was chunky and close-cropped and faintly thuggish looking.

"Yeah," I said, pushing clear of the credenza, and I suffered Lowell's joke about the liquor stores again.

His name was Draper, and he had an actual notebook rather than a scrap of paper. I invited him into my office where I dropped into my desk chair.

"I'm afraid I have some bad news, sir."

His pseudo-sympathy was even less persuasive than Officer Hayes's had been. As he spoke, he tended to an itch on his arm and looked bored and distracted, proved hardly fit for my practiced grim expression. I pressed my lips together, set my jaw and asked him in a throaty murmur, "What?"

I could see Lowell watching us from his office across the hall. He'd rolled over to park himself beside his coat rack.

"It's your son, sir. He's been killed."

I let escape a persuasive groan and tolerated the gruesome details in exquisitely stunned silence.

"My lieutenant would like to talk to you," Officer Draper said in closing. "I'll drive you over. I'm parked right out front."

"Can I have a minute?"

He nodded, flipped shut his notebook and shoved it into his hip pocket. He stepped into the corridor with his shiny oxfords squeaking.

Lowell straightaway lifted his feet to the wallboard, straightaway gave a shove. He streaked backward toward me, steering with his shoe heel, his chair castors chattering wildly. I rose and stepped around my desk, swung shut my office door.

They had agreed upon noon, and the vault was being set as they arrived. The backhoe operator covered his pile of fresh red clay with a green tarpaulin before withdrawing a discreet distance, behind a stand of cedars, where he throttled down and shut the motor off.

Ray and Kit waited by the curbing, opposite the ornate cemetery gates. The chief rolled up in his Country Squire wagon and joined them, checking his watch, saying nothing. Together they watched Mrs. Sizemore perform some manner of horticulture in her yard. She stood out on the hardpan in her muumuu. In her free hand, the one without the cigarette and the tumbler of gin, she held a jagged scrap of broomhandle which she jabbed into the barren ground.

Again, the chief checked his watch. It was precisely midday when his aunt's front door swung open and she stepped out into the sun. Evelyn swept down her stairs in a handsome black suit.

Pearls, Ray noticed, a hat and half-veil. She managed a smile as she approached. It was remarkably broad, quite wholly unembarrassed.

"Miss Carson. Mr. Tatum," she said.

"Mrs. McClendon."

"Please." She rested her fingers upon Ray's arm. "Evelyn."

The chief held out his hand and offered his aunt the screwback opal earring on his palm. It was his part of the agreement they had reached, the meager price he had exacted. "I believe this is yours," he said.

Her smile tightened slightly as she reached for that item, as she examined it. "Perhaps," she allowed.

The preacher was stout and flaky, was littered about the shoulders with discharged scalp and hair. He rested his Bible upon his ample gut. "Now may the God of peace who brought again from the dead our Lord Jesus, the great shepherd of the sheep—"

Ray stole a glance at Evelyn, her head bowed devotionally, at the stone Confederate soldier up the way.

"—by the blood of the eternal covenant, equip you with everything good that you may do His will, working in you that which is pleasing in His sight. Through Jesus Christ, to whom be glory for ever and ever. Amen."

It was Kit who threw the toggle and engaged the motor, releasing the slings that lowered Antony Smalls's handsome brushed steel casket into the ground. The chief excused his aunt with a nod, and she retired across the cemetery, picking her way between the stones. The chief chatted briefly with the preacher on the sidewalk before rolling away from the curbing in a puff of blue Country Squire smoke.

Ray and Kit lingered in the graveyard, watched together the backhoe driver fill the hole and tamp it, saw him shove the spike of the temporary marker into the dirt. Ray managed a sour little smile. "War dead," he declared.

She studied them from her parlor, still in her suit, her hat and her veil. The metallic tang of bile lingered in her throat as she watched them emerge from the cemetery, looked on as Kit drew open the driver's door of the Blazer.

"Want me to drop you at the station?"

"No. I could stand some air."

"So."

"Yeah. So."

"I'll call you tonight. Around seven?"

"Seven's good."

Kit flattened a wayward tuft of Ray's hair with her palm. "Are you going be all right here on your own?"

Ray nodded. "I've got a cousin in Roanoke. Haven't seen him in years. Ought to run down, I guess."

"And you know where to find *me*? Right, Delray?"

"Yeah, I wrote it down." Ray patted at his pockets. "You're over there by the—"

Kit grabbed two fistfuls of Ray's shirtfront along with enough chest hair to gain his full attention. She kissed him thoroughly before releasing him with a shove. "So find me," she said.

Kit slipped in beneath the wheel and turned the key while Ray shut her door and reached in to lock it. "Be sweet," he told her, and she sneered at him as she lurched away from the curb, as she rounded the corner and traveled out of sight. By the time

Ray had turned toward Evelyn McClendon's house, the brocaded draperies—unswagged and flung shut—were swaying
still, but gently anymore and without violence.

He struck out toward town, whistling as he walked, a rendition of *I Can't Get Started* in the style of Lester Young. The
sky was clear. The sun was bright. The air seemed ripe with
promise.

Paul served Spanish peanuts and corn chips, served runny salsa
and alarmingly orange cheese. By way of making his manners,
Ray had stopped at a grocery store just north of Roanoke and
had bought a bottle of rather pricey California wine which Paul
removed from its sack and admired before they agreed on bourbon instead.

Paul's house was not quite what Ray had expected. It was
cramped and dowdy, a bit slovenly and going resolutely to seed.
As Paul fetched ice and glasses from the kitchen, Ray wandered
the cluttered front room with its strewn magazines and yellowing newspapers, its Bakelite coasters scattered about the dusty
tabletops. Ray counted five blue socks on the floor, a pair of
loafers, a crumpled napkin, a lone nappy bedroom shoe.

The glass Paul gave Ray was not altogether clean. Even the
ice cubes were dingy and discolored. "To health," Paul said and
raised his drink in wan halfhearted salute.

They chatted aimlessly for a time. Ray gagged on a papery
peanut hull, sampled the salsa and brought himself to sniff a
sliver of cheese. Paul retired to the kitchen in order, he said, to
put their pork chops on to cook and check on the progress of his

roasted potatoes, but he only saw fit instead to fetch the bourbon from the counter, and he set the bottle on a side table he'd shoved clear of magazines.

They exchanged scathing assessments of a relation they both detested as Ray yanked out his shirttail and wiped clean with it the rim of his cocktail glass. At length, Paul rose a little unsteadily off the settee and lurched over to pause on the sill before the storm door, turning to beckon with his fingers.

"Walk with me, Ray," he said.

They passed together through the weedy yard and off the curbing into the street which was quiet and untraveled, which was overhung with trees. They paused to watch a couple in a house across the way argue hotly behind the gauzy draperies on their front bay window—he snarled and jabbed his index finger while she stood, arms crossed, and seethed.

"Seeing anybody?" Paul asked, sitting down upon the asphalt as he spoke.

"Sort of. You?"

"Not really." Paul slapped the pavement by way of invitation, and Ray dropped down alongside him. "Met a girl up in New York. She made a wicked gimlet." Paul stretched out on the blacktop with a hand beneath his head.

"Back when you lost your boy?"

Paul nodded.

"Did they ever get the guy?" Ray checked for traffic, overcame his misgivings and sprawled beside Paul in the street. The pavement was warm, the August night buggy and thick.

"Nope. Say they probably won't."

"Shame."

"Could be worse, I guess. I mean, I never really knew him."

"I can't imagine that much matters. Your boy's your boy."

Paul nodded and gestured vaguely with his unemployed hand. "Funny," he said. "Somehow I thought it would."

A gangly wirehaired mutt came loping down Paul's neighbors' driveway, barking as he ran, sharply and insistently. He circled full about them in the roadway, plopped down onto his haunches by the gutter and yapped. Ray glanced at him uneasily, but Paul ignored him altogether, occupied himself instead with study of the night sky through a thatch of overhanging maple limbs.

"How long does it take?" he asked Ray after they'd gone for a time without speaking.

"What?"

"You lost your little girl—seven, eight years ago now?"

"Ten."

"So how long before I'm finished with it? Just tell me that."

A light breeze kicked up out of the west. Luther stretched out by the curbing with a groan and gave over his barking to nip at a troublesome tuft of foreleg hair. Leaves fluttered overhead. Limbs shifted and swayed. Ray lifted an arm and pointed toward a scrap of sky littered with stars. "Look," he told Paul. "Jupiter," he said.